love buzz

inked duet two

PERSEPHONE AUTUMN

Between Words Publishing LLC

Love Buzz

www.persephoneautumn.com

This book is a work of fiction. Names, characters, establishments, organizations, and incidents are either products of the author's imagination or are used fictitiously to give a sense of authenticity. Any resemblance to actual events, places, or persons, living or dead, is entirely coincidental.

If you're reading this book and did not purchase it, or it was not purchased for your use only, or it was purchased on a site I do not advertise I sell on, then it was pirated illegally. Please purchase a copy of your own on a platform where the author advertises she distributes and respect the hard work of this author.

ISBN: 978-1-951477-20-2 (Ebook)

ISBN: 978-1-951477-21-9 (Paperback)

ISBN: 978-1-951477-48-6 (Hardcover)

Editor: Ellie McLove | My Brother's Editor

Proofreader: Rosa Sharon | My Brother's Editor

Cover Design: Persephone Autumn | Between Words Publishing LLC

To every reader who keeps choosing my books.
You mean the world to me! I love you!

books by persephone autumn

Bay Area Duet Series

Click Duet

Through the Lens

Time Exposure

Inked Duet

Fine Line

Love Buzz

Insomniac Duet

Restless Night

A Love So Bright

Artist Duet

Blank Canvas

Abstract Passion

Devotion Series

Distorted Devotion

Undying Devotion

Beloved Devotion

Darkest Devotion

Standalone Romance Novels

Depths Awakened

Sweet Tooth

Transcendental

Poetry Collections

Ink Veins

Broken Metronome

Slipping From Existence

Standalone Horror Novels

By Dawn (published under P. Autumn)

one

. . .

Autumn

I CAN'T BREATHE.

Did Leo just say what I think he said? That he has filed for custody of *my* daughter. Swear to God, I must be hearing things because Leo hasn't spent a day of his pathetic adult life near *my* daughter. Why would he suddenly want to now?

Leo waltzes toward his car, and I lose focus, gripping Jonas's arm tighter.

An evil cackle floats through the air and robs all but my hearing. His wicked laughter will no doubt haunt me for days and weeks and months to come.

All I want is to wake up from this nightmare. Because this has to be my mind playing a sick trick. An attempt to rip away the only true happiness I have in my life.

My vision focuses enough to see Leo slip into a white Mercedes sedan. He starts the car and revs the engine—which is a joke because the car isn't equipped to sound threatening. Then he rolls down the driver's side window as he rolls past us slowly. One corner of his mouth tugged up. Brow cocked. Hoity-toity sunglasses over his eyes.

"Until we see each other again." He throws a flippant wave and drives off.

For the first time in minutes, I breathe fully. But it doesn't last long. My deep, full breaths turn to short gasps. Come faster and faster. Pulse pounding so powerfully, I clutch my chest to smother the pain. Fist my shirt and tug at the cotton.

Then I lose it.

I drop my arm from Jonas's, stammer in place, then tip my face to the sky and scream. Belt out my anger and fear and frustration. I scream for all the bullshit I have dealt with since Leo up and abandoned me. Scream for all the pain and heartache I have endured. And I scream at the universe for doing this. For inflicting me with this level of misery.

What the hell did I do to deserve such duplicity?

From the moment I learned I was pregnant; I have been a good mother. A really good mother. I have given up everything for my daughter. Forfeited every part of life not revolving around her. Sacrificed everything so her life won't feel any less with only one parent. Given up on love—until Jonas.

Yet here I am, still on the receiving end of punishment. And I don't get it. Why? Why me? What past blunder has put me on the chopping block? Haven't I endured enough?

Jonas places a hand on my back—warm and

comforting—and draws small circles with his thumb. My anxiety settles down a notch. Just barely. Every nerve ending sparks with unrelenting fury. And I hate it. Hate how easily Leo gets under my skin after so many years apart.

The worst of all… I have been so stuck in my head the last five minutes, I forgot Jonas stood less than a foot away. The man I care deeply for; I mentally abandoned him in a blink. If that doesn't make me a horrible girlfriend, I don't know what does.

Jonas steps closer—close enough, he is all I see—and frames my face in his palms. Brow pinching at the midline, he holds my gaze. His eyes a mix of concern and fear, strength and courage.

"Autumn, what can I do?"

The backs of my eyes sting as I slowly shake my head. "I don't know." Then the first tear spills and slips down my cheek. Jonas swipes it away. "Jonas, I don't understand why he is doing this. Why the sudden interest in her? He didn't care before. Threw us out like trash. So, why now? What triggered this?" As if the first tear granted permission for the others to fall, the floodgates open and flow uninterrupted. My body trembles crown to heel.

Jonas drops his hands to my waist and hauls me closer to him, swathing me in his strong arms. I snake my arms around his waist and cry into his shirt. He shifts one hand to the back of my head, strokes my hair, and shushes me.

"I got you. Just let it out."

We stand near his Jeep for minutes or hours. I cry

gallons of tears as I bury my face in his cotton tee. My eyes puff up painfully. I fist Jonas's shirt, push off his chest, and add distance between us. Slowly, I peer up at him. His iridescent hazels hold my gaze and silently ask if I am okay.

No, I am nowhere near okay.

Honestly, I don't know if I will be for some time. But none of my feelings matter right now. Time to put my selfishness on the back burner. Again.

Inside the apartment, there is a little girl whose feelings matter more. Whose will always matter more. And I plan to do whatever it takes to protect that little girl. Protect her from a man who never cared for her or even the idea of her. Protect her heart from the pain this situation may inflict on her.

"We should check on Clementine," I say, emotionless.

Jonas nods then swipes at my cheeks. He studies me with worried eyes. "Yeah. Let's check on her."

I step up to the Jeep and check my reflection in the window. *Jesus, I look like shit.*

Taking a minute, I swipe at my cheeks to clear as much of the trailed mascara off them as I can. Then I slip my sunglasses on and smooth my hair. Not as if Clementine won't notice the difference in my appearance, but if I can make it as subtle as possible, I will. I need to.

Taking a deep breath, I square my shoulders and step back from the Jeep. Jonas wraps his arm around my waist and presses me into his side. Warmth and strength pass from his touch throughout my body. We walk to the apartment door, a couple united.

But in my head, I slowly lose my mind as I question every circumstance in my life. Including my relationship with Jonas.

For now, I shake it off. My focus needs to be on my little girl and no one else. Not myself. And not Jonas.

We walk inside the apartment and shut the door. Penny sits on the couch beside Clementine. Thankfully, Clementine is oblivious to any disturbance as she watches *The Nightmare Before Christmas* at a deafening volume. My guess is Penny turned it up after I brought her inside and she caught the ghostly expression on my face.

Bless you, my friend.

I slide my sunglasses to the top of my head and Penny's eyes widen. "You okay?" she mouths. Subtly, I shake my head and clamp my lips between my teeth to fight the tremor of my chin.

Jonas walks us over to the couch and we sit. For the first time since we strolled through the front door, Clementine peers over at us. Her sweet, innocent face nothing but smiles and love and cheer. She crawls across the small space between us and hugs me. I have no idea why—maybe she senses I need her little arms wrapped around me—but I hug her closer than ever.

When she unhooks her arms, she sits back and smiles up at me. "Mama, who was the man outside?"

In my periphery, Penny cocks her head and scoots closer to the couch edge. She picks up the television remote and turns the volume down. I peek over at her and give a subdued smile.

Inhaling deeply, I prepare for the grocery list of questions Clementine will have after I answer. "No one important, pumpkin. Just someone I knew a long time ago."

Ever the intuitive, Clementine gauges my expression. Studies my face longer than typical. But by some divine miracle, she appears pleased with my response. "Oh, okay. A friend?"

It takes every rational atom inside me to not rebut her terminology. But I remain tight-lipped. "Pumpkin, will you stay here and watch your movie? I need to talk with Jonas and Aunt Penny alone for a minute."

Clementine smiles up at me and nods. I swallow the emotion slowly building in my mouth. Bite back the tears that threaten to fall. And force it all past the boulder in my throat.

"Yeah. Can I turn it back up?"

I love how her sole concern lies in the volume of her movie. That her little seven-year-old mind knows no other worries. "Sure, pumpkin." I hand her the remote. "Stay here. We'll be back out soon."

Glancing at Penny, I tip my head toward the kitchen. The apartment isn't necessarily closed off in the main living spaces, but at least a partial wall blocks the conversation we need to have. Penny, Jonas, and I rise from the couch and head to the kitchen. In the small space, I drag us as far from Clementine's eyes and ears as possible.

"What is going on?" Penny whisper-shouts.

"Leo was by my car when we pulled up." I tuck my lips between my teeth and blink back the tears threatening to make an appearance.

Now is not the time to break down, Autumn.

"What the hell did he want?" Not too often will anyone ever meet a pissed-off Penny. But when she hits that point, people instantly know. Being on Penny's bad side isn't pretty. Not pretty at all.

I tip my head back and stare at the ceiling. For the umpteenth time since I spotted Leo outside, I fight the anger and frustration and fear boiling in my veins.

Hold it together, Autumn. Crying and screaming right now will not help anything. Just say what needs to be said.

Lowering my chin, I level my gaze with hers. "Said he's filing for custody of Clementine. I will be served tomorrow."

Penny slaps a hand over her mouth and slowly shakes her head as her eyes widen. After she marinates on the outlandish news, she opens her mouth. For a moment, she doesn't say anything. She snaps her jaw shut, then opens it again. "This makes no fucking sense. After all this time. After walking away without worry. So, why now?"

"Question of the day." I laugh without humor.

Beside me, Jonas remains silent with his arm around my waist. No doubt he is as baffled with what happens next as I am. His thumb draws lazy circles on my hip, his gentle reminder so I know he is here for whatever I need. That he supports my decision, whatever it may be. That he will be a leaning pillar of strength through this rocky time.

And I love how much he cares. Love how he will do anything for me, even after such a short time together. His level of love speaks volumes and resonates deep in my bones.

Penny continues to shake her head while tapping a finger over her lips. "Why?" she mumbles. The question not directed at anyone or meant to be answered. Just pure curiosity.

The three of us stand in the kitchen, staring at each other and nothing. My mind wanders as I search for some hidden reason or an obvious resolution. And honestly, I have no idea where to begin.

If Leo is filing a lawsuit through the court system, should I obtain legal counsel? Is an attorney my first step in handling this? Not as if I have friends or family who have been through this. Will I be able to afford an attorney? Especially on such short notice. How much does it cost to hire one? Will Leo drag out the matter and slowly drain my savings?

Panic hits my bloodstream anew and a tremor vibrates my body. Not enough for Penny to notice, but Jonas does. His hold on me is stronger as he leans in and kisses my temple.

Why the hell is Leo suddenly so interested in Clementine? After jumping ship close to eight years ago, telling me he had no idea how to be a father—nor did he want to be—why is he so eager to fill the role now? And how does he know where we live? What I named her?

Something had to have provoked his interest. It's the only logical explanation. But what the hell changed?

Then the answer hits me like a wall of summer humidity. Steals my breath and robs my heart. Jonas. Jonas is the only difference in my life after all these years.

What if Leo has secretly kept tabs on me over the years—kept tabs on Clementine—and recently learned Jonas and I started dating? Although he has no desire to be with me or be a father, is this his way of saying, *I don't want them, but no one else can have them either*?

My stomach balls into a knot and twists my gut.

If this holds true… one—this is fucking bullshit. And two—in order to not lose my daughter, I need to do something harsh. Something I may regret for the rest of my life. Something that has me queasy and on the verge of vomiting.

I need to distance myself and Clementine from Jonas. If my being with Jonas prompted this whole debacle, I need to back off. At least until I consult with an attorney and everything clears up.

Bile rises and burns my throat as I pinch my eyes closed. Jesus, I am going to be sick.

As if Jonas senses my dismay, he squeezes my hip and I open my eyes. I peek up at him and every molecule of love I hold for him slumps with sadness and heartache.

I don't want to do this. Can't do this. But what other choice do I have? Leo has dumped my worst nightmare in my lap and I see no other way out of it. Not yet, anyway.

"How am I supposed to handle this?" I whisper more to myself than to Jonas or Penny.

Jonas takes both my hands in his and lifts them to his chest. Beneath my palms, his heart thumps the rhythm I recently memorized. A rhythm I tucked away for safekeeping. And now it seems as if I will be unlocking that vault sooner than expected to play the recorded rhythm.

Because I am about to change everything. I am about to break both of us.

I stare at Jonas's chest as my fingers gently rumple his shirt. He places a finger under my chin and tips it up until our eyes meet. Golden to hazel. In his eyes, I see promise and hope and love. The knife twists harder beneath my diaphragm at seeing his unconditional support.

I will miss him. So goddamn much. Every second and minute and hour. Every day and week and month. I mentally clench my fists and pinch my eyes.

"We will get through this together. Okay?" Voice soft and tender and barely audible. It shreds my heart further. "No matter what happens, as long as we have each other, we will survive this."

The backs of my eyes sting, but I don't dare let the tears break free. Tears may be what gives me away. And me putting distance between us won't happen if he picks up on my plan.

For now, I keep this tidbit to myself. I trudge forward and let him believe everything will be okay with us. I pray, in the end, it will be better than okay. So, I nod and force past the pain piercing my heart.

Regardless of my feelings, I must remain strong. Not just to get through whatever bullshit Leo is about to deliver, but also to protect my daughter. Above any person, Clementine matters most. And since the moment I learned I would be a mother, I swore to do whatever it takes to keep her safe and feeling loved.

Even if that means losing the only other person I have ever loved. Even if that means losing Jonas.

two

• • •

Jonas

THE ALARM CLOCK WAILS ON MY BEDSIDE TABLE AND, FOR A moment, I ignore it. Ignore the blaring tone as it changes every ten seconds and becomes more frantic. When Spartan nudges my ribs, I roll my eyes and slap a hand in the general direction of the clock. After a few blind slaps, silence consumes the room again.

Silence and darkness.

After leaving Autumn's apartment last night, I couldn't shake the sudden pain in my chest. This sinking, drowning, I-can't-pull-in-enough-oxygen sensation. No matter how much I assured Autumn I'd be at her side, that we would get through this, a nagging pinch lingered beneath my sternum.

All night, I laid in bed and stared at the ceiling. Studied the minor imperfections in the plaster. On occasion, I drifted off. Only to be woken fifteen, twenty, thirty minutes later.

The pang beneath my ribs didn't exist solely from Clementine's father making an appearance—although he royally pissed me off. The stab persisted because something was off with Autumn. With us.

When Autumn, Penny, and I went to the kitchen to talk, I *felt* the rift start. Our relationship may still be young, we may not know much about each other, but I have never been more hyperaware of anyone. Not even Cora. And seconds after we stepped into the kitchen, something in Autumn changed.

Can't pinpoint exactly what, but the ground shifted beneath us. The tectonic plates holding our hearts started slowly drifting apart. And the crack between us swallows me whole.

The snooze alert booms off the walls and I slap the clock again. As exhausted as I am, sleep evades me. No matter how many times I close my eyes, my mind refuses to shut down and let me sleep. But the energy to leave the bed won't come either.

Spartan noses my elbow and groans. "I'm getting up. Just give me a minute."

I roll over to turn off the clock, inhale Autumn's scent on the other pillowcase, and close my eyes. Fisting the pillow to my nose, I drag in the smell of her. Allow it to lessen the sharp sting between my lungs, if only for a minute.

When I drop the pillow and sit up, the pain throbs anew. This is going to be a long fucking day. I feel it in my bones.

Out of bed, I go about my typical morning routine. Taking Spartan for a walk—thank god he knows our route because I am mentally dead on my feet. Shower faster than usual. Dress for work robotically. As I take out items to make breakfast, I spot Clementine's juice in the fridge.

The knot in my stomach twists tighter. Has me nauseous. I cook half my normal breakfast and barely eat any of it. Before leaving the house, I brew a pot of coffee and fill my work thermos to the brim.

Today is going to snail by.

With Spartan secure in his crate, I turn on the radio for him and head out. I opt to ride the bike today and, since it is still pretty early, drive aimlessly for almost an hour.

The cold air stings my skin as I ride around the city. I welcome the frigid burn. The bite of cold air better than the uncertainty clouding my every thought.

I drive aimlessly. Focus on the road. The vibration of the engine between my legs. The heat from the pipes near my calves. When I need to change gears and steer the bike, I focus on what I can control.

After an hour of aimless riding, I park behind the shop and amble into the office. Dad sits behind his desk, his stack of invoices thin as he peeks up when I enter.

I don't miss how he checks the clock above the door. How he scans my face after noticing I am only thirty minutes early rather than my typical hour-plus early. And I definitely don't miss the brief droop at the corners of his eyes and lowered edges of his lips when he scans my face and notes my sullen demeanor.

I never need to tell Dad something is wrong. He just knows. Until Autumn and I got close, I thought no one would be able to read me better than Dad. His parental superpower is sensing when his children aren’t one hundred percent.

And right now, he more than senses something is off.

Giving a wave, I hold up the thermos. “’Morning. Coffee?”

He tilts his head slightly and gauges my stilted greeting. But he doesn’t mention it. Doesn’t shine a light on it and probe for further explanation.

“Please. Thanks, son.”

I nod then turn my back to him, grabbing mugs, creamer, and sugar before parking it all on the desk. Filling the mugs with coffee from my thermos, I hand him his mug without meeting his eyes. Once he adds cream and sugar, I follow suit. It all feels routine… and robotic.

The slowest first ten minutes of my workday tick by. We drink our coffee in silence as Dad wraps up the last of his paperwork and I stare at a framed picture Mom suggested we add to the office. A mountainous landscape at sunset. *“You need more than bare walls and automotive posters in this place.”* At least I have something to lose focus on while I sit here. A place to mentally get lost in.

“Want to talk about it?” Dad prompts after he stacks the day’s invoices in a wire basket.

Dropping my gaze from the picture, I face him and shake my head. “Not yet.”

Dad nods as his chair legs scrape the tile and he stands. Starting for the door, he pauses beside me and lays a hand on my shoulder. “Whenever you’re ready,

I'm here." Before I respond, he pats my shoulder, strolls out the door and into the garage.

I finish my coffee, wash the mug, and set it in the rack. Grabbing a fresh pair of coveralls, I slip them over my clothes, pick up the thermos, then mosey out to the garage. I survey the roster and see the majority of the schedule is full. A busy day is good. A busy day is exactly the distraction I need.

Three oil changes and a full set of new tires later, I would swear it should be closing time. No such luck. Still another thirty minutes until lunch. Then the back half of the day.

Dad has not so nonchalantly checked on me five times. At minimum. I understand his concern, but his constant overshadowing doesn't make matters better. If anything, it constantly reminds me why my mood is sour.

After I replace a starter, Dad orders me to take lunch. My stomach growls for me to feed it, but my head shoots down the idea. Instead, I lie on the couch in the office and close my eyes. Although I won't sleep, my exhausted body will rejoice at being horizontal.

I jolt awake when Dad nudges my shoulder. "Jonas, you should wake up."

Rubbing my palms over my eyes, I stare up at him. "How long have I been in here?"

Dad glances at the clock on the wall. "Little more than an hour."

Shit. I may have needed sleep, but now I will be the chump not returning on time. The one screwing up everyone else's lunch break. The day just keeps getting better.

"Sorry. Be out in a minute." I drop my feet to the floor and sit up, propping my elbows on my knees as I further rub the sleep from my eyes.

"Take your time, son. Garage has been slow since you been in here. I sent one of the other guys to lunch shortly after you."

I nod. "Thanks, Dad."

Without another word, Dad pats my shoulder then exits the office. Once the door clicks shut, I drop my head in my hands and groan.

Why is it when life is going great, time whizzes by? But when life isn't all it's cracked up to be, time barely ticks. And to reaffirm the statement, I glance up at the clock and see I still have another four hours left to work.

Fuck.

I comb my fingers through my hair, tugging at the ends. "Just get off your ass and get the day over with." Besides, I still have dinner to look forward to. Dinner with my girls. Just the idea of dinner, of seeing Autumn and Clementine, perks me up.

Rising from the couch, I grab a cold bottle of water from the fridge and guzzle half of it before I head back to the garage. I will make the rest of the day better. Even if I have to fake it.

~

Dad and I roll down the bay doors and I sigh. The entire day crept by, but thank fuck all is said and done now. Dad checked on me just as much after lunch as he did before. And as we lock up the shop and head to our vehicles, he surprises me with a hug. Not just any hug, but one of his *I'm always here for you, son* hugs.

"Drive safe, son. See you in the morning."

"You, too. Thanks, Dad."

Dad hops in his truck, cranks the engine, and waves to me as he drives off. Once out of sight, I straddle the bike and pull my phone from my back pocket. As with the last hundred times I have checked my phone today, there are zero notifications. At least none I want to see. Which doesn't help the pang since leaving Autumn's apartment last night.

Inhaling deeply, I open our text history and type out a quick message.

Jonas: Hey, scarlet. Still coming over for dinner?

I hold my breath as I stare, stare, stare at the screen. Silently willing Autumn to read my message and respond.

The screen dims and I tap the glass to wake it. Twenty painstaking heartbeats later, the little gray bubble pops up and those three magical dots dance inside it. Finally, I exhale.

Too soon.

Autumn: Not tonight. Got served today and I just want alone time with Clementine.

Her rejection hurts, but I understand the reason behind it.

Jonas: Want to talk about it?
Autumn: Not tonight. Please. But soon.

God, I wish we were face to face. I desperately want to wrap her hand with mine. Want to comfort her and take away the heartache she must be suffering with all this. But I won't thrust myself in her face. Won't annoy her with my anguish. She has enough on her own plate; I shouldn't add to the list of things to worry about.

Jonas: Sure. Talk to you later.
Autumn: Later.

Can't imagine what Autumn must be feeling right now, but God how I want to hold her. Tuck her snug in my arms and reassure her everything will be fine. That it will all work out, in her favor. It has to. After everything she has endured as a single parent, how can this not end favorably for her?

I tuck my phone away, start the bike, and drive home. Mindlessly, I weave through the evening traffic. See other drivers on the road, but pay them no attention. The trip is a blur of early sunset colors and bright red and white lights.

The second I set foot in the house, Spartan barks incessantly and bounces around as per usual. Once out of his crate, I open the back door and let him roam the yard while I kick off my boots and grab a beer.

The entire day—and now the evening—feels forced. Mechanical. Lifeless.

I feed Spartan dinner and polish off beer number one. Every few seconds, Spartan stops eating to peer over at the door. His heart hopeful a specific small human will walk through the door and shower him with hugs and conversation.

"Not tonight, bud." I rough his fur up as I grab the throw blanket from the couch.

Spartan finishes eating in record time. I snag a fresh beer from the fridge and walk out the back door with him hot on my heels. He bolts past me and scavenges the yard for who knows what.

While he forages for lizards that aren't there, I grab the lighter from the cabinet beneath the fire bowl, crank the gas, and ignite the rocks. Kicking back on the lounger, I sip beer number two and stare up at the black sky.

Tonight, the sky is absent of bright, twinkling lights. No stars to guide me. To lead me in the right direction. To guide me down this new path.

It is just me in the darkness with only man-made fire to light my way. The irony isn't lost on me.

Maybe I should have called Autumn rather than texted her. At least I would have heard her voice. Gotten an idea where her head is after being served. After she read the painful lines on the scariest document. I may be reading the whole situation too deeply, but even her texts felt *off*. Clipped. Glum. Harsh.

God, I just want her in my arms. To be by her side and help make this all vanish. Figure out a way to fix this for her. Make it so she never worries about someone trying to take away the most important person in her world.

Long after I empty my beer, Spartan nudges my elbow. His way of telling me he is bored and wants to go inside. I sit up from the lounger and extinguish the fire. "C'mon, bud. Let's go."

Woof, woof, woof.

Although the muscles in my face have refused to let me smile all day, this dog brings one out of me anyway. Never have I met or owned a dog like Spartan. Wild and crazy and my main man. Perfect.

And with the uncertainty revolving around Autumn, I am grateful to have Spartan to cuddle me when home. To keep me company and drive me up the wall on occasion.

I toss the brown bottle in the recycling bin then heat up a small portion of leftovers. I eat to satisfy my stomach—seeing as I have eaten next to nothing—and not my taste buds. After I clean my plate, I turn off all the lights and go to my room.

I tug my shirt over my head and toss it in the hamper. Then my socks and jeans. Spartan hops on the bed and settles where he normally sleeps when it is just us.

Statically pulling back the comforter and sheet, I slip under the covers. But as soon as I bring them to my chest, a waft of Autumn's scent hits my nose and takes residence. Her cherry vanilla perfume floats up my nose and drowns me.

And all I do is drag the bedding closer to me. Close

my eyes and inhale deeper. Picture her in the bed next to me—hair loose and framing her face as she leans in to kiss me. The warmth of her skin as it melds with mine. Her soft lips as they brush mine and take me prisoner.

I groan into the darkness as the throb in my chest expands and I fist the bedding. No matter what it takes, I will make this better. Because, *fuck,* there is no way I can live without her.

three

. . .

Autumn

HOW DOES FOUR DAYS FEEL LIKE A LIFETIME?

The whirlwind makes me dizzy. Sick to my stomach. The earth never felt this lopsided. This uneven and unpredictable. My life flipped upside down Sunday and I no longer know which way is up.

The day started out perfect. Full of warmth and love and everything I have missed out on as a woman. Waking up with Jonas beneath me in bed was nothing short of bliss. *God, I miss him*. Miss his heat and heart and whispered affection. His arms wrapped around my waist. We spent the day together like a normal couple. We enjoyed life. Simply being near each other—breathing the same air, sharing blissful smiles, and walking hand in hand.

Every facet of our weekend was sublime.

Then our bliss was stolen. Our bubble popped. Yanked out from beneath our feet and knocking us on our asses.

Leo. Fucking *Leo*.

Never have I been a violent person. Never have I sunk so low as to intentionally hurt someone. Physically, mentally, or emotionally. It isn't in my makeup. Inflicting hate makes me nauseous.

But since *Leo* waltzed back in and threatened my livelihood, threatened my sanity, I have conjured up countless ways to make him disappear from the world. Allowed my mind to adventure into some dark places.

None of the horrible ideas will come to fruition, nor will I speak them aloud, but they continue to pop up like an uninvited guest.

The funniest, nonviolent idea so far… tattooing "commitment issues" on his forehead. Or better yet, instead of his forehead, the best place is just above his dick. So every woman sees it when he strips bare. So every woman questions why. Questions him. No doubt Rex and Reznor would be up for the challenge.

Beside me, Clementine stirs and slowly wakes. And I envy this little girl right now. How she remains oblivious to what's happening with her sperm donor and the obstacle he threw our way. How she continues each day with a smile on her face and love in her heart.

And as long as there is breath in my lungs, I will keep her in oblivion. Keep her safe—physically, mentally, emotionally—from whatever tricks Leo has up his sleeve.

No matter what stresses life hands us, it should be me who loses sleep and worries about the outcome. In time, I will need to share everything with her—who her birth father is and what he is trying to do. But the time hasn't arrived. Not yet. And I plan to keep her life normal and full of the routine she knows.

Her eyes flutter open and peer up at me. "'Morning, Mama."

I love her sleepy voice. Sweet and raspy and innocent. Not a care in the world. A perfect mix of angel and groggy.

"'Morning, pumpkin. Did you sleep good?"

She nods, slow and steady. Then she stretches out her tiny hand and paints small semicircles beneath my eyes with her fingertip. Her lips turn down at the corners and sadness shadows her eyes.

"Mama, why do you look so tired?" My sweet, sweet girl.

Generally, Clementine is happy-go-lucky. Smiles and laughs and goofs off. But she has the biggest, empathetic heart. She may not understand the trials and tribulations adults deal with, but she senses when something is amiss.

"Just didn't sleep well." I bop her nose with my finger. "Nothing you need to worry about, though."

"Okay, Mama." A soft smile plumps her cheeks. "When will we see Sparty again?"

Over the last few days, I have dreaded the moment Clementine would ask about Jonas or Spartan. One of the reasons I didn't want her getting attached. Because if shit hit the fan—which it did, just not the shit I expected—she wouldn't understand why we didn't see each other anymore.

For now, as painful as it is, I just need things between me and Jonas to slow down. Dramatically. As in, press pause. For now, I need to spend all my time with Clementine. Because the possibility of Leo taking her from me seems inevitable.

Not that I will go down without a fight.

"Soon, pumpkin." And I hate how easily I make the promise to her. Hate how I don't know if I can fulfill said promise. "I have to take care of some special Mama-only tasks first. Okay?"

I love and hate how her little golden eyes narrow as she tries to read my mind. To find falsehoods in my words. I pray she doesn't. "Okay. But I really miss Sparty."

"Me too, pumpkin." I bite the inside of my cheek and smile halfheartedly. "Now, though, it's time to get up and get ready for school."

And just like that, conversation over.

Clementine and I go about our morning routine of dressing and styling and eating breakfast. Thankfully, she doesn't mention Spartan again. Before long, we hop in the car and drive toward her school. She bops and sings to the music and I savor every moment from the corner of my eye. Her dark hair in a ponytail with a bandana tied around the elastic. The snug black long-sleeve top with cherry print, loose jeans, and saddle shoes. My sweet girl.

I will not lose her. I refuse to lose her.

After I drop Clementine off and watch her enter the school, I drive to the appointment I have dreaded all week. An appointment with a family law attorney.

After being served Monday morning, I read through the not-so-thin packet of paperwork. Overwhelmed doesn't remotely cover the whirlwind spinning in my head. I am no idiot, but legal jargon is not a language I speak. It was easy enough to decipher Leo requested sole custody of Clementine. The rest of the documentation was jibber-jabber.

Parking in the lot, I stare up at the building and read the large placard on the wall. *Theresa Chang, Esq. Family Law Attorney serving the community for over 20 years.*

Twenty-plus years has to count for something, right? No one flourishes and stays in business if they have no idea what they are doing. God, I hope so.

I double-check I have the folder of documents tucked in my purse, take a deep breath, then exit the car.

After setting an appointment over the phone, the receptionist gave me a rundown of what today's appointment would entail and what I needed to bring. My sole wish is this attorney will be the one to represent me. Time and money are tight. Bad enough I have to shell out thousands of dollars to deal with Leo in the first place. I don't need to waste any of the limited time I have.

The building is a subtle gray with large white pillars along the front, giving an outward appearance of a small courthouse. Two large oak trees shade majority of the building while ferns surround the trunks. An array of colorful flowers planted in large terra-cotta pots sit near the entrance and give an inviting vibe to an otherwise daunting structure. For a law office, it holds enough charm to appear less unnerving.

I fist the strap of my purse tight, take a deep breath,

and stroll toward the entrance as I mumble self-assurances to settle my nerves.

Two feet from the door, I freeze and stare at the handle as if the metal will scald my skin. A delusion that holds no truth, but since Sunday evening, most of my thoughts have been a mishmash of chaos. How could they not be? Anyone in my shoes would freak out. Scream and tug at their hair. Ask why this was happening. Hell, plenty of people would behave much worse. Turn physically violent.

But I rein it in. I have to. For Clementine.

I clench my palms then release the tension and stretch my fingers straight again. You got this. No one will take Clementine from you. No one. Just breathe.

For days, this has been my mantra. What has kept me moving forward every time I want to crawl in a hole and wither. Fingers crossed this attorney will give me good news. I *need* good news.

Reaching out, I clasp the handle and open the door. *See, Autumn. Nothing to fear.* I step inside and meet the gaze of a young man behind the reception desk. His short blond curls bouncy. Periwinkle button-up undone at the collar. Bright smile on his face as he sits taller and faces me.

"Good morning. How may I help you?"

I step up to the counter. "Good morning. I have an appointment with Ms. Chang. Autumn Rooker."

He reads the computer screen and clicks the mouse a few times. He nods then faces me again. "Yes, Ms. Rooker. If you'll have a seat, Ms. Chang will be with you in a moment. Feel free to grab some water, coffee, or tea."

I thank him and amble over to the waiting area, taking a seat and foregoing the drink. Last thing I need is to fill my bladder then excuse myself in the middle of my appointment. Not only would I embarrass myself, I would probably pay for it—literally—since most attorneys are paid via time put into the case. Every minute counts. Every minute costs.

I weed through a handful of junk emails on my phone before I hear my name called. "Ms. Rooker?"

I lock my phone and shove it in my purse, then look up to meet a petite Asian woman. Her long black strands up off her neck and swirled into a prestigious bun just above the base of her skull. Although she appears of similar height, she stands taller. Fearless. Formidable. Her black pantsuit with an ivory silk top screams *powerful woman* and immediately boosts my confidence. She extends her hand.

"Theresa Chang. Thank you for waiting."

I shake her hand and rise from my seat. "Autumn Rooker. Thank you for seeing me on such short notice."

She guides us down a short hall and steers us into a conference room. At the opposite end of the room, a floor-to-ceiling window illuminates the room. Outside the window, plush green shrubs and colorful flowers add to the view. A hint of shade from one of the oak trees balances the bright morning sunlight. A large, refurbished oak table with a small potted plant in the middle occupies the heart of the conference room. The ivory walls decorated with framed art that has nothing to do with law and everything to do with family. A watercolor of a woman at the park pushing a child on the swings. A photograph of two men side by side, each of them holding a baby. Hand-drawn crayon pictures of stick figure families. And so much more.

My eyes blur. Pulse turns wobbly. Breath comes in jagged bursts.

I chose the right woman for the job.

"Have a seat Ms. Rooker and we'll get started."

Over the next hour, Ms. Chang—who insists I call her Theresa—reviews the documents I received. She asks several questions regarding me, Clementine, and Leo. After our thorough discussion, she addresses the financial end of things—which is hefty, but not as bad as I originally expected. All in all, the appointment wraps up with me less stressed and a strong woman standing at my side. A woman who has every confidence we will walk away from this better than before it began.

After I pay the retainer fee and sign documents to allow Theresa to start the proceedings, I walk out the door and unlock Betsy. I start the car and crank up the heat while I gather myself. For the first time since Sunday with Jonas, I smile. Not one worthy of awards, but a smile nonetheless.

Dealing with this lawsuit won't be easy. Fortunately, I found a woman who will fight to the bitter end beside me. Her confidence the exact boost I needed. And now, it's time to share the good news.

I dig through my purse until I locate my phone.

Without giving any thought, I open the text history between me and Jonas and type out a message.

Autumn: Spoke with an attorney. She is optimistic I won't run into trouble.

I hit send, tuck my lips between my teeth and stare at the screen, impatiently waiting for Jonas to respond. Glancing at the time, I remind myself he is at work and might not be able to answer. But as the thought crosses my mind, the indicator bubble pops up.

Jonas: Glad to hear. How are you?

He doesn't seem upset. Thank god. I have put him through the wringer since this started. And I worried my putting distance between us would upset him. Without a doubt, I'm sure he misses me as much as I miss him.

Autumn: Better now, but still a little frazzled. I miss you.
Jonas: Miss you too, scarlet.

As soon as the term of endearment flashes on the screen, I audibly exhale. With everything going on, I have been so laser focused on how to handle things with Leo. Meanwhile, I dropped all interaction with Jonas. Granted, I did it because I thought it was the appropriate thing to do. But Theresa told me to live life as we have been. Knowing Jonas still holds me close to his heart is a major relief.

Autumn: Can we have dinner tomorrow?
Jonas: Definitely. Mine or yours?
Autumn: Your house. Clementine misses Spartan. And you.
Jonas: See you tomorrow, scarlet.

Four days have passed since I last saw Jonas. Four very long, painstaking days. I miss him on an unhealthy level. A therapist would undoubtedly tell me this. Doesn't matter, though. Can't tell your heart what to feel. It also isn't wise to deny your heart what it wants. Even if what your heart desires may hinder your future.

Theresa told me to live life how I had been. And I want to. More than anything.

But something niggles at my subconscious. Tells me Leo will use my life and how I spend my time as a weapon. Hold it over my head and taunt me.

Sure, several factors of my relationship and history with Clementine weigh in my favor, but Leo—and his family—have money. More money than fathomable. If Leo wants something bad enough, he will have no issue paying the "right" person to get the job done.

I toss my phone back in my purse, grip the steering wheel, and take a deep breath. I stare at the jagged bark on the old oak tree and lose focus. Taking this fraction of time for myself, I let my thoughts roam free.

How do I live life normally? Is there a way to blend

how life was before I dated Jonas with us being together? A middle ground.

The last thing I want is to alienate Jonas—and Spartan—from my and Clementine's life. In such a short period, they mean so much to us both. But I also don't want to become complacent. Don't want to rely on the assurances of my attorney—not that she isn't brilliant, but I haven't seen her in action yet—especially when the livelihood and well-being of my daughter is on the line.

Middle ground. At least for now.

Somewhere in the middle is better than nowhere at all. Right?

four

. . .

Jonas

For the first time all week, the workday doesn't feel forty hours long.

I cash out the final customer of the day, walk them out, and give my practiced business goodbye. Once they drive off, I lock the office door and join Dad in the garage as we close everything up for the night. Currently, we stow one vehicle as we work on extensive repairs, but most of our recent clients have been easy same-day jobs.

As I stash the last of the tools in bay one, Dad coughs to get my attention.

After Monday, I have kept to myself most of the week. Conversations with me have been nonexistent. I arrive at work, spend fifteen or so minutes in the office, work until lunch, sleep on the couch at lunch, then work until the garage closes. I mind my own business and only speak when absolutely necessary. Today may have been the only exception. I probably spoke a few more sentences. And I blame it all on the fact I will see Autumn and Clementine soon.

I glance over my shoulder at Dad but don't say anything. His cough was intended to get my attention. Attention does not equal spoken words.

"How're you holding up?"

I shrug. "Been a rough week. Haven't seen my girls since Sunday night. But they're coming over for dinner tonight, so…" I trail off and finish my task.

Unexpectedly, Dad sidles up to me and hugs my side. "Sorry you're having a rough patch. And I know you don't want to talk about it. But if that changes, you know we're here for you."

The Thompson family unit. Although all adults, we are a tight-knit bunch. We stand by each other no matter what. Mom and Dad instilled that in us. Even at their most annoying stages, Jasmine and Jillian have always been there when I needed them. Have given me the female perspective I sometimes require. And vice versa.

"Yeah, Dad. When Autumn is comfortable with me sharing, I'll explain."

Dad gives me another hug, this one front facing and more constricting than an anaconda. And I let him squeeze the air from my lungs as I revel in the love he passes on. And for a brief moment, I close my eyes and embrace him with equal fervor. Then he pats me on the back and releases me.

"Just keep reminding yourself everything will work out in the end. All you need to do is be there for her, however possible. Now get out of here and go home. I hear you have a date with two special ladies."

A small smile curves up one corner of my mouth. "Thanks, Dad. Tell Mom I say hello. Have a good weekend."

"Will do. You too."

After I strip out of the coveralls, I throw on my jacket, zip it up, and hop on the bike. Helmet on, I spark the engine to life and drive home. The road mild with traffic as the wind whips the exposed skin between my helmet and collar. I don't move to raise my collar and shield my neck. Instead, I let the bite remind me I am alive. Not only alive, but that I also get to see my girls tonight.

My girls.

Fuck, I have missed the hell out of them. Autumn's cognac eyes and natural radiance. Clementine's boisterous tendencies and sweet laughter. The way Autumn holds me close and breathes me in as if she never will again. How Clementine has full-blown conversations with Spartan as if they speak the same language.

Saying I miss them doesn't seem sufficient enough. More like an afterthought or brush-off. No, being apart from them has me missing a piece of myself. A huge piece. An absence. And I will do whatever it takes to have them back. To make us whole.

I park the bike in the garage, set my helmet on a shelf near the door leading into the house, then head inside. Spartan immediately loses his shit the moment I set foot in the house. But this is typical, even if I leave for fifteen minutes. Spazz is his middle name.

"Chill out, I'm coming." I shut off the radio and open the door on his crate. He flies out as if a wasp stung him in the hindquarters. "Wears the fire at, little man. Come on." I point to the door that leads to the backyard. "Let's go outside a minute. Then Dad needs to get to work."

Spartan bolts outside the second I open the door. He locates the perfect blade of grass, lifts his leg, and does his business. Typically, he runs off after, but tonight he dashes back into the house. Like he knows his new best friend is coming over and he needs to prepare himself.

Me too, buddy. Me too.

Back in the house, Spartan goes to the couch and grooms himself. Suppose licking his coat clean is his form of preparation. Whatever. If it keeps him out of my hair while I make dinner, I won't complain.

I get to work on dinner. Tonight's meal will be easier than usual, so I get more time with Autumn. From the freezer, I grab a bag of waffle fries. Then grab the turkey burger patties I set in the fridge to thaw. After setting the temperatures on the oven and stove, I toss the fries on a baking sheet and take the burgers out of the package.

Once both start cooking, I grab the pretzel buns and burger toppings. I slice up tomato, onion, and pickle, then tear up a few leaves of lettuce.

Just as I close the oven door after stirring the fries, Spartan barks like a banshee. *They are here.* I turn down the burner and head to the door. The second I open it, Spartan shoves past me, practically knocking me on my ass, and runs for Clementine.

"Sparty!" Clementine hugs his neck while Spartan licks her like a fiend.

"Let's go inside, pumpkin."

"Sparty, come on. You heard Mama, let's go inside." And just like that, Spartan runs into the house with Clementine on his haunches.

I open the door farther and let Autumn pass. She looks like my girl but exhausted as hell. Maybe more drained than me. The dark half-moons under her eyes appear tattooed like permanent makeup. Her cognac irises more transparent than usual; as if the fire in them almost burned out. And her frame seems thinner, cheeks more hollow, lips less pouty.

Seeing Autumn like this wrecks me. Tears me limb from limb. Going forward, I don't care what the hell is happening, we won't spend this much time apart. Not when it slowly crushes us all.

I shut the door and turn to face Autumn. Before either of us says a word, Autumn steps into me and wraps her arms around my waist. Without hesitation, I snake one arm around her center while the other presses her close to my heart. Resting my cheek on her hair, I inhale deeply and bask in her perfume. One that has slowly faded from my sheets. One that reminded me she was here not so long ago. Time ticks on as we stand unmoving near the door. We shift to inch closer together but don't move otherwise.

Too soon, I lift my cheek from her hair and inch back slightly. Autumn peeks up, her lips a breath away from mine, and I see a hint of the fire returning to her intoxicating irises.

"Hey," I whisper, gaze locked on hers.

"Hi," she whispers back. "Missed you."

"Missed you more."

A small half smile perks up the corner of her mouth before she pushes up on her toes and presses her lips to mine. Warm and soft. Exactly as I remember.

Autumn kisses me sweetly as she curls her fingers in the cotton of my shirt. I frame her face and trace my tongue across the seam of her lips. As if we kissed thousands of times, Autumn opens up for me and tangles her tongue with mine. The kiss is slow and meticulous while we taste each other for the first time in far too long.

Far sooner than preferable, I break the kiss. Autumn slowly opens her eyes and stares up at me with hunger for something other than food. As much as I want to gift her that, now is not the time.

"Come on." I take her hand and start toward the kitchen. "Help me finish dinner."

I flip the burgers one last time and add cheese to each. Autumn gets plates from the cabinet and starts assembling toppings and condiments for everyone. Once the fries come out, we add the patties and fries to the plates and sit down to eat. Spartan whines as I go to sit, reminding me he needs his dinner too.

Over dinner, Clementine shares all the school stories I missed throughout the week. She tells me about one boy who always picks on her—says her clothes are weird or she doesn't have normal hair. I softly chuckle and tell her that is what boys do when they secretly like girls. The face she makes—as if a foul smell sits under her nose—is the cutest thing ever. Oh, how I missed my girls.

Once we finish eating, I set the plates in the sink and tell Autumn to ignore them. Clementine and Spartan get cozy on the chaise as we find a movie to watch. As the intro of *Finding Nemo* lights up the screen, I lie on the couch and create space for Autumn to lie beside me. Rather than lie with her back to my front, she settles in so we are face to face.

Minutes pass and neither of us says a word. We simply lie here and study the patterns of the others' irises. I get lost in the swirl of honey and cognac and love. Memorize the fan of her lashes and arch of her brow. Autumn leans in, lifts her hand to cup my cheek, and I close my eyes a beat before our lips connect.

The kiss is soft. Gentle. A reminder of the connection we share. It isn't lust driven. Not one ounce of it. The root of our bond is incomprehensible. Stardust and luster and vitality. An invisible force of life and love.

I break the kiss and hold her gaze. Although I could keep my lips on hers for days, I also want more than just the physical. I need to know her heart. "How are you?" I whisper-ask.

Her eyes drop to my lips as she swallows. "Better now. Until my appointment yesterday, I couldn't catch my breath. Thought everyone I loved would be stolen from me."

I lift a hand to her cheek and stroke a thumb across her more prominent cheekbone. "Won't let that happen." And I mean it. With every ounce of strength I possess—mentally, emotionally, physically—I will not let anyone hurt Autumn. Or Clementine. Ever.

"How can you be so sure?"

I lower my hand and press my palm to the left of her sternum. For a moment, I stare at my hand as it cradles her heart. "Autumn, you and Clementine mean more to me than anyone. *Anyone*." Her eyes glass over as she tucks her lips between her teeth and swallows. "No matter what obstacles pop up, I will be here to help you, to help us, overcome them."

She releases her lips as a tear rolls over the bridge of her nose and splashes on the couch. "But what if he t-takes her?" she croaks out.

Leaning in, I kiss her forehead. "Between me and you and your attorney, and probably anyone who knows you and Clementine, no one is taking her from you. No one."

"God, I want to believe it. Been telling myself the same thing since Monday morning. But every once in a while, doubt creeps in. With his money, the possibility of him pushing me hard is plausible."

I tuck fallen strands of hair behind her ear. "Scarlet, all things are possible. Even the outcome being in your favor. Although it's difficult, you have to believe you will win. Put the positivity out into the universe. You are a wonderful mother. Have done everything right by Clementine. You may not have an overflowing bank account, but money does not make a good parent. Providing a loving and safe home for them does. Making sure she goes to school and smiles and is happy, those are what matter most."

"But..."

I press a finger to her lips. "No, Autumn." I tip her chin up so her gaze meets mine again. "You are a terrific mother. Please believe it. Tell yourself you are. Make a list of why you are and read it when you doubt yourself."

She nods as her eyes drift back to my lips. I close the space between us and press my lips to hers. They taste salty and sweet like kettle corn at the state fair. I savor the taste and remind myself this sadness is only temporary. A hiccup.

As long as Autumn and I are together, we can get through anything. And we *will* get through this.

five

. . .

Autumn

Being back in Jonas's arms again is nothing short of bliss. Not even a full week passed and yet it felt as if we spent months apart. With every brush of his lips, the idea of taking our relationship slower becomes more of a challenge. With every calloused caress of his fingers along my skin, I question how I will take a step back.

Then I shut down my inquisitive mind.

We should slow down. I *need* us to slow down. Spending less time with Jonas will be difficult. But fighting to keep my daughter supersedes my personal needs. I only hope I don't let Jonas drift too far and lose him in the process.

Seven-plus years have passed since I last saw or spoke with Leo. The Leo I knew in the past also didn't remotely resemble the Leo I met last weekend.

Thinking back, I don't recall Leo as pretentious and mighty. When we were together, he held a softer side. He had yet to be influenced by the patriarchy of his family. But life changes. Who you surround yourself with alters your perception of the world. And Leo has several larger-than-life people circling him.

What do I have? A group of overprotective tattoo artists, a goofy-ass friend, and a man who will do anything for me. Who will do anything for my daughter.

Is that enough? Is my small, yet consequential, circle of people enough to go up against Leo's army. In all honesty, I don't know.

Before visiting the attorney yesterday, I spent several hours online. Searching for anything and everything on Leo. News articles focusing on him and the business he and his family own. Is business good or bad? Has he been seen with women? His dating status was vital for several reasons.

One… if Clementine did spend time with him, who else would she be spending time with? What is Leo's family like now? In our time together, he never spoke much about them and introductions never happened.

Two… is he in a long term committed relationship or does he play the field? Important because my daughter does not need to be subjected to a revolving door of playmates. And after my history with Leo, I don't picture him committing to one woman for years.

Three… what types of women does he date? Are they bitchy and pretentious? Do they like children?

Ugh!

The questions constantly trickle in. The more research I did, the more questions I scribbled on paper.

One photo of him, in particular, continues to throw gasoline on the slow-things-down-with-Jonas fire.

A professional photo of Leo alongside his father and two brothers, all wearing tailored five-piece suits that ooze money, smiling at the camera as they cut the grand opening ribbon on their fortieth luxury hotel in the state. Four-zero.

How do I compete with a family like his? How do I keep the most important person in my life when I have nowhere near the same resources as he does? His net worth is more than I will make in my lifetime.

Jonas runs the tip of his nose along the side of mine before dropping a chaste kiss on my lips. My eyes refocus and lock with his.

"What has you thinking so hard? Your cogs are in overdrive."

A brief glance over my shoulder, I check on Clementine. In her own world, she curls up with Spartan, her head on his belly. Her little fingers wiggle in his fur as she watches the movie. And I take a mental snapshot of the moment. Of her happiness with her new best friend. Of her innocence.

For as long as I am able, I want to shelter her from the case. Shelter her from all the bullshit. The last thing Clementine needs is to stress over a battle she cannot fight. Or worry about a man she has never known.

I roll back to face Jonas again. His fiery hazels lock with mine, studying every move and expression. Gauge every fissure and twitch and almost spoken word, patiently waiting for my response.

God, I have never met someone so patient. Someone who will lie beside me, unspeaking for hours, and wait. Wait for me to find the strength and courage to speak or act in my own time.

How the hell did I get so lucky?

"He's so different from how I remember him," I whisper.

"How so?"

Where do I even begin? A major gap exists between now and then. Suppose the start is as good a place as any. How else can I explain the old versus the new Leo to Jonas? Explain how we met—two people from polar opposite lives.

Taking a deep breath, I dive in headfirst. "Leo and I met at nineteen. Neither of us knew much other than high school and a glimpse of adulthood. We both still lived with our parents. Parents who forced us to attend a fundraiser in Tampa." I pause to lick my lips, small snippets of the evening flashing in my memory. "Even then, Leo had the capability to get whatever he wanted. Always the smooth talker." I roll my eyes. "Mom and Dad insisted I attend the fundraiser with them. The church mentioned the event would raise proceeds to help a fellow member with MS. Each ticket cost a fortune, but the money went to a good cause. But the major influx of money came from auctions."

I close my eyes and take slow, methodical breaths. Jonas trails his knuckles softly over my cheek. "Stop anytime you want. Please don't feel obliged to tell me everything."

Nodding, I take another second to rein in my

emotions. Meeting Leo wasn't necessarily all bad—when things were good, they were really good. Plus, Clementine wouldn't be the most astonishing part of my life if not for Leo.

Slowly, I open my eyes and study the staggering man in front of me. A man who wants nothing other than my happiness. My heart. I lean forward and press a tender, quick kiss to Jonas's lips.

"About an hour into the event, Leo approached me and introduced himself. We chatted briefly—two bored teens, forced to attend an event with their parents—before he asked me to dance." I didn't know how but agreed. It was better than sitting at the table with my parents.

"Before the night ended, we exchanged phone numbers. The first few weeks, we texted back and forth. Nothing important. Just idle chitchat. After a month, we went on our first date. He didn't ooze money then, but you could tell by his clothes and car he wanted for nothing. Not that my family was poor, but we didn't have anywhere near the same means."

I take a moment to catch my breath. To settle the bubbling anxiety beneath my diaphragm. "Anyway, we went on a date and really hit it off. One date led to another, and it wasn't long before we'd been together six months. It was close to New Year's, so we decided to celebrate. Although neither of us could buy alcohol, he had access to plenty. The both of us were so drunk, and we forwent a condom."

When I stop to gather myself, Jonas kisses the tip of my nose as his fingers toy with the length of my hair. I love his supportive nature. How he lets me set the pace while he holds me close. And the small gestures and touches to remind me he's still here.

Taking a deep breath, I mentally prepare to trudge through the ugly part of my relationship with Leo.

"A week before my twentieth birthday..." Jonas's eyebrows shoot up, silently asking the date. I chuckle. "Top secret. But I'll tell you soon." He shakes his head, kisses my nose, then gives me a nod to continue.

"A week before, it dawned on me I hadn't gotten my period since mid-December. Needless to say, I freaked out. Went to the store and bought every pregnancy test brand on the shelf, embarrassed as hell." I didn't have a job, unless you counted my measly pay from helping Dad at church, and I still lived at home. College was a bust because my parents convinced me art wasn't a notable major. The thought of becoming a mother with no future made me nauseous.

"Days before my birthday, we went on a date and I broke the news to Leo. At first, he remained quiet. Speechless. He didn't seem mad, except maybe at himself. The rest of the date felt awkward and ended sooner than usual. After that night, I never heard from him again. He either blocked me or got a new phone number. I had never been to his house, so I had no idea where he lived. By the time I pieced together he'd abandoned me—us—I told my parents. Telling them turned into a vicious cycle of one-sided conversations where they told me how disappointed God was with me. So, I packed up what mattered most and left."

As painful as I thought it would be telling Jonas this

piece of my past, I harbor no apprehension. If anything, relief enters my veins. A major chunk of burden weighing down my shoulders lifts away. Some of the ghosts from my past vanish as the hurt I subconsciously held on to releases.

"How did you meet Penny and the guys?"

I close my eyes as love blooms beneath my breastbone. Although life hadn't been easy after I left home, I wouldn't change anything. Not even the times when I questioned whether or not I'd be able to eat.

"For a week, I stayed at a shelter for women. They had resources for jobs and provided me with so much love and support. With my love for art, I read over every art-related ad first. An ad for the shop popped up."

Clear as day, I see the ad in my head. *Tattoo shop seeking artist to help draw intricate pieces.* I had never set foot inside a tattoo shop. My parents would probably have a heart attack at the mere thought of it. Which is the exact reason I applied.

"Penny worked the front then too, and I instantly fell for her spunk and I-don't-give-a-fuck mentality. She may be a year younger than me, but even then, she had her shit together. The more we talked, the closer we got. I still lived at the shelter and she found out. From that day forward, we lived together. After Clementine was born, Reznor took me under his wing and taught me how to ink."

As weeks and months passed, everyone at the shop became my family. They cared more for me and Clementine than my actual blood relatives. For a time, this ideal made me sad. But as more time passed and I learned what it's like to care for someone else, the memories of them drifted. The way I see it… their loss.

Jonas holds my gaze. Intrigue and awe and admiration spark his fiery irises. "Wow." He doesn't say another word. Doesn't need to. His wide eyes and slightly parted lips say more than enough. His wonderment has the chambers of my heart working overtime as I fall a little more for the man a breath away.

"Leo made a choice back then. Whether it was out of fear or anger or selfishness, he decided. I shouldn't be punished—again—for his decision. Neither should Clementine. And I plan to do whatever it takes to make sure he doesn't hurt *my* daughter."

Jonas snakes his arms around my waist and draws me into his chest. I fist his shirt, inhale his familiar scent, and sigh as every muscle in my body calms. This man is my mojo. My lucky charm. The only person who soothes my soul just by being in the same room. When Jonas holds me in his arms, nothing else matters.

"He won't take her from you, scarlet. A judge would have to be insane to allow it. Especially with his past taken into account and everything you have done for Clementine. You may not have forty hotels and a couple commas in your bank account, but you are an exemplary parent. You always put her first. Always. And that counts more than anything."

I gather his sentiment, hold it close to my heart, and bask in the heartfelt meaning. Our relationship may still be fresh and young, but I savor every kind word and gesture from Jonas.

During my appointment yesterday, Theresa stated the same. Just using different words. She also emphasized most mothers maintain custody of children unless deemed incompetent. The fact that Leo popped up out of nowhere is suspicious and concerning, and Theresa plans to dig up as much dirt as possible. Plans to see if there is an ulterior motive to his sudden appearance.

I snuggle closer to Jonas and breathe in the peacefulness he exudes. Let it fill my lungs and add life to my veins. With each passing minute, I feel more serene, more at ease. My confidence may not be tipping the scales in my favor, but it certainly weighs heavier on my side now than it did hours ago.

The music indicating the end credits echoes throughout the living room. I sigh heavily as Jonas kisses the crown of my head. The last thing I want right now is the absence of Jonas's arms. Or to go home.

But a voice in my head has me hesitant to stay. Whispering ways Leo will use my relationship with Jonas against me to obtain custody of Clementine.

And how did Leo know where I live? Has he been watching me all this time? Following me? I shiver at the invasion. If that's the case, he more than likely knows where Jonas lives too. Where I work.

My stomach rolls as if I just stepped off the Tilt-A-Whirl. I swallow down the urge to vomit.

Every bone in my body opposes, but I pull away from Jonas and sit up. Rest my elbows on my knees and drop my face in my palms.

Why has this become my life? Why am I the one nauseous over being with someone I care for? Deeply.

This is horseshit. I shouldn't be made to feel guilty over wanting companionship and affection. And I shouldn't be punished—nor my daughter—for wanting more out of life.

I take a deep breath. Then another. And another. Jonas softly strokes up and down my spine. Soothes the pain a fraction. Again, I hate that we have to leave. But I suck it up and sit taller.

"Pumpkin, we need to head home."

Clementine snuggles closer to Spartan. "Why can't I stay with Sparty?"

"Not tonight. Maybe we can see Sparty again tomorrow."

Clementine groans and reluctantly slides off the couch. "Fine."

I watch my daughter pout as she puts her shoes on slower than any other time in her life. Occasionally acting as if the shoe doesn't fit her foot. She takes it off, loosens the laces more, then does it all over again. God, if she behaves this dramatically at seven, no telling what nonsense I will deal with when she is a preteen or teenager. Someone better rescue me.

Ten minutes later, Clementine finally has her shoes on and is ready to leave. She hugs Spartan so hard I hear him exhale. But he doesn't seem to mind. Jonas walks us out to the car. After Clementine hops in and buckles up, I start the car. As I shut the door to say good night to Jonas, Clementine mutters something about kissing and I shake my head.

Jonas tugs me close and bands his arms around my

waist. "After having you here, I don't want to let you go."

"Me, either."

"Let me know when you get home. Would love to see you tomorrow. We can talk about it in the morning."

I fist the back of his shirt before leaning away and tipping my head back. Without hesitation, Jonas lowers his lips to mine and kisses me breathless.

In the kiss, he tells me how much he cares, how he will be at my side through thick and thin, and how we will get through this together. I match his fervor and pray he is right. Pray this ordeal with Leo ends quickly. That Clementine remains with me and comes out of this whole scenario unscathed.

Our lips break apart and Jonas places one last kiss on my nose. "'Night, scarlet. Talk to you in the morning. We'll plan the day then."

I nod, opening the car door. "'Night. Talk to you in the morning." And I almost slip up. Almost drop the *L*-bomb, but catch myself as I duck into the car.

Jonas closes my door and pats the roof. After buckling my seat belt, I throw the gearshift in reverse and back onto the street. Jonas waves and waits for us to drive off before going into the house.

I thought I should slow our relationship down, but I haven't the slightest idea how. And if I am honest with myself, I don't want to slow down. Quite the opposite, actually. The urge to sprint forward screams from every corner of my mind.

But the dark cloud that is Leo hovers over me with

threats of robbing me of my joy. A joy no one can replace.

What the hell am I supposed to do? Standing at the proverbial fork in the road, I ponder which direction to take. As I steer the car left, I pray to whoever listens.

Please let this be the right decision.

six

• • •

Jonas

Coldness jabs my elbow. I groan and tuck my elbow more securely to my side. Just as I drift off, wetness replaces the jab. Poke. Nudge. Another round of moisture.

Argh!

I bolt upright, swatting the air. Spartan grumbles when I connect with his furry chest. With each breath in, disorientation fades as reality comes into focus.

I'm in bed. Spartan has been trying to wake me. And I actually slept. Not the best sleep, but sleep nonetheless.

"Give me a minute, bud."

I swipe a hand over my face and widen my eyes a few times. The sun bleeds through the curtains and brightens the room more than usual when I wake. What time is it?

Scooting out of bed, Spartan jumps down alongside me and races out of the bedroom. I grab my phone from the charger and click the side button. A little after eight.

Wow. Sleeping past six thirty is a miracle on its own. Spartan doesn't always let me sleep in, but perhaps he knew I needed the extra time.

I set the phone down, shuffle out of the bedroom and over to the door leading to the backyard, where Spartan bounces like a kangaroo. As soon as I open the door, he flies out and whips across the yard. And just as quickly, he runs back in the house and bolts to his bowl, knocking it with his nose.

"You have way too much energy for me today. Maybe we'll get some playtime in later." Adding a scoop of kibble to his bowl, I ruffle his fur. He stops vacuuming his food long enough to glance up and give me his best doggy smile.

I amble back to the bedroom and flop down on the bed after snagging up my phone. I type out a text to Autumn and hit send. Clementine's energy often matches Spartan's, so I doubt she is still asleep.

Jonas: Morning, scarlet. Up and ready to plan the day whenever you are.

I head for the bathroom and go about my morning routine. While brushing my teeth, I ponder what to do with my girls today. The cooler air outside may eliminate some options, but there are still plenty of alternatives. Indoor options are endless—movies, arcade, bowling, wandering the mall, trampoline playground.

I swish and spit out mouthwash as my phone pings.

Autumn: About to eat breakfast. Give us at least 30 and come by?
Jonas: See you soon.

After a quick shower, I let Spartan out and whip up scrambled eggs and toast. Autumn said thirty minutes, but giving her and Clementine extra won't hurt.

Finished eating, I wash the dishes then grab my wallet and keys. The second he hears my keys jingle, Spartan bolts inside his crate. I hand him a treat and turn on his radio then head out the door.

I type out a quick text to Autumn to tell her I am on my way.

Cracking the window, I shiver at the breeze blowing inside the Jeep. It should reach the upper sixties today, but with the sun beaming down, it will feel closer to mid-seventies. A day at the park may be an option if my girls are up for it. Perhaps a park Clementine hasn't visited yet.

I park outside Autumn's apartment and all but dash to the door. Seconds after I knock, Clementine squeals on the other side.

"Mama, he's here!"

Clementine's boisterous, joyful nature soothes me in an unimaginable way. Her radiant smile and sweet laughter cause my heart to swell in ways I never thought possible. It's strange. That exact moment you discover you were missing this odd-shaped piece of yourself. Not the piece that completes you as a lover. But the one that makes you whole as a man.

The door swings open and my girls stand a foot

away with bright smiles warming their faces. And my heart.

“’Morning, girls.” I step inside, squat down to hug Clementine, then stand tall and kiss Autumn.

“’Morning, Mr. Jonas. Where are we going?”

Door closed, I reach down to take Autumn’s hand in mine and walk us to the couch. The simple gesture warms my skin and jump-starts my heart. This feeling —like the start of a summer rainstorm, when two energies collide and turn electric—will never get old. Will never fade away. Not for me.

“Thought I’d ask if there was anywhere you wanted to go. It’s nice outside. The park could be fun.”

Clementine bounces in front of us. “Ooh, ooh, ooh. The park, the park. Can we go to the playground?” Seriously, she and Spartan must have taken the same bouncy pill this morning.

Autumn leans into my side and I inhale her cherry vanilla scent. The fragrance hits me, and I close my eyes. Relish the perfume I have memorized. And delight in the way it relaxes every ache in my body.

“The park sounds nice. Let’s go to a different one. Okay, pumpkin?”

“Only if there’s a playground.” Clementine gives Autumn a look that states she is not to be messed with. I bite the inside of my cheek to resist laughing. Last thing I need is to provoke her sassiness, which reminds me of Dad with Lex during Wednesday night dinners.

“Promise we’ll find the perfect park, pumpkin. Go grab your jacket, just in case.”

Clementine runs down the hall to get her jacket.

Autumn spins to face me and smiles. The dark circles under her eyes not as significant today. Like mine. The luster in her cognac irises glows brighter today. Warmer. More inviting and intoxicating. Her lips perkier.

All from spending time together. One evening. Nothing extravagant. A small increment of time. Enough to see and touch and hold each other. To breathe life back in our hearts.

I reach up and caress her cheek with my knuckles. The second our skin connects, she closes her eyes, leans into my touch and sighs.

"Missed you. So much," I whisper.

Her eyes slowly open as she nods. "Me too." Autumn twists just enough to press her lips to my palm.

Clementine rushes back into the living room, jacket in her clutches and a bright, toothy smile on her face. She grabs Autumn's hand and attempts to yank her off the couch. "C'mon. Let's go!"

The mini bubble of solitude Autumn and I shared seconds ago pops as we stand. Some people would be upset at the intrusion, but neither of us minds. Every moment with Clementine is a breath of fresh air.

"We were just waiting on you, slowpoke," she says, sticking her tongue out at Clementine as she grabs her purse and jacket.

Their banter continues as we exit the apartment and load up in the Jeep. All I think as they carry on teasing each other is how lucky I am. Lucky to have found this wonderful woman. And luckier that she came with a mini version of herself. Someone who makes us both smile, even on the darkest days.

I drive through Clearwater without direction. Unsure where to go. Until an idea pops in my head and I steer the Jeep toward Safety Harbor.

Clementine bops and sings to the song on the radio in the back seat. Autumn lip syncs the rock lyrics as she looks out the windshield and draws small circles on my upper thigh with her thumb.

Nothing has felt more right than the three of us. Nothing has made my heart thump as wildly than the three of us. Me and my girls.

Twenty minutes later, I maneuver the Jeep into Phillippe Park and drive toward the playground area. As I locate a parking space, Autumn spins in her seat to face Clementine.

"Hey, pumpkin." In the rearview mirror, I see Clementine perk up. "After we play on the playground a bit, I'd like to walk around the park. This park is special and I want to share it with you."

I cut the engine and turn to face the back seat. Clementine's eyes are wide as she stares out the window and looks at the trees.

"Why is it special, Mama?"

"A long time ago, this park belonged to the Native Americans. Their homes were here. They also cherished the earth and sun here, so there's a lot of special energy here."

"Really?" Clementine's brows shoot to her hairline while her jaw slackens. Her amazement is adorable. It makes coming here more memorable and special.

"Yep. We'll look at all the special places after we play at the playground."

We unload from the Jeep and Clementine runs to play. Autumn and I locate a bench in the sun and sit. Clementine climbs the ladder and slips down the slide several times. Then she goes to one of the mini rock-climbing walls and navigates the six-foot venture. Next, she hops on a swing and hurls herself back and forth to dizzying heights.

Autumn leans into my side, loops her arm in mine, and rests her head on my shoulder. Our fingers weave together and we both sigh at the contact. Not a single word exchanged. We simply sit here, in this peaceful place, with our eyes on Clementine.

Faster than anticipated, Clementine declares she is done playing and wants to go see the special part of the park.

The three of us wander hand in hand across a grassy patch. Within minutes, we reach a stairway made of large earth-colored flat stones. The couple dozen steps wide and shaded by moss-covered oak trees. We take the steps leisurely as we observe the park from a different vantage point.

On the landing at the top of the stairs, a large story-board shares the history of the land with park visitors. We step up to the wooden sign and Autumn reads the story about the Tocobaga Temple Mound. The story of the Native American village that existed here before a conquistador arrived in the early 1500s. For a time, their cultures coexisted, but it wasn't long until European diseases caused their demise.

When Autumn finishes the story, Clementine's lips turn down as her eyes glaze over.

"That's so sad, Mama."

"Yes, it is. But many people say the energy from the Native Americans still lives here. That it gives them strength or soothes them or protects them."

Clementine peeks up at us, the skin between her brow bunching. "How?"

I squat down in front of her. "Well, the Native Americans prayed to the earth and sun and animals. Thanked them for shelter and food and life. Sang special songs to them and asked for their protection. The energy from their spirits is said to still live here."

Clementine stares off at the trees and whispers, "Wow."

Autumn takes Clementine's hand. "Come on, pumpkin. Let's walk around and see it all." Clementine nods, speechless.

We stroll without hurry down another, steeper set of stairs closer to the Bay. Every five to ten steps, Clementine stops and points to something fascinating her. A crooked tree, squirrels, birds. At a few trees, she steps up and places her hand on the bark as if trying to feel the energy. Who knows? Maybe she does. Children are more in tune with energy and the spiritual elements of the world.

When we reach the bottom of the steps, we walk along the waterway and stop to admire the Bay. I see the appeal Odet Phillippe had to owning this land in the mid-1800s. A glorious view of the water and nothing but peace.

My stomach grumbles and I press a loose fist to my belly to quiet it. Beside me, Autumn laughs as she fishes her phone out of her purse and checks the time.

"Might be a good time to grab lunch. It's almost one."

Time flies when with people who make you happiest.

It's like pulling teeth to get Clementine to leave, but she concedes when we promise to bring her back on a different day. We trek back to the Jeep, hop in, and buckle up. Since we aren't far from downtown Safety Harbor, I suggest we find a restaurant there to eat.

Soon, we walk into a pizzeria on Main and get seated. After perusing the menu, we decide to share a Sicilian pizza. But it's no shock when Autumn orders mozzarella sticks, toasted raviolis, and garlic knots for appetizers. Maybe with three of us here, there won't be as many leftovers. But let's face it, who doesn't love leftovers. My girl definitely does.

The second the appetizers hit the table, we each dive in. Surprisingly, three-quarters of the appetizers are demolished before the pizza arrives. Thank goodness we didn't order a large. I see possibly two days of leftovers in the future.

After our bellies are full and half the pizza gets boxed up, we head out and window shop Main Street.

Our county only has a handful of cute downtown districts and Safety Harbor is one of them. Most of the shops and restaurants here are locally owned. Everyone is friendly as they stroll up and down the sidewalks and visit the shops. Trees drape several sections of street and sidewalk, keeping patrons cool on summer days. Some buildings are colorful and grab your attention. Eclectic and unique, as are most of the downtown areas near us.

Clementine walks a few strides ahead of us. Her eyes scanning every storefront, eager to see what's inside.

I lean in and kiss Autumn's temple. "Today has been wonderful. Especially after seeing you last night."

"Agreed. I slept better for the first time in days."

"Would love to do our dinners again. I miss my girls."

"Miss you, too." I hear the dejection in her voice. Catch the minor twitch of her lips.

All day, I considered mentioning the party Cora and Gavin are throwing me for my birthday tomorrow. More than anything, I want to celebrate with Autumn and Clementine. But something keeps me quiet. Autumn's somber mood has me hesitant.

In all seriousness, why would she want to celebrate anything when her life feels as if it's being ripped out beneath her?

So, I don't bring up the party. As long as I get time with my girls—like today—I am happy.

"But?"

She tucks her lips between her teeth and watches Clementine as she stares inside a candy shop. "But I don't know if us being together right now will hinder things. While this case with Leo lingers, I mean. I can't lose her, Jonas," she whispers at the end.

I haul Autumn into my arms, bundle her close, and

hold her as if she could slip from my reach. "No one will take her from you. Ever."

"How can you be so sure?" I hate how small her voice sounds. Fragile and vulnerable.

I make a silent vow, once this case ends, to never let her feel this way again. To never let another person make her feel helpless or frightened. No one hurts my girls. No one.

"Call it intuition or instinct or a vibe. You have enough love surrounding the two of you to protect you for a lifetime. No way someone like him will tear it down."

Autumn takes a deep breath and fists my shirt beneath my jacket. "Hope you're right."

Clementine dashes over to us and jumps up and down. "Mama, can we get candy from there?" She points to the shop. The all-window storefront displays hundreds of chocolates and taffy and tons of other confections.

"Sure, pumpkin. But not too many."

"Yay!"

And just like that, we mosey about as if our conversation was background noise since we don't discuss Leo and the case around Clementine. I just pray Autumn doesn't continue to believe shutting herself and Clementine away from the world is the best solution.

I will never leave her side but fear she may try to abandon mine.

seven

. . .

Autumn

OUR DAY HAS BEEN ABSOLUTELY WONDERFUL. BUT ALSO offbeat.

Spending time with Jonas lifts my spirits and eases some of the agony festering in my head. In the same breath, time with Jonas leaves me exposed. Wide open to what-ifs and dreams. Unfortunately, with all the shit Leo is stirring up, I cannot afford to live in the world of what-ifs and dreams.

Jonas parks in front of my apartment. After our conversation outside the candy shop, neither of us has spoken much. He means well and speaks the truth when he says I have a small army of people ready and willing to help me. But how will my family compete against Leo? Against everything his family has to offer? Money may not buy love, but, for the right price, it buys other things—including legalities.

When he cuts the engine, Clementine unbuckles her belt. "Wish we could have dinner at Mr. Jonas's house so I can see Sparty." The blend of sadness and sarcasm in Clementine's voice doesn't go unnoticed.

I twist in my seat and half smile at my daughter. "We'll see Spartan again. Just not tonight, okay?"

She huffs in the back seat and turns away from me. Why is it every time I feel I am making the right choice—not just for me, but also for Clementine—I appear the bad guy? Yes, she has bonded with Jonas and Spartan. Their connection should make me smile like a fool. And it did until Leo popped up. Now, their connection adds another pang in my heart because I have kept them apart.

But how do I tell her it's just until the case concludes? Which, fingers crossed, won't be long. What happens if I throw in the towel? What happens if I live "normally?"

If I live life as I did before Leo made an appearance, I have a sneaking suspicion my and Clementine's relationship with Jonas will be dragged through the mud. Become tainted and damaged. With his money and resources, Leo has the ability to dig up dirt—or create his own. The last thing I want is for me or Jonas to question each other. Our pasts or some fabricated version.

Seems easier to lay low and dial our relationship down until everything passes. Theresa never gave a specific timeline as to when this would end, but the way she explained the process, I foresee it wrapping up sooner rather than later.

Would I miss the hell out of Jonas? Undeniably, yes. In such a short period of time, he has become so much more than the man I date. He has brought me back to life. And with this minor hiccup of time apart, at least we will come out clean on the other side. Or so I hope.

I peer over at Jonas; his fiery hazels stare back at me with questions. Questions I wish I had the answers to. Sentiments I hug close to my heart.

Will you and Clementine come to the house again? What can I do to help? You know you're not in this alone, right? Please, let me help. Please, don't shut me out.

Before I open my mouth and say something undesirable, I twist in my seat and exit the Jeep. As soon as I do, Clementine opens her door. I extend a hand to help her down. She glances at it briefly, ignores it, and shimmies her way down without assistance. "I'm a big girl and can get down by myself. I don't need your help."

Knife to the heart.

Once her feet hit the concrete, I reach for her hand and stop her. "Excuse me, young lady." I drop down in front of her and wait until she looks me in the eye. When she does, I see fire and heartache. "You're upset, I get it. But that is no reason to be lippy with me. Was I mean to you?"

She bites the inside of her cheek. Behind me, Jonas comes around and stands near us. His stance and energy project his agreeance with me. *Thank, god.* He doesn't say a word, but provides me with the strength to hold my ground.

"No, Mama." Clementine hangs her head. "Sorry."

"Thank you for apologizing. Sometimes emotions make us say and do things we normally don't. So, remember to think about other people before you say mean things. Words hurt too, pumpkin."

She sniffles. "I promise to think harder next time."

Rising to stand, I hold my hand out to her and she takes it within seconds. Clementine is frustrated with the wishy-washy too. One week, we see Jonas every night. Then, without warning, I strip it all away. I recognize this wasn't fair of me to do. Maybe with more time and better explanation—not today, but soon—Clementine will understand my reasons.

Inside the apartment, Clementine dashes for the room we share. More than likely, she will be in there until dinner. She apologized for her behavior but now needs solitude to understand it all.

I step into Jonas and wrap my arms around his waist, peering up at him. "Want to help me in the kitchen?" I ask, praying he says yes. My cooking isn't horrible, but Jonas cooks pasta better.

He plants a quick kiss on my nose. "Sure. Have anything in mind?" I shake my head. "Okay. Well, let's go investigate our options."

We head into the kitchen and riffle through the fridge and cabinets. Within minutes, Jonas has chicken, carrots, potatoes, onion, garlic, and green beans on the counter. After I show him where to find the pots, pans, and cutting boards, he gets to work. He puts me in charge of cleaning and cutting the vegetables to roast in the oven. Then he gets to work on cleaning and cutting the chicken into smaller pieces.

Being in the kitchen with Jonas feels routine. Right. A part of who we are. The way we move around each other. How easily life flows when we are together.

In no time, we have a pan loaded with vegetables

and olive oil, and a sheet pan covered in barbecue glazed chicken. We pop them in the oven—which I didn't realize Jonas preheated—and start cleaning up. He makes dinner seem so effortless. I would have given up sooner and probably eaten the leftovers from lunch. Or found something that required less preparation.

Once the dishes are clean, Jonas dries his hands, steps into me and draws me close. My hands automatically wind around his backside while his rest on my lower back and shoulders. And for a moment, we stand stock still. Silent. Nothing but our uneven breaths and pitched heartbeats filling the room.

I love being in Jonas's arms more than anything. Love how his warmth blankets me, protects me. Love the erratic tick of his heartbeat beneath my ear as I lay my cheek to his chest. I snuggle into him farther, not wanting this moment to end.

Which is the exact moment the voice of uncertainty in my head whittles at my happiness. Eats away at my smile. Steals the hope and joy in my heart. And I hate that I listen to it. Hate that the moment it creeps in, I drop my arms from Jonas and take a step back. That I let it overpower me. That I let it fill my head with hesitation and doubt.

"You okay?" he asks, lines marring his forehead.

I nod, although my internal voice screams *what the hell are you doing?* "Yeah. Shouldn't we check the food?" My excuse is lame, and Jonas is no fool. Since the day we pulled up to my apartment and spotted Leo, everything between us has been off-kilter.

"Set the timer." He peers around me. "Still have another five minutes before I flip the chicken."

And because I am irritated with my unsure mind, I remain tight-lipped and nod. When Jonas steps up to me again, I don't resist his embrace. But I don't give myself over to it as much as I long to. Don't melt into him. Don't clutch on to him as if my life depends on it —which is partial truth.

Until dinner finishes cooking, we hold each other in an awkward embrace. If I sense how odd the energy in the room is, he does too. But he doesn't say a word. He just holds me; his cheek resting on the crown of my head.

Dinner is quiet. Not even Clementine speaks up. The vibe while we eat is stifling.

Clementine is upset and pouts for good measure. I push food around my plate like a picky child, eyes glued to my fork. But even with my eyes downcast, I *know* Jonas is staring. I feel his gaze deep in my bones. Every other minute, he spears food on his plate in my periphery but does so blindly. When I lift my chin and catch his eyes on me, my assumptions are answered.

Before I open my mouth to stupidly ask what is wrong, Clementine speaks up. "May I be done, please?"

I glance at her plate, which is mostly clear. "Sure, pumpkin. Go pick a movie and we'll be there in a minute."

The moment Clementine is out of earshot, Jonas locks onto my eyes. "Did I do something wrong?" His voice so soft, I barely hear him. But in his tone, I decipher hurt.

Gah! I have been so worried and distracted with Leo and the case, I am already messing this up.

This is why separation—temporarily—is the best idea. Because I am screwing up the best relationship, the best man, in my life. All because I don't know how to balance our time together along with raising my daughter and dealing with an ex who gave zero shits about me or Clementine then suddenly does.

What *is* the right choice here? Feels as if there isn't one.

God, I like Jonas. Considering I almost slipped and said the *L*-word, I more than like him. He possesses every great quality I desire in a partner—kindness, affection, warmth, and he cares for Clementine as if she were his own. No matter how you spin it, I am lucky to have Jonas in my life.

But I can't stop thinking about Leo using Jonas as a weapon. What if he tells the courts I didn't give him a chance to be a father to Clementine because Jonas assumed the role? Although the idea is far-fetched, I wouldn't put it past Leo to say such things. Which is why I need my relationship with Jonas to slow down a bit. Not full-fledge stop, but ease off until I have better reassurances from Theresa.

Could the teeter-totter balance in the middle for just a bit.

"No, you've done nothing wrong. But I need you to understand how torn I am right now."

His chair scrapes against the tile before he rises and takes his and Clementine's plates to the kitchen. I follow in his wake, adding my uneaten food to a left-over container with the rest. Once all the dishes are rinsed and in the dishwasher, he spins to face me again.

"Can you please tell me what has you so divided?"

I take a deep breath and step within inches of Jonas. Reaching forward, I fist his shirt and peer up. "I feel… stuck. Like no matter what decision I make right now, it won't be the right one. If we go about things as if nothing has changed, what if Leo digs up stuff and pins us against each other."

"Autumn, I have told you about my past."

"Romantically, yes. But Leo's family can get dirty when they want something. No doubt he picked up the habit. He may not dig up something bad about either of us in the romance department, but what if you got into a physical altercation before? He may claim to the courts you have a history of violence."

"That isn't true, though."

"Yes, but his money will make it true long enough for him to win. Do you understand where I'm coming from now? Why I have been so tossed up? Jonas, I lo— care about you. A lot. And I don't need Leo ruining your life just for the hell of it."

Jonas closes the space between us and swathes me in his arms. "I care about you a lot too, scarlet." He kisses the crown of my head. "The only way he can ruin my life is to take you away from me."

Knife in the heart, twisting and digging deeper.

"Can we talk about this later? Let's go watch the movie with Clementine."

Jonas kisses the crown of my head again, then releases me. "Sure."

We weave our way into the living room and plop down on the couch. Clementine is a good twenty minutes into *The Nightmare Before Christmas* already. She lays sprawled across pillows and blankets on the floor, twirling the length of her hair around her finger. In no time, Clementine will pass out. She fights sleep by twirling her hair.

And as we do every time a movie plays while we are together, I curl into Jonas. Sometimes we spoon—his front to my back—but tonight I want to nestle into his chest. I burrow my nose where his neck and shoulder meet, and inhale his scent. A blend of working in the garage, sunscreen, and Jonas. My favorite smell.

His arms snake around my backside to press me closer while I hold on to him for dear life. Legs tangle. Breathing spikes little by little. Hearts thump, thump, thump to a vicious rhythm. But we don't move. We remain close, encased in our own little bubble of bliss.

When the familiar jingle plays for the credits, I quietly huff into Jonas's chest before separating us.

"Stay here," he says. "I got her."

I scoot to sit up. Jonas eases off the couch, crouches down, and gingerly scoops a sleeping Clementine off the floor. As he tucks her close to his chest and her little arms cling to him, I melt into the cushions. When he rises from the floor and snuggles her closer to his chest, Clementine reaches for his hair and plays with what her little fingers reach.

I stop breathing. While Jonas walks her down the hall to the bedroom, he whispers in her ear and she hugs him tighter. My heart melts and puddles on the floor. Doesn't matter what he said to her. His whispered words were meant solely for my daughter.

Jonas is so good with her. Cares for Clementine more than I ever imagined possible. More than I pictured any man caring for my daughter.

Which makes my indecisiveness that much more difficult.

A moment later, Jonas returns to the living room empty-handed. He sits on the couch beside me and picks up his shoes with hesitance. Jonas doesn't want to leave. I don't want him to leave. But until we know what type of Leo fire we need to extinguish, us sleeping apart is for the best. At least this is what I continue to tell myself.

When he finishes tying his laces, we rise from the couch as I walk Jonas to the door. We stop a foot away and Jonas closes the space between us. He brings one hand to my cheek, then the other. For a beat, he just holds me there, his gaze locked with mine. His face inches away, I swear he will kiss me any second.

He brushes the tip of his nose along the length of mine, and I close my eyes. Then his lips drop to mine. Warm, soft lips press to mine as I wrap my fingers around his forearms. His lips caress with such tenderness and devotion. Our breaths swirl in the air as we gasp between every other kiss. Then he slowly brushes the tip of his tongue over my lower lip. A shiver ripples through me before I open up and invite him in.

A hand slides into my hair while another drops to my hip and squeezes. I skim my hands up his chest, over the column of his throat, and into his hair, fisting the dark locks. We kiss until we need to come up for air. Even then, I need more of his kisses.

Foreheads pressed together, we work to settle our erratic breathing and hyper heart rates. I wish for this blissful bubble to never burst. Wish me, Jonas, and Clementine could stay in this happy place forever without disruption. But, right now, this wish won't be coming true.

I pinch my eyes closed and wish I felt confident enough to *not* do what I am about to do. Maybe I will get lucky and someone will smack the obvious against my skull. Until then, this is the only way.

"Jonas," I whisper between us. He inches back enough to see my face. To see the worry lines marring my forehead. The pain in my pinched eyes.

"Scarlet, open your eyes." It would be so much easier if I didn't have to *see* his pain when I say this. But I deserve to feel the impact. "Talk to me."

I tuck my lips between my teeth, take a deep breath, and swallow. "Until I get more details from my attorney, about Leo and any possible leverage he may hold, I think it's best we slow down more."

Jonas flinches as if I slapped him. "Slow down more? Yesterday was the first time I saw you in almost a week. After we…"

Now I flinch. I deserve the virtual slap to the face. He was going to say after we made love over the weekend. More than once.

"Please, Jonas. I can't lose her, or you. But I don't know how to navigate down this path. The only person who can guide us safely is the woman I just handed half of my savings to. And she's currently digging to find me answers. Until she does, I shouldn't jeopardize any chance I have of keeping my daughter."

Jonas drops his hands to his sides and steps back. The second step back hurts worse than the first. His eyes dart between mine, looking for any semblance of misunderstanding. When he doesn't find any, he shakes his head and takes another step back. God, why won't he say anything? His speechlessness kills me just as much as the pain smeared across his face.

He pats his back pockets before pulling his keys from the front. "I need to go," he mumbles.

"Jonas, please tell me you understand," I croak.

The longer we stand like this, the more pained Jonas appears. The backs of my eyes sting. I blink and blink, begging my eyes not to betray me while he stands here. Why did I believe this was the only viable solution? I need answers. Now. But all reasonable thought has left the building.

"Wish that was possible, Autumn." He shakes his head. I don't miss how he calls me Autumn instead of scarlet. Twist the knife a little more to the left. "Not like I have a choice. I'll be waiting in the wings. Let me know when I'm allowed to care for you and Clementine again. Hope it's not too long."

He steps around me, opens the door, and storms out. The door hangs open and I follow him with my eyes as he unlocks the Jeep, jumps in, cranks the engine, and whips out of the complex.

What did I just do? What the hell was I thinking? He's gone. Jonas is gone. And I did this.

I shut the door, lean my back against it, and slide down until my butt hits the ground. As soon as it does, a torrent of tears lets loose, soaking my cheeks and shirt.

Don't know how, but I need to resolve this mess. Quickly. I need answers from Theresa. Because this isn't like last weekend when Jonas and I parted. This isn't like after the bowling alley when I told him about Clementine.

No, this is a million times worse. And I fear I permanently messed us up. Ruined the best thing, other than Clementine, to happen to me… all because I am too scared to take a risk. Too scared to let love stand up and fight.

eight

. . .

Jonas

"DID YOU ACTUALLY PAY ATTENTION IN BODY SHOP CLASS, Ken? Or did you just watch videos on YouTube?"

Ken shrivels under my harsh criticism, but I don't give a fuck. Feels as if it has taken him ten times longer than usual to replace the rear quarter panels on the sedan he's working on.

"Jonas," Dad barks from the door leading into the garage office. "Office. Now." He doesn't wait for me to answer. Just pivots on his heel and heads inside.

I throw the wrench in my hand in the general direction of the toolbox, the metal on metal clangs and echoes off the concrete walls. Just as I open my mouth to snap at Ken again, Dad hollers from the office. "Now, Jonas."

Weaving between the cars in the bays, I head into the office. I shut the door and huff as I cross my arms. "What, Dad?" I bite out.

Dad steps up to me and points a finger in my face. "Don't you take that tone with me, son. You may be a man, but I don't deserve the shit coming out of your mouth."

I flinch, not used to hearing my father speak to me in such a harsh manner. He lowers his finger, then walks over to the couch and sits down. Eyes on me, he doesn't ask me to sit down, but his narrowed lids imply I do so. Taking a deep breath and dropping my arms, I amble over to the couch and sit.

"You need to talk to me, Jonas. I have put up with your foul mood for more than a week now. I've let some things skirt by because you are obviously upset. But yelling at the employees for no reason, I draw the line there."

I rest my elbows on my knees and drop my head in my palms. *Fuck, fuck, fuck.* I am a goddamn mess.

The last time Autumn and I truly spoke was when I left her apartment… ten days ago. After the way we left things, I haven't reached out. She texted once to say she missed me but left it at that. What did I say in return? Nothing. If she still wants to spend time with me, if she still wants our relationship, Autumn needs to be the one to take the leap. She needs to say something more than *I miss you*. Show me some indication she wants to see or spend time together.

"Haven't talked to Autumn in almost two weeks," I groan. "She said things between us needed to go slower because of her ex making an appearance and filing for custody." Beside me, Dad gasps. Not loud, but enough for me to hear. "Autumn thinks if we're together, the ex will use our relationship against her. I don't get her reasoning. And considering the guy ditched her before

Clementine was born, I don't think he has a leg to stand on."

Dad pats my shoulder. "For obvious reasons, I didn't go to law school. But after seeing how friends of ours handled divorces and custody battles, I would side with you on this. If the man has never been around, his case probably holds no weight."

I lift my head from my hands and sit up straighter, peering over at Dad. "This is what I've tried to tell her. Even her attorney said to live life as she had before he showed. There has to be something she hasn't told me. Something else about him that scares her. Which bothers me more."

"Son, all you can do is support and be there for her. Even if it's sporadic. If she hired a good lawyer, this will work itself out soon. And although she asked for distance, don't keep hiding in the shadows. Reach out to her. If she doesn't want to talk, she won't."

This has been one of my fears. After this much time apart and no real interaction, will she just shrug me off? She has handled this without me for more than two weeks since it all came to light. Does she need me for anything at this point?

"Dad, if she doesn't want to talk to me… I don't think I'll handle that well. At all. You think the last ten days have been bad?" I shake my head and leave it at that.

"I don't doubt it, son. But stop for a moment and put yourself in Autumn's shoes. Imagine all the stress and uncertainty she has to deal with right now. Until not too long ago, her life was normal and boring. She went to work and spent time with her daughter. Then you came into the picture and stirred things up." I give him the side-eye and he holds his hands up in surrender. "In a good way. But she was still adjusting to a new way of life with you, then her ex blindsides her and threatens to take away her daughter. Son, she went into protection mode. Like any good parent would do. And I attest to doing irrational things while in parent mode."

"Okay. So, how do I insert myself into her life then? I don't want to overwhelm her. But I want to be there. Right now, it feels as if I don't matter. Like she could live without me."

The more days we spend apart, the deeper the ache in my bones. I can't seem to catch my breath. And the pain in my chest grows stronger each day. Worst of all, I get next to no sleep. So, all I have is time to think. And I just want my brain to shut the hell up. Just one night.

"Text or call her. Without too much detail, tell her how you're feeling. Don't make your chat a guilt-trip. Don't make it all about you. Ask her how things are going. If she's gotten any updates." Dad clasps my shoulder. "Son, it's okay to go at her pace. Just don't lose sight of her."

I nod. *Go at her pace, but don't lose sight of her.* Got it.

We sit in the office in silence for a bit. Dad knows I am marinating on his words. Trying to absorb and digest them. Dad may not have a wall full of college degrees or any special initials after his name, but he has always been a good listener and an even better advice giver. He has the patience of a saint. Who wouldn't after dealing with us Thompson kids?

Dad claps my shoulder and stands. "Heading back out to the garage. Stay in here as long as you need. Come back out once you're levelheaded enough."

"Thanks, Dad. Be back out shortly."

Once he exits the office, I fish my phone out from my coveralls. Unlocking the phone, I open my text history with Autumn and read her last message for the millionth time.

I miss you. Same, scarlet.

I take a deep breath and poise myself to type out a text. My fingers tremble above the screen and I close my eyes and take a few more deep breaths before I type.

Jonas: Sorry I didn't answer before. Miss you too. Terribly. How are my girls?

After I hit send, I question whether or not it's okay to still call Autumn and Clementine "my girls." But as soon as the three dots dance in the gray bubble, my doubt gets shoved aside.

Autumn: Clementine is a grump. Me too. I have another appointment with my attorney Thursday. Hoping for good news.

I don't know much about attorneys and the timetables for legal matters, but two weeks have passed since Autumn last spoke with them. Shouldn't there be updates already?

Jonas: Fingers crossed. I'd love to see you. No pressure, though.

Adding the last part was painful. As if I have ever pressured her into spending time together. If anything, I have been more relaxed than most.

Autumn: Me too. I promise. Soon. Gotta go - client.

I want to text her back and say more, but I stop myself. She wouldn't see it until later anyway. Maybe I should write her another letter. Her work hours are earlier now, so I would have to either drop it at her apartment or give it to Penny or one of the guys at the shop. Maybe I will just leave it at her door.

In the meantime, I should get all the advice I can right now. With my phone still out, I open up another text history and type.

Jonas: Busy tonight?
Cora: No, what's up?
Gavin: Just watching Lord of the Rings for the 361,722,908,639th time.
Cora: Shush, mister.
Jonas: Mind if we hang? Could use some advice.
Cora: Come over when you're done with work. I'll cook.
Gavin: Eat meat ahead of time, if that's your thing.

I laugh out loud, and it feels good to smile a moment. Although my time with Cora isn't as frequent as it once was, I still remember her no-meat diet.

Jonas: Not worried about it. I'll be there a little after 5.
Cora: See you.
Gavin: It's your stomach. Later, bro.

I stuff my phone back in my coveralls and amble out of the office. Work is the last thing I want to do, but I need to pass the time with distractions. Later, I will ask Cora and Gavin the hundreds of questions brewing in my head. Hopefully, they will have answers.

After going home to let Spartan out and feed him early, I ride over to Cora and Gavin's house. At times, I still find it odd calling it *their* place.

Not a full year has passed since Gavin returned to Florida, and yet it feels as if several years have flown by. So much has happened since last April. Most of the monumental moments have occurred in the last two and a half months. In my eyes, anyway. Between Cora and Gavin getting married and me falling for Autumn and Clementine, life has been a whirlwind. And now with the custody case, seems I can't catch my breath.

I pull onto the paved driveway and park my bike behind Cora's car. Kicking the stand out, I rise off the bike and remove my helmet. For a beat, I stare at the small patio area just outside the back door. Most of the decor is small pieces Cora had before Gavin returned, but every now and then I spot new touches. Pieces that reflect Gavin's taste or their combined taste. As similar as the two of them are, I notice the small nuances after knowing my best friend for a decade.

If I get lucky, one day I will see pieces of Autumn in my life.

Taking a deep breath, I head for the back door. Although my family would be more than happy to give me advice with what's happening, my friends are what I need. People who are family, but in a different light. That have no bias because they know my childhood or want to soothe my wounds. Cora and Gavin may not have experienced the same hiccup in their relationship, but they have had hardships.

Just as I lift my hand to knock, the door swings open and a smiling Cora stands on the other side. "Hey." Without warning, she lunges toward me, grabs my hand, and hauls me forward. Her slender arms wrap around me and squeeze with unimaginable strength.

I welcome the embrace and return it. A year ago, Cora's hugs held different meaning. They once held the hope of something beyond friendship. Now, hugging Cora is like hugging Jasmine or Jillian. Full of warmth and tenderness and love, but familial.

"Hey," I say as I peel my arms away.

Gavin steps past Cora and pulls me in for a half hug and shoulder slap. "Hey, man. Come in."

My relationship with Gavin shifted quicker than imaginable. Since our conversation at Dave and Buster's, after he packed up his life in California, Gavin and I developed a slow but great friendship. Until I met

Autumn, I remained envious of him. Now, I envy the bond he shares with Cora. A bond I believe lies buried deep between me and Autumn too.

The back door closes and I step farther into the house, Cora and Gavin following in my wake. As I make it past the short hall, hints of basil, garlic, tomato, and an unfamiliar savory scent flit through the air. After I set my helmet in the living room, I join Cora and Gavin near the kitchen on one of the barstools. Cora stands at the counter, slicing up a baguette. I follow her hands as she saws the serrated knife across the crusty bread. Watch as she mixes olive oil, herbs, garlic, and parmesan.

"Want a beer?"

I snap out of my daze and turn toward Gavin. "Yeah, thanks."

He twists the cap off and hands me the brown bottle before resuming his seat beside me. "So, what's going on, man?"

I lift the bottle to my lips and sip the local brew, the flavor more bitter than I'm used to. Setting the bottle down, I pick at the corner of the label. "Did you know Autumn has a daughter?"

Gavin says "no" at the same time Cora says "yes." Well, at least I am not spilling too much if Cora knows. I assume Autumn sharing with Cora would mean it is safe for Gavin to know.

"I haven't met her," Cora states. "But Autumn has mentioned her when we hung out—just her and me."

After another sip, I take a few breaths. "Her name is Clementine, and she is the cutest little girl."

Across the counter, a soft smile perks up Cora's lips. "What a sweet name."

"Yeah," I mutter as I continue to pick at the label. "I hope you meet her soon. You'll both love her."

"Would be great. Is Clementine the reason you need advice?" Gavin asks before sipping his own beer.

I nod. "Not the only reason." Peering up from my bottle, I glance between my friends. "Also regarding Clementine's estranged birth father's return."

Cora's eyes widen at the same time Gavin's jaw drops. *My thoughts exactly.* The timer on the range buzzes and we all jump.

After Cora extracts a hefty pan of lasagna from the oven, she sets it on trivets to cool before returning to the counter. "Are they back together?" Cora asks, hesitant to hear the answer.

"No," I answer with obvious relief. "He jumped ship while Autumn was still pregnant. Now, more than seven years later, out of nowhere, he has filed for sole custody of Clementine."

"Are you serious?" Gavin stares at me with fire in his eyes. The same fire that roars in my veins every time I mull over this whole scenario. "Why the hell would anyone even give his case merit? He hasn't been around."

"Right there with you, man. But Autumn isn't looking at it the same way. She believes his family's money will hold enough ground to take Clementine away from her. So, she's trying to be the supreme model parent. Which includes spending no time with me."

Without a word, Cora rounds the bar top, sidles up

next to me, and hugs me. "So sorry, Jonas." She drops her arms and steps back. "How can we help?"

This is my dilemma. I don't know how anyone can help. Autumn is so stuck on thinking Leo will use our relationship as a weapon. I have yet to figure out how. So what if Autumn is in a relationship with someone other than the father of her child. This is not an abnormal occurrence in the world. If I were a piece of shit, then sure, it would make sense for Autumn to be concerned. But I care for my girls like no one else. They mean everything to me.

"Autumn is convinced the more I am in the picture while the case is open, the likelihood of her losing Clementine is greater. But I don't understand why. She needs someone to literally write it out that her ex has no chance of winning. And I don't know where to go from here. Dad tells me to be patient, but I'm losing it."

Cora shuffles back into the kitchen and starts portioning out lasagna for the three of us. "Do you want me to reach out to her? See if I can get a girls' day with her? Maybe she will explain her fears to me differently."

"Give it a try. Not sure she'll spend time away from Clementine, though. You may only get her on the phone."

Cora carries the plates to the dining table while Gavin brings the bread and dipping oil. I slide off my stool and join them at the table.

"I'll send her a text first. Check in. Haven't seen her since bowling, so it wouldn't seem odd for me to ask for updates. I won't mention our conversation."

I nod. "Thanks. Appreciate it."

Scooping a portion of lasagna onto my fork, I let it cool a moment before tasting it. The hot cheese melts over my tongue as I bite into something resembling meat. My brows pinch together as the flavors hit my taste buds.

"What do you think of the lasagna?" Cora poses the question with obvious curiosity.

After I swallow the bite and take a sip of my beer, I answer, "Thought you didn't eat meat?" Across from me, Gavin snickers.

"I don't."

I point my fork at the heaping square of layered pasta on my plate. "Uh, this states otherwise. Not sure if Gavin snuck it in, but there's meat in this." Now, Cora giggles and confuses the hell out of me.

"Nope. No meat. In fact, this lasagna is one-hundred-percent vegan. You like it, don't you?"

I startle with a slight shake of my head. "No denying it, but you better tell me what I'm eating before you expect me to eat more."

Gavin full belly laughs before shoveling another forkful in his mouth. Traitor. Not that I expect anything else. He loves Cora enough to eat whatever she cooks.

"Pasta, red sauce, plant-based meat, and cheese." She says the ingredients as if everyone eats them.

"And how exactly do plants equal meat or cheese?"

For the next half hour, Cora goes into a long drawn-out explanation of plant-based substitutes. Although it's not something I see myself switching to, I don't dismiss it either. If I would have eaten this lasagna anywhere else, I'd have guessed it was traditionally made.

The rest of our night is filled with light conversation and talks about upcoming projects Cora and Gavin have. And when I leave their house after watching something other than *Lord of the Rings,* I feel a little lighter. My relationship with Autumn may not be better, but sharing with my friends has helped. Plus, Cora reaching out to Autumn is perfect. Although Autumn has Penny, sometimes talking with someone outside of the situation makes a difference.

I hope it does. Hope it helps Autumn look at the case and us in a different light. That being with me won't hinder her chances. Hell, it might help.

But most of all, because I need her, maybe more than she needs me.

nine

. . .

Autumn

Swiping the dampness from my cheeks, I slip out of bed and tiptoe out of the room. I have another thirty minutes before Clementine has to be up. I intend to use the time to shower away the tears staining my cheeks.

Steam billows throughout the bathroom as I step under the hot spray. Under the stream, I cry for the umpteenth time since this nightmare began. I cry for my daughter—who has been affected in this whole scheme, although she still has no idea what is happening. I cry for the man who cares more for me than anyone, who cares for my daughter as his own, and who I have sidelined.

Damn, I miss Jonas.

I miss the way he presses me against his chest and holds me close to his heart. Miss the warmth of his lips on mine, kissing me breathless and waking up my soul. Miss the fire in his magnificent eyes and the inferno he creates when we are skin to skin. But most of all, I miss having him beside me. His strength and heart and smile.

I am sick and tired of crying. Sick and tired of being punished for someone else's choice. Why the hell am I the one who suffers in all this? Why do Clementine and Jonas have to suffer? None of us have done anything wrong. I may be far from perfect, but I am a good person. Do good things. Make good choices.

The tears stop flowing as I rinse the suds from my skin. Before the bubbles swirl down the drain, anger replaces the tears. Anger for a man who has no right to disrupt my life. To insert himself after abandoning me and his unborn daughter. Uprooting the life we have built.

I crank the shower to cold and allow the frigid water to diminish the fire boiling beneath my skin. Because I need to remain as levelheaded as possible around Clementine. Even if just for show. Once I cool down to a simmer, I shut off the water and towel dry. Wrapping the towel around my torso, I tiptoe back into the bedroom.

As I tug a shirt over my head, the alarm clock buzzes on the bedside table. Clementine groans, rolls over, and slides under the comforter, as if hiding will make the need to get up vanish. I laugh under my breath as I turn off the alarm.

"Time to wake up, pumpkin," I singsong. "Gotta get ready for school." I rub the comforter where her back is and she wiggles.

"I don't want to get up."

"Neither did I, but we both have things to do

today."

"Why can't I stay home from school today?" Clementine never stays home from school unless she feels sick, which is next to never.

"Because you can't stay home unless you're sick. Those are the rules," I remind her.

Beneath the comforter, Clementine starts coughing. "I don't feel so good, Mama," she croaks. *Nice try, kiddo.* I whip the comforter off of her and she yelps. Then, I tickle her. "Stop." Giggle. "Please, Mama. Stop." Snort laugh.

I pause the tickle fest. "Are you going to get up and get ready?"

Who knew a seven-year-old could scowl? Not me. But Clementine scowls for two beats before replacing it with another forced cough. "But I said I don't feel good."

"And you didn't mention not feeling well until I told you it was the only reason to miss school. Plus, you don't have a fever and you wouldn't be laughing if you were sick, even if I tickle you."

In the same fashion as she has for the last couple of weeks, Clementine jerks upright and storms out of the bed. She heads straight for the bathroom without a word. At least I convinced her early on to not slam the doors with Penny sleeping. My daughter may be upset, but she isn't heartless.

Once dressed, she meets me at the table to eat breakfast. I whipped up some quick cheesy eggs and toast. She sits down and eats. After a few bites, she peers up at me.

"When can I see Sparty again? He misses me."

I love how each time Clementine brings up Spartan, she mentions how he misses her and not vice versa. No doubt it holds true, but Clementine misses him more than she cares to admit. And I hate that I have separated them this long.

Yesterday, out of the blue, Cora texted me. When my phone dinged, I half expected it to be Jonas. Especially after he left another note on my car sometime between Tuesday night and yesterday morning. The note simple —*I miss you*. And I have a sneaking suspicion Cora's sudden interest in talking was sparked by Jonas. Either way, I was happy to talk with her. Penny is supportive, but she has too much inside information to give me an outsider's perspective. Which Cora did with perfection.

Our texts weren't anything spectacular, but she started it off with "heard you might need someone to talk with." An hour later and I had spilled my fears to her. In return, she told me I should share the same with Jonas if I hadn't already. Not until the end of our texts did she mention Jonas, and even then it was just that I should talk to him. Cora opted to play the neutral party to help steer us back toward each other.

"I bet he does, pumpkin. After my appointment today, I might stop by Jonas's work to talk with him." Clementine's face lights up. "But no promises." Her face falls again.

For a few minutes, we remain quiet. Clementine scrapes the fork tines across her plate between bites. After she finishes her breakfast, I take our plates to the sink and wash them. While she stomps around the apartment to grab her belongings, I ponder explaining to her why we haven't been to see Jonas and Spartan as often. She may be seven, and her little mind might not grasp all the ins and outs, but she has every right to know why everything has changed so drastically in such a short period of time.

Glancing at the clock on the microwave, I note we don't have to leave the house for another fifteen minutes. I walk into the living room and sit on the couch. Clementine should be out here in a moment with her backpack. And like clockwork, she stomps out and sits to my right.

"Pumpkin, I want to talk to you before we leave. About why we haven't seen Jonas or Spartan as much."

She peeks up with worry lines drawn across her face. "Is Sparty okay?"

"Yeah, pumpkin. He's okay." The lines on her face smooth out as she exhales. "You remember the day we came home from the beach park with Jonas and there was a man outside?"

She looks up and to the left while bunching her lips. After a moment, she nods. "Kind of."

I take a deep breath and prepare for the most adult conversation with my seven-year-old. "The man who was outside when we came home that day, he is your father." I don't use the term dad because I have always seen a dad as someone who participates and spends time with their children.

"Mama, I don't understand."

"Before you were in my tummy, I met that man. Back then, he was nice. And we spent time together like

I have with Jonas now. And after we dated a while, he became my boyfriend. When grown-up people date for long periods of time, they do certain grown-up things to show each other how much they care."

"Like what?" Clementine interjects.

Kind of walked myself into a corner with this one. "Things we will discuss when you're closer to being a grown-up. Anyway, after we showed each other how much we cared, you started to grow in my belly. But your father didn't want to be a daddy, so he stopped being my boyfriend and didn't talk to me anymore."

"He didn't love you?"

My poor sweet girl. Voice so soft and frail. If I tell her he no longer loved me, then she will assume it was her fault.

"Pumpkin, I'm not sure if either one of us really loved each other. We liked each other a whole lot, enough to make a beautiful little girl." I bop her nose. "But there are just some people in the world who don't want to have children, and that's okay. There are still plenty of other people who do."

The skin between her brows bunches. "So how come he was here that day?"

Here is the part I dread telling her, but I need to be open and honest with my little girl. "He said he wants to be your daddy." The confusion still sits on her face as she stares at me with unfocused eyes. "And he wants you to live with him and not me."

At this, Clementine jumps up from the couch and balls her little hands into fists. "He's not my daddy," she screams. "I won't let him be. I hate him." She snatches her backpack and storms to the front door, cutting our conversation off.

Penny comes out of her room, wiping her eyes. "Everything okay?"

"Peachy," I deadpan. "Tell you later." She waves and goes back into her room.

I grab my purse and head for the door. A few feet from Clementine, she unlocks the door and stomps out. Nothing like starting the day with a moody seven-going-on-seventeen-year-old. Can't wait to see her temperament when she actually gets closer to her teens.

The drive to her school lacks conversation, but at least she sings and bops to the music while staring out the window. As soon as we get to the drop-off point in the school car line, she hooks her backpack over her shoulders, grumbles out an *I love you*, and exits the car. I stare after her as she steps on campus and smiles at some of her friends. Sighing, relief fills me that she can at least smile with her friends.

Leaving the school, I steer the car in the direction of the attorney's office. Theresa said she had some updates she wants to discuss, plus a document I need to sign. After dealing with morning traffic for forty minutes, I park in front of Theresa's office. Today, the building isn't as intimidating as on my first visit.

I head inside, wait a few minutes, then am escorted back to the conference room. Over the next hour, Theresa explains how Leo holds no weight in the case. Since he intentionally left before Clementine was born, has never spent time with her or attempted to, and has never contributed to her well-being, the judge will side with us without question. Theresa assures me no amount of money will sway a decision in his favor. There is no justification or evidence to back up such a ruling.

The document I sign is for the court hearing toward the end of the month. *Sooner than expected, thank god.* I sign on the line and Theresa steps out of the room to make me a copy. During the minute of her absence, I go back and forth on an idea I have toyed with. She enters the conference room and I decide to heck with it.

"As I stated at our first meeting, I have no intention of giving up custody of Clementine." Theresa nods. "But I am okay with her meeting Leo's family, if they would like that. Supervised, of course. She would be so scared if I wasn't there."

Theresa smiles. "A kind gesture. Not many would be so nice. Not after everything you've had to deal with on your own."

"I like to offer second chances. We all make mistakes. If Leo's family would like to meet her, it's only fair of me to allow it."

"I will make note of it in your file, but we won't be mentioning this until the hearing. If we bring it up now, they may push for more."

"Sounds good. Thank you for everything you've done so far. Don't know where I'd be without you."

She offers another smile. "I'm here to help you win and relieve you of legal stresses. In the meantime, don't let this wear you down. Enjoy your life. You're an excellent mother and don't deserve any undue strain."

At this, I question my being with Jonas. Now is the

perfect time to ask the proper person. "Theresa, I have a personal-ish question."

"Shoot."

"Does it look bad for the case if I am in a relationship with someone other than Clementine's father?"

Theresa cocks her head and studies me a moment. "Why would you think that?"

At this point, I don't know. "Honestly, I wasn't sure how the court would perceive it. Leo's family has money and can no doubt provide for Clementine. I didn't know if me being in a relationship would make me vulnerable. An easy target. If they could say my time is divided and not solely focused on Clementine."

Theresa scoots the paperwork aside, laces her fingers, and sets her hands on the table as she leans in. "Autumn, you are allowed to be in relationships. Long term or short, doesn't matter. You are allowed to continue living. Allowed to be happy, as is your daughter. I encourage you to be in a relationship. Lean on someone. Share the burden of this situation. Don't take it on alone if you have others willing to stand by your side."

Several people tried to tell me the exact thing Theresa said, but an unsettled part of me needed to hear it from her. Someone who knows the outcomes of cases like mine with different variables. In her twenty-plus years of practicing, she has surely seen every possible case out there. Has fought for women with similar circumstances.

"Thank you. You have no idea how much I needed to hear that. Especially from you."

We stand and she walks me out. "Don't worry about a thing. Do what is best for you and your daughter. If that includes you being in a relationship, then you do it."

I give her a quick hug and am a bit surprised when she returns the gesture. Theresa is more than my attorney; she's a friend too. And more than anything, I am grateful to have her fighting my case.

Leaving her office, I drive down the road with a smile on my face. Minus Clementine's outburst this morning, it has been a great day. Better than the previous twelve. And I hope it continues to get better.

I make a quick stop at the sub shop Jonas and I ate at during one of his lunch breaks. After I study the menu, I order us both sandwiches. Even if I didn't remember the correct sub, he won't care. Once the food is ready, I hop back in the car and drive up the street.

As I pull in the lot of Thompson's Garage, my pulse whooshes behind my ears. My breathing morphs from a walk to a sprint. With the car in park, I close my eyes a beat and work to settle my nervous body.

Our texts have been so abrupt—my fault, if I am honest. And he was so upset when he left my apartment a couple weeks back. Will he forgive me for my irrational fears? Will he take me back with open arms?

God, I hope so.

I turn the key until the engine quiets and look over at the bays, spotting Jonas right away. His gaze locked in my direction. I swallow hard, grab the food bag, and exit the car.

Here goes nothing.

ten

. . .

Jonas

A familiar rumble echoes across the lot. The rumble any mechanic would automatically recognize as a classic car. When cars are created different ways, with different components and materials, they just sound *different*. Most newer cars are quieter—unless they have major issues or added upgrades. But classics have this low purr-like roar.

I roll out from under the pickup I work on and scan the lot. Sure enough, a black Bel Air I know all too well is parking near the office.

Rising off of the creeper, I stand, pull the red rag from my coveralls, and wipe my hands. I stare through the windshield at Autumn as she locks eyes with me. Feels as if I haven't seen her in years.

She breaks eye contact when she fetches something on the passenger seat and gets out of the car. Without a side-glance, I toss the ratchet in the general direction of the toolbox. When a loud clang rattles, I give myself a mental high five.

Autumn walks my direction—cute as fuck in a dress that makes concentrating impossible. The navy material V's at her bust, but doesn't dip too low. It hugs all her curves and stops at her knees. Large white buttons start to curve from her left hip to the base of the fabric at her midline. White accents the base of each sleeve, the neckline, and the waist. And like a cherry on a sundae, two houndstooth bows rest near her shoulders.

Not sure if this is her dressy look—since she had an appointment with her attorney—but I love it.

I meet her halfway. "Hey, scarlet," I whisper. "Happy to see you."

She smiles and my heart hiccups. "Brought us food." She swings a bag in the air.

I glance back at Dad and he tips his head toward the office. "Let's go inside." She nods and I direct us to a more private place to talk.

Once we reach the office, I strip out of my coveralls. "Jonas, what…" Before she gets another word out, I wrap my arms around her and breathe her in. She drops her purse and the bags of food to the ground and winds her arms around me, squeezing me as if I may disappear any minute.

We stand like this—unmoving, not a word spoken—for minutes. Autumn presses her ear to my chest and listens to my heartbeat. With one hand around her waist, I stroke the length of her hair with the other. I close my eyes and rest my cheek on the crown of her head. Breathe slow and steady as I reacquaint myself with her perfume, the feel of being in her arms, her warmth. Everything about this moment feels like returning home after years apart. No matter what, there is no way in hell we are spending so much time apart again. I may have said as much last time, but I don't care. She means too much.

"God, I've missed you," I whisper.

Her arms squeeze me tighter as she fists the back of my shirt. "Me, too. So much."

I lean away and she tips her head back, her cognac irises swirl as she soaks me in. Without hesitation, I lower my lips to hers. As soon as our lips meet, I am home again. Every tear, every spit of anger, every hair pulling moment since I last saw her disappears. Wiped away with the press of her lips.

The kiss isn't lusty or intense but expresses every emotion we experienced in our time apart. Deprivation. Anticipation. Hope. Love. It spins in the air, surrounds us, like a gyroscope.

Reluctantly, I break the kiss and press my forehead to hers. "Can we please not torture ourselves like this again?"

Autumn lays her palm on my cheek and strokes her thumb over my stubble. "No more torture. Promise."

I exhale and pull back to look in her eyes. "Thank fuck." I kiss the tip of her nose. "Let's sit down so we can talk and eat."

After picking the food bag up from the floor, I guide us over to the couch. Rummaging through the bag, I note she went to the sub shop I took her to months ago. And she ordered the exact same sandwich I got that day. Either she has a fantastic memory or she made the perfect wild guess. Either way, I smile at the notion.

We unwrap the brown paper from our subs and dig in. After each of us has a few bites, Autumn sets hers down, wipes the hint of mayo off her lips, and faces me.

"I'm sorry for how things have been between us since all this chaos started. It wasn't fair of me to not include you. Thought I was doing right by Clementine."

I reach for her hand and hold it between mine. "You do not need to apologize for loving your daughter. For wanting the best for her. And with her father showing up, neither of us knew what the best looked like."

She nods. "True. But I have a better grasp now." Autumn tucks her lips between her teeth as her jaw wobbles. "Jonas, it has been terrifying. Not knowing what will happen from one minute to the next." Her eyes glaze over. "I had it drilled in my head that if I wasn't the picture-perfect parent—and who knows what that looks like—I would lose Clementine. And although I have always been there for her, done everything to provide for her, I feared me being with a man other than her father would look bad in the court's eyes."

I give her a minute to catch her breath before speaking. "Not to come across in a derogatory way, but why would you think they'd look down on you for being with another man?"

Autumn sighs as her head slumps an inch forward. "I don't want to get into it too much because it rehashes bad memories, but my parents would be the reason." She closes her eyes a moment and swallows. When she opens them, I see the tears ready to spill. "Long story short, my parents don't believe a woman should be with any other man except the father of her children. Most people call my parents extreme. I didn't know any different until my late teens. In their eyes, when I told them I was pregnant, I should have married Leo. Of course, I got lectured several hours a day and handprints on my cheeks for having premarital sex. Until I left."

Just wow.

Yes, I have heard of people behaving like this. Only seeing the world as one way. Expecting or assuming every man and woman lived their life in this way. But I have never personally known anyone with such perceptions. I haven't met Autumn's parents, but if I ever do—after what she just said—I don't imagine the meeting will be pleasant.

"I don't know what to say. Sorry doesn't seem appropriate."

"It's okay. You don't need to say anything. I haven't seen or spoken to them in almost eight years. But every now and again, small tidbits of how they raised me creep in and fill me with doubt or fear. Make me wonder if I made the right choice when I left their house. Eventually, I remind myself why I chose to leave and the questions and uncertainty fade. But when Leo made an appearance, it was the first time since leaving I let all their hurtful words seep back in. Let them overrule every rational thought. And I don't want it to happen again."

I want to assure her it won't happen again. Not with me supporting her. But now is not the time to make such proclamations. Not when the case with Leo still looms over her like an angry thunderstorm.

"You know I'm here for you, right?" Autumn nods. "Good. Nothing will change that. You and Clementine are my world. My girls." A delicate smile tugs at the corners of my mouth. "Just don't shut me out again. Please."

I have never been the type of man to beg or grovel, but I will do whatever it takes to keep Autumn and Clementine close. Being without them for the last couple of weeks has been torture. The sleepless nights and lack of laughter and joy. My purpose had been stolen. Robbed by someone who holds no significance in any of our lives.

Autumn shakes her head. "I won't. It's been hard dealing with all this Leo stuff. When I sat down and really thought it over, dealing with it all without you to support me is harder."

I take the sandwich in my lap and set it on the table, followed by Autumn's sandwich. As soon as they are out of the way, I scoop her into my lap and just hold her. Hold her until my arms grow tired. Hold her until she melts into me and I melt into her. For as long as I live, I will never have my fill of this woman. Of the love she gives.

A soft knock raps at the door. "Come in," I grumble against Autumn's neck, refusing to let her go.

"Sorry to interrupt. We just had a few more clients pull up," Dad informs.

He won't come right out and say he needs my help.

But he needs my help. "I'll be out in a minute." Without another word, Dad exits and closes the door.

I groan against Autumn before kissing the spot where her shoulder and neck meet. "Why isn't the workday over yet?" I grumble.

Light laughter shakes Autumn's frame and I lean away from her. She lifts her hands to frame my face and leans in. Her lips close enough to kiss. "Soon." Eyes open, she closes the space between our mouths and presses our lips together.

Her intoxicating eyes locked on mine while we kiss makes me dizzy. In the best way.

"Come over tonight. Have dinner at the house. You and Clementine. Spartan has been a mess without his new favorite person."

Autumn laughs. "Clementine keeps telling me Spartan misses her, and not the other way around. Although I know she misses both of you. And yes, we'll come over tonight."

I grab Autumn's hips and slowly shift to stand, planting her on her feet. Then I kiss the hell out of her. Kiss her like oxygen feeding the flame. Kiss her to make up for all the kisses we have missed ever since this fiasco began. And as much as I don't want to stop kissing her, I do. Because I am at work and she probably needs to go to work too.

"See you tonight, scarlet." I kiss the tip of her nose. "Let me walk you to your car."

We wrap up the rest of our uneaten sandwiches, put mine in the fridge and hers in the bag. Then I walk her out. On the way to her car, I catch Dad smiling as he fakes busywork. Somehow, he knew everything would work out. I had doubts, probably because my emotional scale went from jovial to freaking out in point-five seconds.

Everything is better now. I have my girls back. In my arms. And no one will take them away again. No one.

eleven

. . .

Autumn

ALL IN ALL, TODAY HAS BEEN BETTER THAN ANY DAY IN THE last few weeks.

When I picked Clementine up from school, her pouty face dwindled slightly when I told her we were going to Jonas's house tonight. She wouldn't show or admit it, but this news made her day better. Knowing she would see Spartan later, that she would get to cuddle with her favorite furry friend, made a smile tug at the corners of her mouth.

The first question out of her mouth was why we couldn't see them before, but can now. I didn't have a short answer for her, so I just told her I needed my friend—meaning Theresa—to assure me everything would be okay. For the first time ever, Clementine rolled her eyes.

And I gave her a one-time pass.

On the drive to Jonas's, I work to wipe away the discontent Clementine has felt through all this.

"Blinding Lights" by The Weeknd comes on the radio and I crank up the volume.

Usually, she sings at the top of her lungs and dances in her seat when the song plays. At one point, she tried to convince me to make a TikTok video with her to this song. Didn't happen, of course. I hope to get a little bit of her typical energy going. And she doesn't disappoint. Clementine doesn't belt the lyrics out like usual, but she sings loud enough for me to hear it and dances in her seat slightly.

A small win that I gladly take.

Before long, I park behind Jonas's Jeep. The second we exit the car, Spartan starts yipping from inside the house. *He really has missed Clementine.*

Clementine bolts to the front door as fast as her short legs will take her. "I'm here, Sparty. I'm here." Just as she reaches the door, it flies open and Spartan attacks her with slobbery dog kisses. And my little girl giggles and giggles. The most perfect sound in the world. A sound I missed these last weeks.

When I reach the door, Jonas looks up from the Spartan-Clementine hugfest and smiles. "Hey, scarlet." He takes my hand and tugs me into his chest, hugging me as if we hadn't seen each other earlier. And I welcome every second of it. "Come on, let's go inside."

We head inside and go separate ways—Clementine and Spartan to the couch while Jonas and I go to the kitchen. The simple routine something I more than missed. While Clementine whispers to Spartan on the couch, catching him up on all the stories he hasn't heard over the last two weeks, Jonas and I cook dinner.

"What's on the menu tonight?"

A smile kicks up Jonas's lips. "Thought I'd keep it easy tonight. Pizza."

Across the open floor plan, Clementine hoots. "Yay for pizza!"

"Dad told me about a new take-and-bake place that opened. We'll see how it is. Clementine…" Jonas calls across the room to her and she perks up. "I got you a four cheese pizza. Hope that's okay."

"She loves all cheese," I mention.

Clementine scowls at me a second before looking at Jonas and smiling. "Cheeses is my favorite. Thank you, Mr. Jonas."

"You're welcome, cutie." After Clementine focuses her attention on Spartan again, Jonas turns to me. "What just happened there?"

I purse my lips. "Caught that, did you?"

"Kind of hard not to."

"She's been upset with me for days." Understatement of the decade. Upset doesn't begin to cover how Clementine has acted. I don't blame her, but it also means she has become very much attached to Spartan and Jonas. In some respects, I love the idea of her connecting so easily with them. But I fear the worst if something bad happens. "Today hasn't been as bad since I told her we were coming over."

"Sorry you've had a teenage seven-year-old on your hands." He leans against the counter and pulls me to stand between his legs. "Hopefully the dramatics fade soon, now that we'll see each other more."

"Fingers crossed."

The timer buzzes and Jonas checks the pizzas. As soon as they are out of the oven, the air fills with the delicious scents of cheese, bread, and herbs. After they cool a moment, Jonas cuts the pizzas and sets them on the breakfast bar.

"Time to eat, pumpkin."

Clementine huffs, walks from the couch to the breakfast bar, then pulls out the stool on the far end. She doesn't say a word before she swaps the pizzas—hers and Jonas's. In the past, Clementine sat between us. But she is still upset, and her payback is to not sit next to or acknowledge me unless absolutely necessary.

After Jonas feeds Spartan, we all sit down to eat. Dinner is quieter than any previous time. Part of me worries my former decisions have screwed up my relationship with Jonas. As if he hears my wayward thoughts, he nudges me with his elbow. I peek up from my pizza and meet his gaze. He shakes his head.

"Your thoughts practically scream from your head. Stop. It'll be okay."

"Maybe we should both talk with her after dinner. Since I seem to be the enemy, maybe she'll listen to you."

He nods. "Good idea. Better to nip this in the bud now."

I swoon a little at how effortless it is for Jonas to want to speak with Clementine. How he assumes a fatherly role with her without overstepping. How he wants the best for her—for us—and has no issue doing whatever it takes to make it happen.

We finish eating our pizza in amicable silence. When

Clementine finishes, she hops down and runs back to the couch. After Jonas and I clean up our plates, we join her in the living room.

"What movie are we watching, Mr. Jonas?"

"Not sure. Before we watch a movie, your mom and I need to talk with you."

She rolls her eyes and I lose it. Although this entire ordeal has been nothing but painful, I don't deserve to be treated as the villain in all this.

"That's enough, young lady." Clementine's eyes go wide. "The eye rolling stops now. It's rude and disrespectful."

She crosses her arms over her chest. "Well, you haven't been very nice either."

I have to remind myself that Clementine is seven and not an adult. The way she reacts to situations will be different than me or Jonas. Juvenile. All her little mind knows is I took away someone she cared about, and it hurt her feelings. I take a few deep breaths and calm my nerves.

"Yes, I have made some choices that have upset us all. And I apologize."

Jonas rubs his palm over my thigh. "Clementine, your mom did what she thought was best for you at the time. She didn't know another way yet. Now she does and we can be together more. But you have to stop being mean and hurtful. Being that way will only make everyone stay upset longer, and we want to be happy." Jonas's tone is gentle and nurturing.

Clementine looks between me and Jonas, unsure. She wants to believe him. Wants to believe he wouldn't tell her lies. But after all the back and forth over the last few weeks, it's like grasping at air. My poor girl.

I did this to her. Let her get close to someone. Someone I care about deeply. Then I pulled the rug out without warning. Left her in the dark because I didn't want to burden her with topics a young child shouldn't have to worry about. But it still didn't work. I still messed up. My only hope is it won't take long for her to smile at me again.

"But what if that man takes me away?"

Twenty-four hours haven't passed since I went into a better explanation about Leo to Clementine and she is already worried about the outcome of the case. A burden I did not want for her.

I scoot closer to her and, thankfully, she doesn't back away. "You know all those appointments I've been going to, pumpkin?" Clementine nods. "Those are so I can talk to my attorney friend, Theresa. When I saw her today, she gave me good news." At this, Clementine leans an inch closer. Eager to hear more. "She said because I have been such a good mom and your birth father has never seen you, the judge will let you stay with me." Partial truth. Still have to wait until the judge puts his seal of approval on the paperwork. But Clementine doesn't need semantics. "We just have to wait for the special meeting later this month. But Theresa also said it's okay for you and me to be with Jonas and Spartan. Before, I didn't know if spending time with them would make it harder for you to stay with mommy."

All of this is a lot for Clementine to process, but I

need for her to understand that I haven't done all these things to be mean. Being apart from Jonas hurt us too. Since seeing him earlier today, after agreeing to not be apart again, the ache I experienced since this whole nightmare started has lessened.

I may not *need* Jonas to get through this, but I want him by my side. Without effort, he makes me whole. Lifts me up and keeps me standing strong. Has my heart beating vigorously. My lungs flooding with oxygen. He gives me life.

After a moment, her eyes dart between me and Jonas. "Okay, Mama. Can we watch a movie now?"

"For a little bit. Not too late. We still have to get up early tomorrow." She nods.

And just like that, the conversation ends. We turn on the television and find something to watch on Netflix.

Jonas and I curl up on the couch facing each other. Neither of us says a word, we just lie there, get lost in each other's eyes, exchanging the occasional touch or kiss. Everything about the moment feels right. Meant to be.

Before long, the show ends and I decide it's time to head out. Not that I want to. More than anything, I want to stay in this house, crawl between Jonas's sheets, and never leave. But not tonight. Probably not tomorrow either. But hopefully soon.

Clementine hugs Spartan and whispers in his ear before letting go. As we walk to the door, a smidge of her sulkiness lingers. But this version is much more tolerable.

Jonas walks us out to the car. After Clementine is in

her seat, I start the car and turn the heat on low. "We'll go in just a minute," I tell Clementine. She nods and turns up the radio. Good sign.

With Clementine situated, I close the door and face Jonas. He wraps his arms around me and hugs me tight. "Come over again tomorrow. Feel like we have so much time to make up for." He kisses the crown of my head.

"Yes, we do. And we'll be here."

Jonas brings his hands to either side of my face and holds me as if I am the most precious person in existence. He lowers his lips to mine and lights a fire under my skin as he kisses me senseless. No matter how much time passes, I will never get enough of Jonas. Not his hugs. Not his kisses. Nor his love. Call me addicted, I don't care. All I know is, Jonas is the only person who has completed me. Made me whole. A better version of myself. And I don't want another day without him in my life.

Jonas breaks the kiss and inches back. "Text when you get home."

"I will. See you tomorrow."

"Tomorrow…" And I swear he wants to say more. I see it linger in the air. But he bites his tongue.

Me too, I say to myself. Because I swear Jonas was just about to say he loves me.

twelve

. . .

Jonas

"NOT SURE WHAT HAPPENED YESTERDAY, BUT IT'S GOOD TO see a smile on your face again," Dad says as I stroll into the office early.

For the first night in weeks, I slept without disruption. Yesterday, the stars in my and Autumn's constellation realigned. Everything wasn't back to before Leo made an appearance, but I don't imagine it will be exactly that way again. If I had to guess, I would say our relationship will be better. Stronger. More potent and appreciated.

After our time apart and the heartache we both endured, neither of us will take our relationship for granted. We will cherish it more. Every touch—big or small—will hold more meaning. Every kiss will have deeper sentiment.

"Autumn and I had a lengthy discussion after her appointment at the attorney's office. The attorney gave her the reassurance she needed to be comfortable in our relationship while dealing with her ex."

Dad sets his pen down on a stack of invoices. "Glad to hear things are on the upswing. We all enjoyed meeting her and Clementine. Hope to see them again, when the dust settles."

I brew a pot of coffee and bring the cream and sugar to the desks. "Me too. She loved meeting everyone."

Once the brewer finishes, I pour a mug for us both and sit at my desk. The stack of paperwork on my desk has gotten taller and taller with each day I didn't see or hear from Autumn. Thank goodness I am not in charge of billing, otherwise we would be too far behind. My job is to file away invoices for record keeping. No big shake. Usually finish the prior day's paperwork before the garage opens each morning. But seeing as how I haven't filed paperwork for several days, I may be spending my lunch breaks playing catch up.

I use every minute possible before the garage opens to file invoices. When the time comes to roll up the bay doors, Dad and I head out to the garage.

One after another, customers clamber in with their vehicles. Oil changes. Tire replacements. Dent removal. Windshield replacement. The day whizzes by. The entire time, a painful smile stretches across my cheeks. Nothing can ruin this day.

The back half of the day goes by just as fast as the morning. It boggles my mind how easily my mood changes the pace of the day.

About an hour before closing, I glance up from an engine I'm working on. A familiar white Mercedes drives into the lot and parks near the office.

How can my blood boil and turn to ice simultaneously? I set the ratchet down, grab the red rag from my coveralls, and wipe my hands as I step toward the car.

"Jonas," Dad calls from a bay over. "Everything alright?"

I tip my head toward the car. "Autumn's ex."

Dad sets down the wrench in his hand and steps closer in my direction. "What's he doing here?"

"Hell if I know. Probably stirring up shit. Seems to be his thing."

"You need me with you?"

I subtly shake my head. "No, but stay within earshot in case he causes problems."

Dad pats my shoulder. "I'm here."

Leo steps out of his pricey car wearing an even pricier suit. He scans the garage as if he doesn't see me twenty feet away. When his visual perusal stops on me, a smug grin lights his face. He closes the door and presses the fob, locking it as if someone might steal his precious car with him feet away.

Ten feet from him, I stop. The distance between us intentional. I know next to nothing about this man, but he has done nothing but piss me off and upset my girls. No telling what I will do if I get within a foot or two. So, for now, it is in the best interest of us all if I keep my distance.

"What can I help you with?" I continue wiping the oil and grease from my hands to keep my mind distracted.

He takes another step closer. I don't move. But if he gets much closer, I will have to divert him. Distance from him is best no matter what goes down.

"You need to back off."

I know he refers to my relationship with Autumn and Clementine, but I plan to play coy. "Don't know what you're talking about."

"Maybe you're as dumb as you look."

"Best if you think before you speak."

He cocks his head. "Like I said, you need to back off."

Less than five minutes has passed and I already want to punch him in the face. In my periphery, Dad takes a step forward but doesn't say a word. He will go to bat for me—and the girls—without hesitation. Dad may be a kind and forgiving man, but no one steps on him or his family.

"Well, *Leo,* seems as if you're confused." The skin between his brows bunches then relaxes. "Seeing as you have no claim."

This pisses him off. Within seconds, his posture shifts. He leans in closer. Takes another step forward. Balls his hands into fists at his sides. Curls his upper lip. "Hate to break the news, lowlife. I have more claim than you'll ever have. That little girl… she's mine." His voice climbs an octave. "And if I want Autumn again, she will be mine."

I grind my molars and breathe through my nose. I don't give a fuck what this prick says, he will never get Clementine and he was too chickenshit to stick around for Autumn. His loss. All my gain. And that knowledge alone fuels the beast within.

Throwing my head back, I laugh. When I meet his eyes again, he looks even more pissed. *Good. Asshole.*

"You may have donated sperm to the cause, *Leo*, but you have zero claim on that little girl. You lost that privilege when you left her mom high and dry. Pregnant and alone." I point my finger at him and inch closer. "Your money won't win this war. Best if you leave and crawl back in the hole you squirmed out of."

Leo's face turns a brilliant shade of red. The color nothing to do with the sun beaming down on us. He is livid. Furious I called him out in front of other people. Made a mockery of him. He should be angry—at himself. No one but himself put him in this position. He has no one else to blame.

"Best if you watch your back, lowlife. You think money can't win this war? Who knows, maybe you're right. But it sure as hell can make things highly uncomfortable. Unpredictable. Unsafe."

Now I step forward. Resist every urge inside me that says to knock him to the ground. I have to—for Autumn and Clementine. I lean in closer and laugh when he jolts back. "You threatening me? Threatening Autumn? I'd watch what I say next, if I were you."

He takes a step back. Then another. His shitty smile dons his face. "See you around, lowlife." He unlocks his car, gets inside, and drives off a moment later.

Until he is out of sight I don't move, don't breathe. Dad steps up to me and rests his hand on my shoulder, and I inhale for the first time in too long. "Go sit in the office and cool off. I'll close everything up." I close my eyes and nod. When I open them, Dad stands inches to my left. "Everything will be fine. Just keep Autumn and Clementine safe. Keep them front of mind at all times." Dad gives my shoulder one last squeeze and heads back in the garage.

I go to the office and pace. Think over how I will explain this to Autumn. She needs to know her ex is threatening people. Threatening her and Clementine. She needs to inform her attorney. No way this is acceptable or allowable, especially with the case open.

I will tell her. Later. Not yet. Not when my synapses are firing on overdrive. After I calm down and can properly articulate what just happened. Last thing I need to do is freak Autumn out after we have just returned to a better place. Either tonight or tomorrow, once I have had time to let his words simmer and digest.

Until then, though, Autumn and Clementine shouldn't be alone. Not with him tossing threats around like beads at Mardi Gras. Leo is scrawny. But who's to say he won't pay someone else to do the dirty work. Isn't that what people with money do?

I fish my phone out of my coveralls and unlock it. Pulling up the text history with Autumn, I type out a message.

Jonas: Hey, scarlet. Almost done at the garage. Any dinner requests?

We may have only just decided to pick things up where they left off, but I have to ease into asking things of Autumn.

Autumn: Breakfast sounds fun. Doesn't matter, though.

Breakfast. Perfect segue.

Jonas: What if my girls stay over and we can have 2 breakfasts together.

A minute passes while I stare at the screen. She hasn't responded yet. The indicator bubble to tell me she's typing hasn't popped up. Was it too quick for me to jump on the "stay the night" train again? Things have been off, but I don't think she has reservations about staying. Maybe the doubt her parents cause crept back in. The last thing I want is for her to slow things down again.

Before she responds, I send another message.

Jonas: No pressure. I'd just love to have my girls stay over. Think about it. I'll see you in a little while.

And with that, I leave the decision up to her. Until she answers, though, I am a live wire. Thank god, I have plenty of stuff to preoccupy my time between now and when Autumn and Clementine arrive at the house. Grocery shopping. Spartan. Dinner/breakfast.

Dad steps into the office and tells me everything is taken care of. After we strip out of our coveralls, we lock up and exit through the back. He gives me a hug and pat on the back. "Just stay levelheaded. It will all work out." I nod. "And if you need me, you better call."

"Thanks, Dad."

"Those girls are family. And Thompson's protect their own."

I love how easily Autumn and Clementine have won the hearts of my family. Even through all the craziness, Dad recognizes what I feel. That the love I have for them won't fade. And that I intend to keep Autumn and Clementine for the long haul.

thirteen

. . .

Autumn

PENNY STROLLS INTO MY BOOTH AND PLOPS DOWN ON MY chair. "What's up with you? Look like someone just shredded your favorite dress."

In all the madness, I have been a bad friend and roommate to Penny. Between my grumpy antics and Clementine's tantrums, we have to be driving her insane. If so, she hides it well.

"Jonas just asked me and Clementine to stay the night."

Her brows shoot up as she continues to smack her gum. "So, what's the big deal? You stayed over before."

True, but that was before Leo waltzed back in and trampled over my life. "Things have been off since Leo showed up. Do you think it's too soon? Again."

Penny blows a bubble and pops it. "No. You guys have it bad for each other. Plus, your attorney said to do you. Don't let *him* dictate your life, Auti. That isn't fair to you, Clementine or Jonas."

I huff, tossing the wad of paper towels in my hand

in the trash bin. Nothing about Leo returning has been fair. From the second I saw him standing next to my car, I knew nothing good would come from his sudden appearance. And no matter how I try to let it go, I continue to question why he materialized out of thin air. After no communication in years, why now?

None of it makes sense. Every sleepless night, my mind orchestrates countless possibilities as to why he wants custody of Clementine. Publicity, perhaps? But giving the appearance of a family man to the media, claiming a little girl as yours when no one has seen her previously, would pose more questions and issues than Leo probably wants. So, why?

"It isn't fair. But I just don't get it, Penny. I don't understand his motivation."

She jumps off my chair and skips around it to stand where I see her better. "Auti, maybe you aren't meant to understand. Not yet. But have patience. You have a kick-ass attorney who will dig. And if she doesn't find anything before the hearing, maybe the judge can pull out his reasoning. You have a right to know, but quit letting the whys and what-ifs rule your life. Don't give him your power."

I shift ink bottles around on the shelf in my station. Organizing the bottles then rearranging them. Anything to keep me busy while I mull over Penny's advice. She stares at me while I stall, but I don't rush my reaction or answer.

Every time the topic of Leo and the custody case comes up, it always cycles back to the same result. Everyone telling me to let the attorney do her job and for me and Clementine to go about our lives. God, am I trying. Some things are easier said than done.

But I don't want to regret missing out on life. Of being happy, of Clementine being happy. Regret will eat at my joy more than Leo.

"Guess you're right."

"Damn straight I am. And as far as staying over at Jonas's house, I say do it. You never know what will happen tomorrow, Auti. Live today, and don't have regrets tomorrow."

I throw my arms around Penny, hugging her close and squishing her more than normal. But she gives as good as she gets and has me tapping out of the hug first.

"Love you, Pen."

"Love you, too." Penny slaps my ass and winks. "Now finish cleaning up and get out of here."

Once I finish wiping my booth down and everything is back in place, I snatch my purse and say bye to the guys. Before leaving, I give Penny one last hug. "Thanks again. See you tomorrow."

When I release the hug, she narrows her eyes before tossing out another wink. "Have a good night," she singsongs.

~

"You ready to go, pumpkin?"

Clementine comes barreling out of the bedroom with a tote bag hooked over her shoulder. Shortly after I got home, and Iliana left, I told Clementine we would stay at Jonas's house tonight. Not a second after the words left my lips, she bolted from one corner of the apartment to the next. When I started packing an overnight bag for us, she asked if she could pack her own.

"Mama, I'm a big girl. I want my own bag."

How could I deny her sunshiny smile? Too much time had passed since I last saw that smile. And the fact I stole that from her stabbed me center chest.

"Yep." She pats the overstuffed bag. "Got all the goods."

"What on earth did you put in there? Looks like it weighs more than you."

She purses her lips and narrows her eyes. "My clothes, some movies, and some stuff I want to show Sparty."

I laugh under my breath. Spartan has become her brother, their bond unrivaled. "Okay. If you have everything, let's go. Jonas is making breakfast for dinner."

Clementine's eyes go wide and she scurries for the door. "Come on, Mama. Let's go."

As soon as Clementine learns the dinner menu, she rushes us. Has me shoving our bags in the back and all but snaps her fingers for me to start the car. Thankfully, it's a quick ride to Jonas's house. Music and singing pass the time faster.

I park in Jonas's driveway and cut the engine. Clementine hauls her bag from the back and bolts for the front door. I dash to keep up with her sprint. Before either of us can knock, Jonas opens the door with a wide grin splitting his cheeks. Spartan tackles Clementine with kisses. It all just feels normal.

"Let me take your bags," Jonas offers, taking Clementine's off her shoulder before holding a hand out for mine.

The start of our evening goes much the same as before. Except now, Jonas and I discover every possible moment to touch each other. In the kitchen, while we eat, when we curl into each other on the couch. His fingers sweep stray hairs off my cheek. Arms around me as he demonstrates how to cut the fruit "easier." My knees grazing his over and over as we eat our meals. And now, his fingers splayed on my belly, thumb drawing small circles, reminiscent of the movie night we shared in the park.

The movie plays on the screen, but I don't see or hear any of it.

Eyes closed, I focus on my breathing. His breathing. The rapid uptick in each pattern. From shoulders to toes, our bodies mold as one. Heat radiates off him, burning through layers of clothes, and scorches my skin. And a rhythmic cadence I memorized, one I called to mind several times while we were apart, beats fierce in his chest and thumps between my shoulder blades.

A light sheen of perspiration prickles my skin as Jonas skims his palm higher and higher, slow and steady up my abdomen. When he traces the underwire of my bra, I stop breathing. When he kisses the sensitive skin behind my ear, I grind my hips into him. Jonas exhales a soft growl, his breath hot on my neck.

"Cannot wait for this movie to end," he whisper-growls in my ear.

I open my eyes, peek at the screen before shifting my gaze to Clementine. The movie is almost over, but she is wide awake. Time to offer alternative solutions.

Rolling over to face Jonas, I bring my hand to his cheek and run my palm over the stubble. "She's still awake. Might need to put on another movie to watch, flip the lights off, and we can go to bed." He lifts his head to spot Clementine then nods.

For the last fifteen minutes of movie one, Jonas and I kiss and touch and reacquaint ourselves with simpler contact. When the movie ends, I pop off the couch. "Pumpkin, what other movie do you want to watch? Jonas and I are going to bed, but you can stay up and watch."

"The Nightmare Before Christmas." I should have known.

"You got it. Go change into your jammies while I set it up."

She jumps off the couch and bounds down the hall with pajamas in hand. While out of the room, I start up the movie while Jonas sets up the couch for her to sleep. A few minutes later, she plops back on the couch in her movie-themed pajamas with Sally on her limbs and torso. She wiggles her way under the blanket, Spartan curls up beside her, and we kiss her good night.

Jonas and I stroll back to the bedroom, hand in hand. The second the door clicks shut, the energy changes. Grows heavier. Potent. Feverish. I freeze and Jonas steps up to my backside. Hands on my biceps.

Fingers traipsing down until they weave with mine. He inches closer. Heat swirls in the air, licks my skin, and blankets me. His breath comes faster, hotter, sweeping across my neck.

He brings one of our joined hands to my abdomen and grazes the skin above the hem of my jeans. Presses me into him. Rocks his hips against my butt. I tip my head back and rest it on his shoulder. A slow moan on my lips.

"Missed you so much," he growls and trails kisses up my neck. Along my jaw. Consuming my lips.

I unweave my fingers from his and spin to face him. "Missed you more."

Pressing my hands to his pecs, I trail my palms down his chest, relishing the dips and ridges beneath my fingertips. When I reach the hem of his shirt, I fist the material and tug up. The cotton hits the floor as I lean forward and press my lips to his skin.

He hisses in the dimly lit room, hands clutching my hips as I navigate the terrain with my lips. Each clavicle, left then right. The dip at the base of his throat. Down his sternum—paying extra attention to the flesh protecting his heart. I kiss my way across his left pec, drawing circles with my tongue around the nipple before pulling it between my teeth. Mimicking the same on the right.

As my lips pop off his flesh, he tugs at my shirt and whips it over my head. Before the fabric hits the floor, his fingers tug at the button and zipper of my jeans. In a blink, we flip from hungry to famished. Hands pawing, fingers grasping, lips groping.

When the only thing separating us is underwear, Jonas guides me to the bed. Slides me toward the headboard then yanks the comforter down. He crawls up the mattress, hazels locked on my golden irises. Kisses my knee, my thigh, the waistline of my panties before trailing his lips and tongue up my center to the base of my throat. He nips at my jawline as my back bows off the bed.

My bra unfastens as Jonas trails a finger along my spine. I wiggle out of the lacy material and drop it to the floor just as Jonas takes one nipple between his lips, then the next. A firestorm rages beneath my skin. Scorches me from crown to toe. Builds. Faster. Needier.

"Jonas…" I moan, grabbing at the waistband of his underwear. "I need you inside me."

He rocks his hips and grinds his erection against my apex. His lips crash to mine and he devours me as if he will never taste me again. I shove his underwear down his legs, using my feet to push them off completely.

Jonas breaks the kiss and trails his lips down my center again, painfully slow. When he reaches my panties, inch by slow inch, he peels them away. He crawls back up the bed, locks his thermal gaze with mine, and kisses me with reverence. Cherishes me. Worships me. Then rocks his hips forward and fills me. I gasp and knead his firm glutes.

"Fuck." He rears back and rocks forward again. And again. Building a rhythm until my body remembers his girth.

He flips us over, grabs my hips, and guides me up and down his length while I flatten my palms against his chest and ride him. I pick up speed, rock my hips as he meets me thrust for thrust. Energy builds in my chest, hot and heavy and powerful. Trailing down my spine and seating low in my pelvis. It's liquid fire and hunger and lust and love. And as I dig my nails into Jonas's pecs, body rocking to a feverish rhythm, I shatter around him.

In a blink, he flips me on my back, lifts one of my legs over his shoulder and pistons his hips. His lips crash to mine and I weave my fingers through his hair, fisting the strands. He braces one hand at my shoulder while the other holds my hip, pinning me in place, hitting me deeper and deeper with each thrust forward.

And my body climbs up that mountain one more time. My breath coming in short bursts. Heart pounding. Orgasm building. Heat scorching. Body dripping.

Then my body finds oblivion. And Jonas is right there with me. Kissing me. Caressing me. Whispering how beautiful I am. Holding me in his arms. Stirring me back to life. Loving me.

And that's exactly how we fall asleep. In each other's arms. Blissfully replete.

fourteen

. . .

Jonas

Cherry and vanilla waft around me in a cloud of bliss as I wake from the best sleep in weeks.

On my back with eyes closed, I bask in the heat of Autumn's body draped over mine. Bare skin pressed to my chest and limbs. Cheek nestled between my shoulder and pec. Arm draped across my torso. Leg tangled between mine. Her soft, shallow breaths painting my skin as her chest rises and falls. Heartbeat steady beneath her breast bone pressed to my ribs.

I want to open my eyes, shift an inch or two, and memorize the lines and curves and peaks of her face while she sleeps. In the early morning light, I want to take in the shape of her brows, where they arch and end. Study her lashes as they fan out over the small area just above her cheekbone. Trace my eyes around the edges of her lips until I follow where they join in the center. Navigate the soft edges of her jawline. Regard the movement of her eyes behind her closed lids as she dreams.

But I don't dare move an inch. Don't jostle her awake. Because everything about this moment is as perfect as it should be.

As I listen to the soft cadence of Autumn's breathing, I notice it changes. Takes on a new rhythm. Grows in tempo. Her fingers twitch on my chest. Toes wiggle beneath the sheet. Jaw flexes as she licks her lips. Breasts press against my side. Hips wobble just above mine. Unhurried, she lifts her head to peek up at my face.

When she catches my eyes already on her, a brilliant smile plumps her cheeks. Seeing her like this—not a lick of makeup on her face, hair messy in every direction, lips plump and perky, irises glittery in the morning sun —steals my breath. Jolts the chambers of my heart. Robs me of every rational thought. Has me in a trance.

I return her smile as my fingertips dance up and down her spine. "'Morning."

She wiggles up my body, leans in and presses her lips to mine, slow and sweet. "'Morning. How long have you been awake?"

"Not long." I skirt my fingers up her side, from hip to the curve of her breast.

Her fingertips stroke the stubble along my jaw before she brings her lips to mine again. This kiss hungrier as she lifts her hips and straddles me. Nipples hard, scraping against my pecs. Hands planted on both sides of my face, caging me in. Her hips rock over mine, skimming my erection with her slick lips.

I take hold of her hips. Squeeze them with inexplicable roughness. Match the intensity of our kiss as I rock her core over my erection. A heatwave ripples through my body, scorching every inch of me in its wake. Dampness slickens me from root to crown. The heat converging, pooling, settling in my groin.

I bolt upright, her legs encircle my waist as her hands glide around the back of my neck, into my hair. Curling. Fisting. Tugging at the strands. I scoop my hands under her ass and lift her enough to rock back and glide the crown of my cock against her slick folds. For one, two, three strokes, I tease her entrance. On the next stroke, I lower her on to me with precision and fill her fully.

Autumn tips her head back and gasps at the feel of me inside her. Presses her breasts against my collarbones as she yanks my hair with such force, the ceiling comes into view. I don't move. Not an inch. I wait for her to let me know she is ready. Until she drops her chin, until her addictive cognac irises lock with mine.

Her fingers loosen their grip, just slightly. But I keep my head back. I stare up the column of her throat, lock on to her pulse as it pounds beneath her ear, watch her swallow and drag in a deep breath. Her chin drops lower, lower. Our eyes meet. The tip of her nose brushes the bridge of mine. Lips lock and claim. Licking, sucking, consuming.

Bundling her in my arms, I harden my hold on her and rock my hips. She moans against my tongue, down my throat, and it's a bolt of lightning to my cock.

Her fingers release my hair, ankles unhook behind me, and before I protest, she pushes me down into the mattress. Pins me, fingers digging into my skin. Grinds her hips, moves against and in time with me. Nipples pebbled. Jaw slack as soft whimpers spill from her lips. She tucks her chin, her hair falling forward and framing her face.

I bite my lower lip and groan as every nerve in my body sparks like heat lightning. The electrical current ebbs and flows. Fuses together. Slithers down my spine until it settles in my groin. Expands and pulses with each rock of her hips.

She buries her nails in my flesh as her body constricts. I flip her on to the mattress, lift her legs to rest on my shoulders, grip the back of her neck, and slam into her. Autumn tucks her lips between her teeth before turning her head and biting the pillow. One, two, three more thrusts and my vision hazes as I release. Ringing echoes in my ears as bright lights sparkle behind my lids when I slam them shut.

I release Autumn's legs and press my weight into her. Kiss her fiercely as she combs her fingers through my hair. When I break the kiss, I press my forehead to hers and breathe her in.

"God, I love waking up with you in my arms," I confess.

"Couldn't agree more." She brings a hand to my cheek and strokes her thumb over my stubble. "I don't want to, but we should probably get up. Before Clementine."

I sneak in one last kiss before leaving the comfort of the bed. Autumn sticks out her lower lip, pouting, and it is one of the cutest fucking things I have seen. She rolls on to her belly and groans into the pillow before reluctantly abandoning the bed.

"I want to take my girls out today," I declare as I shrug a shirt on.

"Oh, yeah?"

"Yep. Don't know where. Not sure what we'll do. But we should make today adventurous." Autumn giggles at my proclamation. "And cake should be involved more than once."

"Cake?" Autumn's eyes widen. "Clementine won't disagree with you."

"Lots of cake. We'll call it a belated birthday celebration."

Autumn freezes, hand hovering over the zipper of her jeans. "When was your birthday?" Her question comes out squeaky.

"Couple weeks back." Autumn's face pales as her eyes glaze over. I frame her face in my palms and shake my head. "No, scarlet. No tears. We will have plenty more birthdays to celebrate together. And I'm not upset. Just because we didn't celebrate on the exact day doesn't mean anything."

Autumn works to blink away her tears before taking a deep breath. "I promise to make it up to you."

I lean down and kiss her briefly, tenderly. "You being here, staying with me, has more than made up for missing the day."

Just as Autumn opens her mouth to rebut, the soft sound of little feet padding on the floor, followed by a knock, halts any further conversation. Autumn pats her head in an effort to tame her sex hair before opening the door.

"'Morning, pumpkin. We were just coming out to see if you were awake yet."

Clementine hugs Autumn's waist, then mine. "Sparty needs to go potty," she says as she releases me and walks out of the room.

Just like that, our morning has officially begun. The three of us—plus Spartan—in the same space feels *normal*. And I love every second of it.

After our previous visit to Phillippe Park, Clementine immediately suggested us spending the day at a park. Although I love revisiting parks, I asked her permission to go to a different location since we were celebrating my birthday. When she cocked her head and pondered, it was the cutest thing ever. But she agreed with one condition.

We have lots of cake and ice cream.

Sold!

Foraging through the garage, I locate the cooler and carry it inside. Once we are ready to go, I toss the cooler in the back of the Jeep and we all pile in. On the way to the park, we stop at the grocery store and buy subs, drinks, snacks and a small bag of ice. With everything packed in the cooler, I drive us to a nature preserve at the northeast corner of the county.

Clementine kicks her feet while she sings along with the song on the radio. She sports a pair of black wingtip sunglasses and stares out the window at the passing scenery. The closer we get to the preserve, the less buildings we see. In our part of the state, most of the land is packed with streets, malls, shopping plazas, and homes. More concrete than trees. Thankfully, though, some beautiful stretches of land have been preserved.

As I steer the Jeep into the preserve, Clementine sits up straighter. Scans the land with curious eyes. "Is this the park?"

"Yep," I say, turning down the music. "But this park is different than most parks by us."

"Why, Mr. Jonas?" I love it when she calls me Mr. Jonas.

"This park is ginormous. Bigger than any other park close by. With lots of big trees and trails to walk on and a nature center to learn about the animals."

"Will we see animals here?" she asks as her pitch bumps up.

"If we're lucky. We might see some deer or rabbits or other animals."

She gasps and stares into the passing trees. "I hope we see a deer. Would be so cool."

I glance over at Autumn and match her ear-to-ear smile. Seeing her this happy, seeing Clementine this happy, it brings new meaning to love and life and joy. Clementine may not be my daughter, but she is as equally precious to me as Autumn. *My girls*. I never knew I could be this enamored by a woman and her daughter.

As I park the Jeep, Clementine bounces in her seat, eager to jump out. We hop out and leave the cooler in the back. For the next few hours, we wander through the education center and along the trails of the preserve. The sun beats down on us and keeps us warm in the cool February air. Every once in a while, Clementine has us swing her in the air as we walk.

When our stomachs begin to rumble, I grab the cooler and we sit at a partially shaded picnic table to eat our lunch. For the most part, the preserve has minimal people here. At most, we have seen ten people. During our visit, we see one deer, a few rabbits, several squirrels, and a snake that slithers away. Clementine has been fascinated with it all.

All in all, it's been a peaceful day. Which is exactly what the three of us needed.

With full bellies and tired feet, we decide to head back to the house. But as promised, on the way back, we stop at the store to pick up cake and ice cream.

We stroll into the store and beeline to the bakery. "If I get to pick the cake, you can pick the ice cream," I offer to Clementine.

She taps her lips with a finger and narrows her eyes a moment. How can someone be this adorable? "Deal." Clementine extends her hand and we shake.

After I select a small vanilla and chocolate cake with chocolate frosting, we go to the frozen section. For the next ten minutes, Clementine studies the ice cream selection as if her decision will end a war. Autumn holds her up every other minute so she can see the higher shelves better. I don't rush them.

Instead, I stand back and observe my girls. *My girls.*

Clementine points at a container and Autumn whispers in her ear what the flavor is. Clementine shakes her head and they move down the line. This happens over and over, and yet, it doesn't bother me. Doesn't make me impatient.

If anything, I ask for more time like this. More time to bask in the joy of being a part of their lives. More time to watch the woman I care about dedicate herself to her daughter. To help her with tasks most adults consider menial. To focus on her daughter and forget everything else. Autumn is a phenomenal mother to Clementine. I envy her devotion. Having them in my life… I have never been so lucky.

After Clementine chooses, we check out and leave the store. "Happy birthday, Mr. Jonas."

I peek in the rearview mirror at Clementine. "Thank you. Hope you're ready for cake and ice cream."

She gives a confident nod. "Born ready."

Autumn laughs, slips her hand into mine over the console and squeezes. "Today has been wonderful. And it's still somewhat early."

At the red light, I meet her eyes. "Maybe we can take a nap after cake." I cock a brow.

"A nap, huh?"

I simply shrug and focus my eyes on the road again. A few minutes later, I park in the driveway and we all hop out.

In the house, Clementine tells Spartan about the preserve while we dish up cake and ice cream. And after our plates our clean, I mention napping again. Clementine says she will watch a movie with Spartan while Autumn and I take a short nap.

Once we land on my bed, I close my eyes. Although I can't see her, I *feel* Autumn observe me. "You really wanted to sleep? Interesting. Thought you were using a nap as an excuse for birthday sex."

I laugh and pull her down to the bed. "We can do that later. For now, I just want to lie here and hold you. That okay?"

Autumn snuggles into my side. "Yes, but we should set an alarm. Just in case."

After we set an alarm for forty-five minutes, we just hold each other. And for the first time since yesterday evening, I think of Leo's visit to the garage. I need to tell Autumn what happened. Not just for the sake of telling her, but also because I worry for her and Clementine both. Plus, she should forward the incident to her attorney.

Tonight, I will tell her. After dinner.

"Stay with me again tonight," I whisper against her hair. "I love having you both here."

Autumn stays quiet a moment and I wonder if she fell asleep. Until she gently fists my shirt. "Yes." She lifts her head and rests her chin on my chest. "We love being here."

I sweep a few wayward strands from her brow and tuck them behind her ear. Then lean up to kiss her. We lie in the bed until the alarm buzzes. For the rest of the day, we take it easy. We order Chinese takeout and laugh over fortune cookies, and another helping of cake and ice cream while watching *The Secret Life of Pets*.

When Clementine falls asleep, I extend my hand to

Autumn. "Come sit out back with me for a bit." She takes my hand as I lead her to the patio.

I light the fire bowl before sitting on the lounger and nestling Autumn between my legs. We stare at the flames and weave our fingers together. I close my eyes and breathe in her cherry vanilla scent, letting it center and soothe me as I muster up the courage to tell her about yesterday.

Inhale. Hold it. And exhale. I do this a few times. "Autumn," I say softly. "I need to tell you something, but don't want you to freak out."

As the words leave my lips, she locks up. Not moving for ten rapid beats. Then she breathes again and twists to look at me. "What is it?"

I swallow, trying to dampen the sudden dryness in my throat. "Leo stopped by the garage yesterday."

She sits up straighter and spins to face me full-on. "What?" she exclaims, eyes wide with fear. "Why? What did he want? How did he know where you work?"

All questions I wanted answers to as well. Honestly, I think he was looking to start a physical altercation with me to make Autumn appear bad in the court's eyes. Too bad for him, I am not a dumbass.

I relay everything that happened. How Leo flaunted his tail feathers and acted possessive. How I kept my cool but put him in his place. And how Dad stood in my peripheral the entire time and had my back. When I finish, Autumn shakes her head. Not because she doesn't believe me, but more as if she doesn't understand his sudden interest.

"Just let your attorney know as soon as possible. Sometimes, little things add up in the end."

We stay out by the fire a while longer, enjoy the quiet as our minds run wild. When I extinguish the flame, I guide us back in the house and to the bedroom. As soon as we step over the threshold, I pull Autumn into my arms.

"In here, we don't talk about anything but you and me and, occasionally, that little girl in the other room." I trace along Autumn's jaw and tip her chin up. "Okay?"

She nods. "Yes." Pressing up on her toes, she leans in and kisses me. On her next breath, she says, "Let's go to bed." And I let Autumn guide me to the bed as we peel away our clothes.

fifteen

. . .

Autumn

Jonas snores softly beneath me. His chest rises and falls in a slow, rhythmic pattern under my cheek. Palm over his heart, I fan out my fingers, tempted to draw patterns into his skin with my fingertips. But I lie unmoving, eyes closed, mind unable to shut down.

New questions run wild in my head. Questions asking what Leo aims to accomplish with his relentlessness. What is his endgame in this scenario? What is he out to accomplish? I just don't get it. If he would have stepped back into the picture within the first two years, I might have understood the desire to be a part of Clementine's life easier.

But too much time has passed. Too many circumstances in both our lives have changed. For someone who ditched me—us—without a backward glance, Leo's newfound persistence worries me. His pursuit of sole custody of Clementine is tied up with something. Something just out of my reach. And it twists my insides in a nauseating pretzel.

I *need* to learn what's behind his motivation and soon. I need the truth behind his sudden desire to be a father. Not just for the sake of knowing, but because Clementine's well-being hangs in the balance.

Curling farther into Jonas's side, I work to match my breathing pattern to his. Inhaling his unique scent, my body relaxes more. And before long, I dream about Jonas at my side until we are old and gray.

What's better than a great night of sleep? Waking up with Jonas's lips on my skin. God, if every day starts like this, I will never leave this bed.

After he ignites every inch of my skin and liquifies each molecule in me—three times—we stumble out of bed and dress. My legs are noodles walking on gelatin as we exit the bedroom and I slap a hand over my mouth to stifle my laughter.

Clementine lays curled in a semi-fetal position with Spartan as a partial pillow. But it won't be long before she wakes.

Jonas and I step into the bathroom, brush our teeth, and groom enough to not look as if we have spent the last hour trying to yank each other's hair out. I skip putting on makeup and twist my hair into a topknot.

Stepping up behind me, Jonas locks eyes with me in the mirror over the vanity. His hands secure on my hips, lips grazing the shell of my ear. "I love waking up with you in the morning. Seeing you like this." He kisses the spot below my ear, grinds his hips against my low back, then locks his gaze with mine again. "Natural and perfect and more stunning than ever."

I spin around, tip my head back, and lace my fingers at the nape of his neck. "You trying to flatter me, Mr. Thompson?"

His intense, addictive hazels lock me in place and I stop breathing. Heart thrashing against my ribcage. Limbs tingling as heat courses through my veins and sparks new life. Jonas drops his chin an inch, his lips so close I practically taste the peppermint on his tongue. He traces the tip of his nose along the ridge of mine and I stutter an exhale.

"How can I not?" he whispers against my lips. "Hope you let me flatter and compliment and kiss you every day."

I press my lips to his in answer just as a knock on the door disrupts the moment. "Are you almost done? I need to go potty," Clementine states from the hall.

"Just a second, pumpkin." I peek up at Jonas. "As long as you can handle the two of us, you may dote upon me any day of the week."

"Wouldn't want it any other way." He steps back, adjusts himself in his sweatpants, and opens the door with a smile on his face. "'Morning, sunshine."

Clementine narrows her eyes with suspicion. "Why are you both in the bathroom? That's weird."

"We didn't want to wake you while we brushed our teeth," Jonas answers without delay.

And as if his answer needs no further questioning, Clementine shrugs and relaxes her expression. "Okay. Can I go now?" She points toward the toilet.

"Sorry, pumpkin."

We scurry out of the bathroom and leave her be. Heading into the kitchen, we start our morning like a family. Jonas and I take out ingredients to make chocolate chip pancakes, cheesy scrambled eggs, and turkey bacon. We move seamlessly in the small space as if this normal task happens daily. While I whisk the eggs, he ladles batter on a hot skillet and sprinkles it with mini chips. The bacon sizzles in the oven as I pour the eggs into a pan.

Jonas deposits the first batch of pancakes on a plate, butters the skillet again, and adds more batter. Spatula midair, he glances my way. "I don't want this to come out the wrong way, but you and Clementine shouldn't be alone. Not until the case ends."

I stop scraping the eggs from left to right and peer over at him. He means well. Wants to protect me. Protect us. But if I am supposed to live my life normally, that means I will be alone from time to time. Or with only Clementine. How can I not be?

"Jonas, I get where you're coming from. I understand it. But how am I supposed to follow a regular routine—work, school, errands—if I" —I pause and take a deep breath— "we need a bodyguard all the time."

He flips the pancakes, sets the spatula down, and steps closer. I peek over my shoulder and check Clementine isn't eavesdropping. "We'll find a way. Between me, Penny, everyone at the shop, and our friends, we can make it happen. We need to." I roll my eyes and shake my head. Jonas grazes his knuckles down my cheek. "It's only temporary. And if something happens to either of you, I won't be able to live with myself."

I turn the heat on the stove to low and face him fully. His eyes bore into me, glassy and a tinge red. Concern written in the underscoring on his forehead. I snake my arms around his waist and rest my cheek over his heart. Warm arms envelop and hug me with renewed strength. "It won't be easy."

"Doesn't matter," he mumbles into my hair.

"How will we get everyone in on the plan?" A legitimate question, considering not everyone knows the details of my past.

Jonas kisses the crown of my head and releases me, stepping back to the skillet. "The shop is closed today?" I nod. "Let's invite everyone over for an impromptu cookout. We can use my birthday as the initial excuse."

Not a bad idea. The guys will definitely be down for a gathering if we involve food and drinks. Penny will get Iliana on board. The last time we all did something outside of work was too long ago. Years ago, we'd hang out a Sunday per month. Nothing special, just enjoying life and seeing each other somewhere besides the same four walls.

"Okay. After breakfast, I'll get the ball rolling with everyone from the shop. What time?"

"Is five good? We can chat a bit while I get the grill going. Eat around six."

"Should be fine. Clementine will also get to play with Ashton, Rez's little boy."

Jonas cooks the last of the pancakes while I take the

bacon from the oven. We plate up the food and sit at the breakfast bar with Clementine, sharing our plan for the day. A lazy morning, followed by house cleanup and a trip to the grocery store before having friends over. She chimes in with food she wants added to the grocery list and tells Spartan he will meet one of her friends today.

After texting our friends and watching hours of Sunday morning cartoons, we decide to vacate the couch and get to work. The inside of the house sparkles within the hour. A candle lit in the living area wafts the scent of fresh cotton around the house. Jonas goes outside to check the grill, making sure we have enough charcoal.

The trip to the grocery store goes quicker than expected, but we walk out with more than our list of items. Every time Clementine pointed to something and begged, Jonas caved and added it to the cart. Thankfully, she only did this a handful of times. She picked good things, though—s'mores making supplies, a couple movie night candies, and berries to go with our leftover cake.

Back at the house, Jonas marinates chicken and forms burger patties while I cook pasta and potatoes for salads. Clementine digs out colored pencils, crayons, and a coloring book from her stuffed overnight bad. Sneaky girl brought everything.

We finish prepping whatever possible. Every opportunity we get, Jonas and I exchange touches. A forearm graze. A kiss on the cheek as he reaches for a gadget. His front brushing against my back as he moves past me. My fingers tracing his low back as I set the strainer in the sink.

Will it always be like this? The constant need to touch each other. For me to feel his warmth and strength and love. To be near him, to see him, to smile with him. Some may consider our attachment unhealthy. Clingy. I say, when you find the person who connects all the dots perfectly, the person who makes you see the whole constellation and not just a mess of stars, do what makes your heart happy.

Yes, I pushed us apart when Leo made an appearance. But it was maternal instinct to shut everything down and protect my daughter. Little did I know, Jonas was equally willing to go to battle for her to stay. And no matter what is thrown at us going forward, I won't make the same mistake.

The doorbell chimes and snaps my attention to Clementine, who peeks out the window and waves like a loon. "People are here."

That she doesn't mention names has me heading for the window. Glancing out, I spot Cora and Gavin. Walking up the drive is Erin, Shelly, and Micah. "Those are my and Jonas's friends. The ones we went bowling with." Clementine nods.

Jonas opens the door and invites everyone in. I introduce Clementine to everyone and she gives each of them a hug. The guys loiter in the kitchen and catch up while us ladies sit in the living room. Less than five minutes pass before Clementine bolts up from her spot at the coffee table and peeks out the window. The recognizable low rumble of Reznor's car echoes outside.

"They're here," she exclaims, jumping in place. "Can I open the door?"

"Wait until they walk up, so Spartan doesn't run out."

Jonas excuses himself and joins us at the door. Clementine peeps up at me and I nod. She flings the door open and runs up to everyone, giving them hugs. I stare after her a minute, watching as she plays mini hostess. "Come on, guys. Let's go inside." She takes Ashton's hand and helps him up the porch stairs.

Once everyone steps inside, I introduce my tattoo family to everyone already here. Gavin shakes Reznor's hand and gives a more in-depth introduction to Cora. I learn Reznor inked Cora's name on Gavin's chest before I inked bands on their fingers. Small world. Reznor introduces Tatyana—his long-term girlfriend—and Ashton, their son. Before everyone settles, Jonas suggests we head out back and start grilling.

Cora deposits a small cooler on the counter and takes out a few items. When she sees me staring, she explains. "Vegan burger and sides."

"You should've said something. We would've got stuff at the store."

"No worries. Kind of used to bringing stuff when we go places." She hands the patty to Jonas and says to cook it like a normal burger.

Everyone heads out back, Spartan on Jonas's heels, praying for him to drop something. The kids share a lounger and pull up a side table to color. Spartan runs around the yard, sniffing the grass and searching for lizards. I light the fire bowl while Jonas mans the grill.

Beforehand, we brought out extra chairs from the garage, and now have more than enough seating for the large group.

The guys shoot the shit by the grill while us ladies talk on the outdoor L-shaped couch. Cora tells me about an upcoming wedding she and Erin are shooting. Erin has slowly transitioned from an assistant to a photographer over the last year. She continues to learn, but Cora is the perfect teacher. Since the change, the two of them have tweaked the business. A fresh name—Hunt-Wallace Enterprises—and new faces. They reach more clients, hired assistants, and have the ability to take time off. Cora says she couldn't do it without Erin, while Erin disagrees.

Shelly talks about the floral industry in ways I have never heard. Quotas and sales and deadlines. Sounds like a nine-to-five corporate office gig. But I suppose all industries have this. I never think of the tattoo industry like this, but I suppose Oscar—the shop owner—does. He pops in once a month to check on us but leaves us be for the most part. He owns several shops in the state but designates a manager for each location to make on-the-spot decisions. That would be Reznor for us. He keeps the shop going with ease.

Penny chimes in on occasion, but otherwise chills beside me with our arms hooked at the elbow.

Once the food is ready, we all gather around the fire bowl and eat. Smiles and laughter and shoulder bumps flow like the beer in our bottles. When people start leaning back and patting their stomachs, I glance up at Jonas and nod.

"Thanks for coming on such short notice, everyone," Jonas announces. "We brought you here under the guise of a makeup birthday celebration. While that's true, there's more to it."

All eyes turn my direction. The men with an air of concern and the women silently questioning what the hell is going on. Penny glances down at my abdomen before meeting my eyes again and I shake my head. She laughs.

"Some of you know," Jonas continues, looking to Penny before scanning the group, "and some of you don't. But Autumn's ex has started stirring up trouble." This causes Rex and Reznor to sit taller. "He filed for sole custody of Clementine and has since made verbal threats to both of us. We have maintained our cool and done everything through the appropriate channels. But it seems he is stepping up his game. So…" Jonas smiles and my favorite dimple appears. "We are enacting Operation Don't-leave-Autumn-and-Clementine-alone."

Everyone nods except the children.

"What does this look like?" Penny asks.

"Basically, someone is with them around the clock. Doesn't matter who. Even together, someone should be with them. Obviously, when here, they'll be with me."

"And with me at the apartment and work," Penny chimes in. "But if our schedules don't align, we'll sort it out ahead of time."

The conversation flows for another hour before people leave. Beforehand, we all exchange phone numbers and sort out tomorrow's schedule for now.

Since Penny rode with Reznor, Tatyana, and Ashton, she stays to ride home with me and Clementine.

We clean up the back patio and kitchen. The closer we get to clean, the tighter my stomach twists. After a wonderful weekend with Jonas, I don't want to leave. I want to crawl into bed and snuggle with him. Listen to his soft breaths as he sleeps. Fall asleep to the thumping cadence of his heart beneath my ear. Wake up to the scent of his skin and the warmth of his embrace.

But we aren't there yet. Aren't to the point where we spend several days straight in the same place. Should we be? Would it be odd this early on? Some would say yes while others would suggest there is no correct timeline.

Reluctantly, Clementine and I gather our bags and trod to the door. Penny holds out her hand for my keys. "I'll start the car so you can exchange good nights." After I hand them over, she walks to the car and starts it.

Clementine hugs Jonas around the waist. "'Night, Mr. Jonas."

He hugs her small frame. "'Night, sunshine."

She clings to Spartan a moment. "Night night, Sparty. See you soon. We can have more slumber parties." Giving him one last squeeze, she trots down the drive and gets in the back seat of the car.

"I don't want to leave," I confess, peering up at Jonas.

He pulls me into him, wraps one arm around my waist while he braces the length of my spine with the other, fingers in my hair. "Don't want you to go either.

After we figure out schedules, we'll be together more nights. Guaranteed." He kisses the crown of my head.

"Music to my ears."

We inch apart. Jonas frames my face in his palms and drops his lips to mine. He kisses me sweet at first, then traces my lower lip with the tip of his tongue. I deepen the kiss, devouring him as if I won't see him for days again. When he breaks the kiss, I brace myself on his forearms.

"See you tomorrow, scarlet."

"Tomorrow." I give him one last kiss before walking to the car.

I toss my bag in the back, then get behind the wheel. As we back out, Clementine and I wave goodbye.

A block from Jonas's house, Penny twists in her seat to face me. "I foresee needing a new roommate in my future."

I slap her arm without looking. "Shut up," I joke. But I don't fight the painful smile. Nor do I dispute her accusation. Because I see it too.

sixteen

. . .

Jonas

NOTHING LIKE STARTLING AWAKE TO A COLD NOSE AND wet tongue in your armpit.

"Argh! What are you doing?" I croak, arms flailing in a desperate attempt to stop Spartan.

Woof, woof, woof.

I peek up at the husky hovering an inch from my face. "You don't behave like this with Clementine," I accuse.

Woof, woof.

"I see how it is. Well, I'll remember this conversation next time you beg for treats."

The alarm buzzes and Spartan jumps off the bed. I slap the clock and roll into Autumn's pillow, smothering myself with her scent. Not quite the same as her in my arms, but it will make due for now.

I fall out of bed, slip on sweatpants and a hoodie, and use the bathroom before clipping Spartan's leash on. We trod out the door and walk our normal route around the neighborhood.

Five houses down, an odd sensation washes over me. A fluttery twitch in my solar plexus. I stare down the sidewalk and across the street but spot nothing out of the ordinary. When Spartan stops to sniff a mailbox, I glance behind us and scan where we came from. Being five in the morning, I don't usually see neighbors during our morning walk. And this morning is no exception as I spot nothing. But the uneasy tremble in my gut begs to differ. The sensation screams at me that I am not alone.

Unable to shake the feeling, I cut our walk short.

Back in the house, I go about my morning weekday routine. After eating a quick breakfast, I pour the pot of coffee in my thermos, grab my wallet and keys, then put Spartan in his crate and turn on his radio.

"Be good. See you later, bud." I ruffle his fur through the grate.

I lock up the house and walk to the Jeep. As I peer up and press the fob to unlock it, I notice a slip of paper pinned beneath my windshield wiper. Approaching the Jeep, I scan up and down the street for signs of anyone but see nothing odd or notable.

Once the paper is within arm's reach, I tug it out. I check the street one last time before unfolding the paper and looking down.

She doesn't belong to you.

What the actual fuck?

My fingers curl as I start to ball up the note. But before I wad the note or rip it to shreds, I take a deep breath and relax my digits. I walk to the end of my driveway and scan the street again as I stuff the note in my pocket.

I scrutinize every car along the street. Peek through the windshields for people or movement. Scan the length of the sidewalk, searching for anyone on foot. Glance up the nearby trees and stare through every shrub within a fifty-foot circumference.

Not a goddamn thing.

"Come at me, motherfucker," I growl. "You won't touch her."

Not sure who this asshole thinks he is, but there isn't a chance in hell he will lay his hands on Autumn. He is damn lucky I restrain myself from beating his ass.

I get in the Jeep and start it. While the engine warms up, I take out my phone and type a message to Autumn.

Jonas: Morning. After you drop Clementine at school, please call me.

I send the message, connect my phone to the Jeep, and drive to work.

When I step into the office, I stash away my concerns about the note for now and smile when Dad looks up. He matches it with one of his own. "'Morning, son. Glad to still see a smile on your face. How are the girls?"

"Good. We had a nice weekend together. Created a plan to make sure they're safe."

Dad rises from his desk and walks to the dish rack

to grab his mug for coffee. After mixing our morning caffeine, we sit behind our desks. "Glad you're taking care of them. Raised you right," he states with pride in his voice.

Shortly after the garage opens for the day, my phone rings. I wipe my hands and retrieve it from my coveralls. "'Morning, scarlet," I say, walking toward the office.

"Good morning. Everything okay?" Concern laces her words and I hate that I have to deliver more unsavory news.

"Are you driving?"

"No. Penny is. We just dropped Clementine off."

Once I step inside the office and close the door, I tell her about the note. "As I left for work this morning, I noticed a piece of paper under my wiper blade. It was a note." The line goes silent for too long. I check the screen to make sure the call didn't drop and see it hasn't. "Autumn?"

"Yeah, sorry." I picture her with her eyes closed, taking deep breaths. "What did it say?"

I swallow and relay the message. "When I took Spartan for a walk earlier, I felt as if someone was following me. But I never saw anyone."

"This is ridiculous," she mumbles. "Will you take a picture of it and send it to me, please?"

"Of course." At this point, I have no idea what steps we should take. But she should definitely tell someone. "Should you send it to your attorney?"

She huffs into the line, exasperated over the whole

scenario. "Probably. I don't know. When we get off the phone, I'll call her."

I don't want to upset Autumn with how I feel right now, but I refuse to hide or run from the stabbing pain in my chest. When it comes to Autumn and Clementine, everything needs to be out in the open. She needs to hear where my head and heart lie. "Autumn, please be safe. Both of you. Keep your eyes open and stay vigilant."

"I will," she whispers. "Promise."

"Thank you." I sigh. In some respects, I am glad Autumn and Clementine didn't stay over last night. They would have been witness to the note this morning and Autumn might not have been able to keep her cool in front of Clementine. Then again, maybe the note wouldn't have been there if they stayed. Who knows? "Call me back when you know more."

"Okay." Her voice travels from miles away, quiet and somber. "Talk to you soon."

The need to tell her I love her hangs from the tip of my tongue now more than ever, but I don't say the words. I want to. God, do I want to. But now feels so far from appropriate. Her thoughts are probably all over the place with worry. I don't want the first time I express my love for her to be during a moment of stress. I don't want it to be over the phone, where I cannot see her face and vice versa. Plus, I don't want her to feel obligated to return the sentiment just because I put it out there.

So I bite my tongue and project my love into the

universe in her direction. Send her every ounce of positivity and love she has stirred in my veins.

"Soon. Stay with Penny."

"I will. Bye."

"Bye, scarlet."

The call disconnects and I stand staring at the wall a moment. I zone out, close my eyes, and beg to the heavens for all of this madness to end soon.

Then I remember to take a picture of the note and send it to Autumn. Once she receives it, she texts her thanks.

I stay in the office a moment to drink another mug of coffee. When I head back into the garage, Dad catches my eye and waves me over.

"Everything alright?"

I nod. "Just more drama. Autumn is calling her attorney to figure out what we do next." I tell him about the plan for the girls to not be alone and about the note this morning.

"Keep me up to date."

I agree and amble over to the car I was working on before the call. Picking up the socket wrench, I get back to work. Thankfully, I can work on the engine without one-hundred-percent focus. Because my mind is far from this garage. My arms mentally around Autumn as we navigate through this nightmare.

seventeen

. . .

Autumn

"WHAT'S GOING ON?" PENNY ASKS WHEN I GET OFF THE phone with Jonas.

I huff and drop my head back on the seat. "Jonas found a note on his car this morning." My phone pings with an incoming text. I open it and see the note. The handwriting too boxy, as if someone put extra effort into disguising their penmanship. "And he just sent a picture of it."

"Can I see?"

"In a minute. Let me call Theresa first."

I scroll through my contacts and tap on the attorney's office, bringing the phone to my ear. On the second ring, the young man at the front desk answers. "Good morning, attorney Theresa Chang's office. How may I assist you?"

"Good morning. This is Autumn Rooker. I need to inform Theresa of some new information regarding my case. It's somewhat urgent."

"Let me check if she's available, Ms. Rooker. I need to place you on a brief hold."

"Thank you." Jazzy café music floats through the phone line while I wait. Not a minute later, Theresa answers.

We exchange pleasantries, then she turns all business. Asking if Clementine and I are okay. Once I assure her we are physically safe, I share the incident of Leo stopping by Jonas's work on Friday afternoon and the note on his car this morning. She asks me to send her the picture, but to get the actual note from Jonas. When I have it, I am to bring it to her after I file a police report.

Not that I didn't foresee this happening, but dizziness starts to swallow me whole. Everything whirls around me in the passenger seat as I take deep, relaxing breaths. Beside me, Penny reaches over and clutches my arm.

"Auti, you good?"

I nod, slow and unsure. Lifting the phone away from my mouth, I whisper, "Go to Jonas's work." She gives me a thumbs up.

Theresa informs me she will spend the day trying to get the hearing moved up in light of this new information. I thank her and promise to see her soon.

"Talk to me," Penny states as soon as I hang up with Theresa.

"The note says *she doesn't belong to you*. Jonas thinks it's about me, but I think it refers to Clementine." I take a deep breath then continue. "We need to get the note from Jonas, go to the police station and file a report, then take the note to the attorney as evidence." I press my palms to my eyes. "How am I supposed to work today? And how am I supposed to get around if you have to work today and I shouldn't be alone?"

"Call Rez. He'll understand. As for me, I'll tote you around as long as possible. My shift doesn't start until noon. Hopefully, we can knock this out in the next couple of hours."

While Penny drives, I call Reznor and explain the situation. He waves off my worry and tells me to take the day off. With everything going on, his empathy is bar none. At least I have one less stressor to bog me down.

Penny parks in front of Thompson's Garage and I jump out. Jonas dashes over to me and we exchange a brief kiss.

"Hate to cut this short, but I need the note to file a police report and take to the attorney's office."

Jonas fishes the note from his jeans pocket beneath his coveralls. When he hands it to me, he kisses my forehead. "Let me know how it goes." He waves at Penny. "And if you need me later when Pen goes to work."

"I will." We exchange one last kiss. "Call you when I know more."

Penny whips out of the parking lot faster than she pulled in. We speed down the road, but I miss the blur of the buildings and trees.

I stare down at my hands in silence. Stare at the ivory paper between my fingers. Rub the vellum with the pads of my thumbs. The subtle roughness familiar, but can't place from where. I unfold the paper with ease, eyes glued to the shaky block letters. Tracing the slight swoops and lines and edges of the letters, I study the print for any indication of who wrote it.

The answer is there. Just out of reach. On the tip of the tongue. But it retreats back into my mind, mimicking a frightened child.

Folding the note back together, I tuck it in my purse before eyeing the road. We are blocks from the police station now. Any other day, I would reprimand Penny for her lead foot. But today, grateful doesn't begin to cover her speediness.

She parks the car in the police station visitor lot and stands at my side the moment we step out of the car. For a beat, I contemplate telling her to wait in the car but know I won't win the battle.

After checking in with a receptionist too bright-eyed and smiley to work in a police station, we sit in the waiting area. With the early hour, I pray we get in and out quickly. Minutes later, the gods answer my request and send an officer to call me back. Since we're in the station, Penny opts to sit in the waiting area while I speak with the officer.

I have never seen the inside of a police station but didn't picture it looking like an open area call center. Cubicle central with low glass walls dividing clusters of desks. Weird.

The female officer directs me to have a seat. Unyielding plastic digs into my hips as I sit down. Minus a few framed photos of her with fellow officers or superiors, her workspace appears as sterile as my booth at the shop.

She extends a hand across the desk and I shake it. "Officer Martinez. I was told you need to file a harassment report."

"Yes. I'm in the middle of a custody suit and my daughter's birth father has begun harassing my boyfriend." Opening my purse with shaky hands, I retrieve the note. "Friday, the birth father went to my boyfriend's place of business and provoked a verbal altercation. This morning, when my boyfriend left for work, he found this on his car." I hand the note to her. "My attorney advised me to come here and file the report before giving her the note."

Officer Martinez takes the note and studies it momentarily. "Bear with me, I need to ask you questions and document everything. Shouldn't take long. Please answer as openly and honestly as possible."

For the next thirty-plus minutes, Officer Martinez prattles off question after question. Some in regards to Jonas, others in reference to Leo. I provide her with as much detail as possible. She scans the note into the digital file and hands it back. With the note being touched so much this morning, she said the likelihood of lifting prints from someone other than me or Jonas is low. Before she walks me to the front, she prints off a copy of the report and hands it to me along with her business card.

"If anything else pops up, reach out." She points to her contact information on the card. "I may not respond immediately, but will as soon as possible." I nod. "In the meantime, I suggest being vigilant. Stay aware and steer away from any possible interactions unless your attorney is present."

"Thank you, Officer Martinez." We shake hands again.

"You're welcome. Stay safe." With that, she leaves me in the reception area.

Penny peeks up from her phone, locking it and rising when she spots me. "Done?"

"Yeah. Now, to Theresa's office."

I tuck the report and note in my purse on our way to the car. The second I click my seat belt in place, Penny backs out of the parking space. I prattle off the address for the office and direct her where to go. Thank goodness, the drive to Theresa's office takes less than ten minutes.

Inside, Penny does the same as at the police station and waits out front. In the conference room with Theresa, I relay what Officer Martinez said, then hand over the police report and note. An unfortunate side effect of no prints or detectable handwriting, the police cannot point the finger directly at Leo without further evidence.

Theresa keeps the original documentation but makes copies for my records. "I submitted a request for an earlier hearing date. Should receive a response soon. As soon as I do, I'll reach out to you. Meanwhile, steer clear of Leo, if possible. If he approaches you or Jonas, call the police. With a report filed, it will reflect poorly on him if an officer arrives on scene." We rise from our seats, and before leaving the conference room, Theresa gives me a hug. The embrace comforts me and I return it. "We'll get through this. Until then, stay strong and lean on people you trust."

"Thank you," I say, breaking the hug. "Doing my best."

She walks me back to the front and reminds me she will be in touch. Stopping here hasn't wiped away all the anxiety and stress, but knowing I have a team of people on my side helps ease it slightly.

Penny and I stroll out to the car, the adrenaline buzz from the morning fading as it inches closer to midday. We get in the car and sit quietly. Penny doesn't start the car or turn the key to kick the radio on. For a moment, we just breathe in strength and exhale the bullshit.

Until Leo reappeared, life had been low-key and kosher. Yes, my romance life was snore-worthy until Jonas came into the picture, but I had been content with sharing all my time with Clementine. She is the most important person in my world and her happiness is more important than my own. Little did I know, me being in a loving relationship boosted her happiness.

After a deep breath, Penny starts the car and steers us out of the lot. "Don't know about you, but I'm ready for this day to be done."

"Me—" My phone buzzes in my purse and I dig it out. Clementine's school name flashes on the screen. I rush to answer. "Hello?"

"May I speak with Ms. Rooker, please?"

"This is she."

"Hi, Ms. Rooker. This is Daniel in the front office of Clementine's school. We have a gentleman here, not on the approved list, who is trying to take Clementine out of school early. He will not identify himself. We have denied him, of course, but need to notify you."

I stop breathing. *What the fuck is going on?!* I have no clue what the hell is going on in the world, but all the walls are caving in. Seems if it isn't one thing, it's another. Like my and Clementine's life are some big game to toy with.

"Is the man still there?" Penny glances at me, wide-eyed.

"Yes, ma'am. He refuses to leave without Clementine."

I inhale deeply and ball the hand not holding the phone into a fist. My nails bite the skin and I welcome the reality check. "If possible, don't let him leave. I'm on my way. He is *not* to leave with her."

"We will keep him here as long as possible."

"Thank you." I disconnect the call and face Penny. "We need to get to Clementine's school. Now. A man is trying to withdraw her from school."

"What the actual fuck?" Penny belts out as she changes course and speeds toward the elementary school.

"My thoughts exactly."

I scroll through my contacts and tap on Jonas. He answers on the second ring. "Hey, scarlet. That was quicker than expected. Everything go alright?"

For a beat, I stay silent. I clench and relax my fingers a few times. "Jonas, please don't freak out. Because I'm freaking out enough for the both of us."

"You're scaring me. What's going on?"

I pinch my eyes together so tight, a sharp jab shoots from the midline out. After a deep breath, I answer. "Penny is driving me to Clementine's school right now. An unidentified man is trying to withdraw her."

Deafening silence. Then a bang so loud I hold the phone away from my ear. "Motherfucker," Jonas growls. He remains quiet a minute. "Want me to meet you there?"

Part of me wants to say yes. To ask him to meet me there and help protect me and Clementine from all this craziness. But it isn't sensible. More angry tempers will not fix this. And without seeing his face, I *feel* the pain and anger radiating off Jonas. He loves my little girl as much as he does me and is willing to do whatever necessary to protect us both.

"No. We're pulling in now. I'll check in soon. I—" I cut myself off. *Not the time, Autumn.*

"Me too, scarlet."

The call disconnects just before Penny parks the car. I jump out while she waits in the lot. My feet carry me faster than ever before as I run for the office. Daniel from the front desk buzzes me through a locked door and I step inside the warm office.

"Autumn Rooker. You called about a man trying to withdraw my daughter from school."

Daniel smiles as if a stranger wasn't just here trying to steal my child. And it pisses me off. But I bite my tongue and breathe through my anger and frustration.

"Yes. He left a few minutes ago after we wouldn't comply."

"Did you get a name?"

"No, ma'am."

The heater kicks on and ruffles papers on the countertop between us. Daniel's clipped answer bumps my irritation up a notch. The whole situation isn't his fault and I don't want to take my problems out on him, but the fact he seems so nonchalant about this annoys me further.

"Can you tell me what he looked like?"

"A few inches taller than you, gray hair, balding on top. Short-sleeve dress shirt. Khaki pants. Older, but I'm not good with age." He winces. "Until I asked for his identification, he was overly polite."

"Did he say anything else? Besides asking to pick up Clementine?"

He shakes his head. "No, ma'am."

Well, at least my daughter is still here and safe. "Thank you, Daniel. While here, I'd like to review and update who may pick up Clementine."

"Sure thing."

With each tap of the keys on his keyboard, I lose my cool a little more. Why the hell is this my life right now? Why are people trying to steal my daughter? Whoever came to the school today was not Leo. His father, perhaps. No one I know fits the description Daniel provided. Nicely dressed fits Leo's family.

All I want to do is tip my head back and scream at the sky. Scream loud and violently. Scream until my throat becomes sandpaper and my larynx shrivels.

As I update Clementine's approved pickup list to include Jonas—just in case—I decide to withdraw her from school early. At this point, she has less than half the day left. Once she arrives in the office, I take her hand and hold it tighter than usual.

When we walk out of the building, she glances up at me. "Why did you pick me up early, Mama?"

My daughter doesn't need my stress, so I choose to skirt around the truth. "Today has been a crazy day. Just need to have you with me." She hugs my side but doesn't say a word.

I open the back door for her and she hops in. Sitting in the passenger seat, I face Penny. "Not there," I mumble. "Left before we got here. But it wasn't him. Someone older." Parallel lines wrinkle Penny's forehead. "Will you drop us off at Jonas's work? You can keep the car."

"Of course."

In my short-lived life, I have experienced a lot. Not in regards to travel. But actual life experiences. Hope and adoration. Despair and worthlessness. Love and joy.

Today, in this very moment, is the first time I encounter extreme vulnerability. Today is the first time I feel my and my daughter's safety is at risk. And I have no clue where to go from here.

eighteen

. . .

Jonas

WHEN I PLUCKED THE NOTE OFF MY JEEP THIS MORNING, fury slithered in my bloodstream. When Autumn stopped here earlier to collect the note to take to the police and her attorney, her red eyes and withered stature nearly crippled me. But when Autumn called forty-three minutes ago to tell me an unknown man was trying to remove Clementine from school, I lost my shit. Literally.

Once our call disconnected, I threw a wrench at the back wall of the garage. Then, stormed into the office, grabbed a pillow off the couch, and screamed into the stuffed material. More than once. Although the action was cathartic, relief didn't follow.

The measures this man takes to hurt Autumn, emotionally more so than physically, blows me away. Disgusts me more than comprehensible. Makes me violent and irrational. I aim my rage at inanimate objects, but it boils beneath the surface, begging to seep out. I remind myself this is probably all a ploy. A way for him to provoke me or Autumn. And as much as I am dying to take my aggression out on him, I won't.

I refuse to stoop to his level and be a lesser man. Money may buy you fancy things, but it doesn't make you a decent human. People choose to be decent. From what I have seen so far, Leo has made his choice and it is nowhere near respectable.

For the last five minutes, I have laid on the creeper and stared at the same oil filter. If today were a good day, I would have removed it four and a half minutes ago. I have yet to lift a finger.

Just as I do, the familiar rumble of Autumn's car garners my attention. I roll out from under the car, point to James and ask him to finish the job. After my outburst earlier, everyone here is on edge. So James nods and shifts his attention. After this is all over, I need to treat the staff to beers and burgers.

I jog over to the car. Autumn and Clementine both get out, opposing expressions on their faces. Autumn looks as if she just went ten rounds in a fight and came out visually unscathed. But I know her insides are pulverized. Clementine is all smiles and sunshine. Obviously, she has no idea what all has happened today. Which is good. Children don't deserve to bear the brunt of adult issues.

With as much enthusiasm as I can muster, I haul both my girls in for a hug. "Hey," I whisper in Autumn's ear. "Been worried about you both."

Autumn squeezes me with more oomph. "Can we

stay here until you're off work? I-I don't feel safe going anywhere else right now."

"Don't even have to ask." I unravel my grip on them and squat down in front of Clementine. "Hey, sunshine. Let's go sit in my office for a bit. Is that cool with you?"

Clementine nods and scrunches up her nose. "It smells funny here."

Autumn and I laugh. "Yeah. Sometimes the stuff in car engines smells weird. But I promise the office smells nice." I cup a hand around my mouth and lean into her. "My dad sprays flower air freshener in there sometimes." She giggles and I love how unaware she is of the chaos.

I lead them into the office and tell them to use whatever they need. Before I head out to the garage, I order lunch for the three of us and promise my girls to be in when it arrives.

Back in the garage, Dad wanders over. "Everything okay?" He tips his head toward the office.

There is no use in sugarcoating it. Because shit is definitely *not* okay. "Not really." I relay what happened at Clementine's school. Relay how unsafe Autumn feels. Share how she is doing her best to not let Clementine hear all the nitty-gritty details because it isn't fair to worry her over something she ultimately can do nothing to fix.

Out of nowhere, Dad hauls me in for a hug. "Sorry you're both dealing with this. Let us know if you need help. Even to watch Clementine so you two can run errands or go to appointments."

I nod. "Thanks, Dad."

Taking back over my job, I thank James and work until lunch arrives. Now that Autumn and Clementine are here, I breathe easier. Focus without difficulty. Relax with less effort.

When the food is delivered, Dad tells me to take as much time as I need. I carry the bag into the office and enjoy the next hour with my girls. Clementine has been busy doing schoolwork while Autumn occupied herself with the internet, reading old magazines in the office, and occasionally helping Clementine with her work.

We munch on sandwiches while Clementine tells us about the art project they are doing—a collage made from magazine clippings where each image must represent a letter of their name. Needless to say, her collage will have lots of pictures. While Clementine eats french fries and does a sheet of math equations, I take the opportunity to talk in hushed tones with Autumn.

"Might be a good idea if we update everyone later. We can visit the shop after work, then text everyone not there."

Autumn nods and leans on my bicep while resting her head near my shoulder. "Good plan." I kiss the crown of her head and she closes her eyes. "Just want this to be over."

"Me too. Soon." I take one of her hands between mine in my lap. "Until then, definitely don't want either or both of you alone. Not even at home."

May seem like drastic measures, but when it comes to my girls, no measure is too extreme. I will protect them until my last breath. And that breath won't come anytime soon.

Wetness hits my collarbone, and I tip my chin to look at Autumn. She stares at Clementine with silent tears rolling over the bridge of her nose and down her cheek. I drop a hand from hers to reach up and wipe away her tears. She leans in to my touch and kisses my palm.

Autumn tilts her head on my shoulder, pressing her lips to my neck, my jaw, beneath my ear. My eyes roll back as my jaw falls slack. We have kissed several times with Clementine in the room, but right now, I want to kiss her fiercely. Much stronger than any PG suggested rating.

I cup her jaw and meet her lips in the middle. Warmth and tenderness and intimacy collide as our lips move in time. Soft and gentle at first. But the moment she paints the tip of her tongue across my upper lip, I gasp and tug her closer. Inhale her heady cherry vanilla aroma. Taste the cola on her tongue. Tremble as she adjusts her position and fists my hair. Scoot her closer when she moans down my throat. Groan in return when I brush over her pulse and feel how viciously her heart thumps for me. For us. For this kiss.

When her hands untangle from my hair and drop to my chest, I break the kiss but don't lift my lips from hers. "If she wasn't here right now…"

Autumn presses her lips to mine again. "Same."

Reluctantly, I inch away from her and groan. "I have to get back out there, but only a bit longer. Do you need anything? You can use the computer if you want." She shakes her head. "Be done soon." I kiss the tip of her nose before getting up, adjusting myself as I do.

When I get back to work, Dad and James take their lunch. For a Monday, the garage is slow. Then again, we are caught up on the few labor-intensive jobs we had, which helps other jobs go quicker. While Dad has lunch, I finish a routine oil change James started, plug a tire in no time, and schedule body repair for a crumpled fender.

As a new customer pulls up, Dad exits the office/customer waiting area. I check the wall clock between two of the bay doors. He took twenty, maybe twenty-five minutes for lunch. At minimum, we take thirty. Been that way since day one of Dad buying this place.

After collecting basic information from the customer, I show them to the waiting area while we work on their car. When I walk back into the garage, Dad is gearing up to take over.

"Hey, old man. I got this. You should finish your lunch."

He laughs and shakes his head. "When James gets back, you head out for the day."

What? Although I'm grateful for the offer, I don't want to ditch everyone and overwhelm them. "Why? I can stay longer."

Dad steps closer and rests a hand on my shoulder. "Of course, you *can*. Doesn't mean you *should*." He points his thumb over his shoulder. "They need you more than me right now. And we'll be fine here. Been slow." He taps my shoulder one, two, three times. "Son, there are times when the people you care about are more important than work. You need to recognize those moments and do what's right. And being with them while all this is happening, it's the right choice."

Who knew my dad was philosophical? He is a good man. Always has been. Puts those he cares about above everything else. Which is exactly what he tells me to do now. How can I not be proud of the man who raised me with heart? Hopefully, I meet his expectations when it comes to being a good man. Tough shoes to fill and all.

I pull him in for a hug and hold him longer than our typical hugs. "Thanks, Dad. For everything you've done and always do."

"Love ya, Jonas. Now, stop being all sappy. We have work to get done before you go."

I laugh and slap the back of his shoulder before I release him. We work in sync for almost thirty minutes before James returns. Once he jumps in, I say my goodbyes and collect the girls from the office.

We make a quick stop at my house—which is easier said than done when Clementine and Spartan get together. Once Spartan has done his business, we pile back into the Jeep and drive toward the shop. Autumn has been quiet since we left the garage. More than likely, overwhelmed with everything happening. If my nerves are shot over this whole Leo debacle, I only imagine how crazed she must feel. I just wish there was more for me to do to make it go away.

Monday appears to be an all-around slow business day when I park the Jeep behind the shop. Autumn leads us inside through the back entrance. When we round the front desk where Penny sits, she pops her gum, bolts out of her chair, and hugs Autumn with undeniable strength.

Penny steps back, holding Autumn at arm's length. "Any updates from earlier?" Autumn shakes her head, still silent.

"We thought it might be a good idea to come update you guys in person."

She nods. "Rex should be done in a few. Rez is indisposed."

Autumn walks us over to her booth and plops down on her stool. I pick Clementine up and sit with her in my lap. Understandably, Autumn is upset and frustrated. But since the day we met, I have never seen her like this. One hundred percent in her head. I would give anything to know what she's thinking right now. To help her trudge through all the *what-ifs* and *whys* and *where do we go from here* moments. None of us have all the answers, but we will find them easier together.

Rex finishes up and wipes down his booth. Once everyone comes together, we give the simple version of what happened today. Clementine acts as if she isn't listening, but I notice her ear perk up on occasion.

Everyone is on the same page when it comes to Autumn and/or Clementine always being with someone. The only exception is work and school, which happen by default. For the first time since I met her, Penny stopped chewing gum. Her face never more serious.

"Why don't the two of you stay with me until this settles," I suggest.

Autumn turns to me, eyes wide and jaw slack. "Don't you think that's extreme?"

"Quite the opposite."

"Jonas, I love being at your house. But being there nightly, without everything I need, or everything Clementine needs, it's more of a hassle."

Ouch. I see her point—us picking up their belongings frequently—but it still stings. "Can we at least compromise?" Last thing I need to do is give Autumn something else to worry over.

She tucks her lips between her teeth and rocks her jaw side to side. Her cognac irises have dulled today. Darkened. They dart between mine, glassy and indecisive. I hate that she has to make these choices. I hate that she fears stepping foot outside, worried who might be waiting. Hate that she questions every decision about their lives.

"We should do at least two to three nights a week at the apartment." Her decision lacks confidence. She may change her mind. Make it more time at her apartment. Or… possibly more time at the house. Fingers crossed for the latter.

"Whatever you feel most comfortable with, scarlet. You good with Spartan tagging along?"

Clementine bounces up from my lap. "Sparty!" She rushes Autumn. "Please, Mama."

Autumn tucks a strand of Clementine's hair behind her ear. "Sure, pumpkin." She meets my gaze. "Tonight, let's stay at my place."

I lean in and kiss her forehead. "Fine with me. We should grab dinner soon."

The group disburses. After saying our goodbyes, the three of us pile into the Jeep and pick up a quick bite to eat. We stop at my house, feed Spartan, and gather everything we need for the night.

No matter how many trips it takes, no matter how uncomfortable the arrangement, I will protect my girls.

nineteen

. . .

Autumn

I TOLD JONAS WE WOULD ALTERNATE BETWEEN STAYING AT my apartment and staying at his house. That was Monday. Monday, we stayed at my apartment. Now it is Thursday, and we haven't been at my apartment since, with the exception of packing stuff to bring to Jonas's. To be honest, I would more than love to stay here every night. Question is, am I ready?

Two very different voices clamber inside my head. Take up space and want to be heard. One claims to be reason, while the other claims to be reality. Both make me seem certifiable.

Believe it or not, reason is the temperamental one. The loudest and most annoying voice. Reason spews off all the what-if questions. Reason makes me second-guess myself and the choices I have always made. Makes me paranoid and uneasy. Before reason came into play, I never felt this uncomfortable in my own skin or mind.

Now, reality… she sits in the corner. A quiet spectator. She only speaks up when reason gets a little out of hand. But when reality voices her opinion, everyone stops to listen. Reality stands tall and fierce. Is a force to be reckoned with. Reminds me I deserve to live a life full of love and passion and exultation. I deserve to smile and laugh and joke around with people who lift me up and stand strong beside me. I deserve to live the life of my choosing, not what someone else deems fit.

Some days, reality rises above. Other days, reason stomps her foot and knocks reality down a notch.

Since the note and incident at Clementine's school on Monday, nothing else has happened. Seventy-two-plus hours without a peep. I want to be excited, but worry something crazy will happen if I get ahead of myself. Celebration is an invitation for chaos.

Clementine sits beside Spartan on Jonas's couch, reading her book to him as part of her homework assignment. Jonas stirs a pot of pasta sauce on the stove while the noodles boil and meatballs bake in the oven. I offered to help, but he shooed me away.

"Need me to pack anything for you? Seeing as I have nothing to do."

He side-eyes me over his shoulder. "Already packed. You just stay on the stool. It's okay to just be sometimes."

I roll my eyes at him. "Says the man who hasn't sat still in days."

When Clementine and I stayed over on Tuesday, the house looked different. At first, I had difficulty putting my finger on what changed. Wasn't until we headed to bed, walking down the hall, that I noticed more light in the second bedroom on the way to Jonas's room. I never toured the office set up in the room, but the desk grabbed your attention when walking by. Now the desk was gone.

I just stood in the hall and stared into the room. Jonas stepped up behind me, wrapped his arms around me, and told me he hadn't used the desk in a while. So, he donated it. The bookshelf had been moved to the living room, which is what was different.

But that wasn't such a big deal.

Nope.

Not by a long shot.

I rest my elbow on the breakfast bar, chin on my palm, and smile at Jonas—well, his backside. The man who took it upon himself to clear out a room less used. To repurpose it and put it to better use. Not better for him, though. Better for Clementine.

Two nights ago in the hall, he steered me into the second bedroom, closed the door, and flipped on the light. I didn't see the white-framed twin bed in the dark, but with the light on, I saw it perfectly. It wasn't only a frame and mattress. It was so much more. *Is* so much more.

"Do you like it," he had whispered in my ear. "It's for Clementine. So she has her own bed here. But don't tell her yet. I want to surprise her."

When Jonas told me this two nights ago, I cried the happiest tears of my life in his arms. With the exception of the day Clementine was born.

In that moment, when Jonas confessed his selfless act, I fell even harder for him. Me telling him I love him was there. Right there. Ready to dive headfirst off my tongue. But reason slapped me in the moment and I didn't profess anything.

But the resistance in me is fast fading.

Yes, it terrifies the hell out of me to tell Jonas I love him. It terrifies me to cut myself open, expose my heart, and pray he knows how to handle the beating organ with compassion and tenderness. That he won't abandon me when times get rough. That he won't jump ship because something doesn't go according to plan. Since Leo appeared, Jonas has stood strong at my side. Fought for me, even when I pushed him away. But reason whispers doubt in my ear. Tells me different circumstances create different responses. Maybe next time around, whatever pops up will push Jonas over the edge.

"If you think any louder, I may actually hear what's brewing in that head of yours," he teases as he strains the pasta.

"Just thinking about the room." As promised, I have not told Clementine. If I refer to it as *the room*, she won't make the connection if she eavesdrops.

Still, Jonas glances over his shoulder at her. She flips the page of her book and points out a picture on the page to Spartan. Oblivious.

"Anything in particular?"

"No. Just the room itself." I tuck my lips between my teeth. "What might look good in there."

Jonas blends the pasta and sauce together, then takes the meatballs out of the oven. He sets the pan on the stove, then steps my way while they cool. "Throw some ideas my way."

He tosses me a wink. A wink. Have I ever seen him wink in my general direction? Not so much. Smile? Yes. God, I love his smile. Especially when his dimple makes an appearance. But winks are not a Jonas thing.

I narrow my eyes. "What are you up to?"

"Just making dinner," he says, a wide smile plumping his cheeks and displaying my favorite dimple. *Way to distract me—for now.*

We plate up dinner and eat earlier than usual. Spartan crunches on his kibble and tries to get Clementine to sneak him pieces of meatball. Thank goodness, she doesn't give in to his cute whines and grumpy groans at her feet.

Once we finish dinner and clean up, I check my email while Jonas grabs his things. An email from Theresa is the bearer of good news.

"Guess what," I say as Jonas walks back out to the living room.

"What's up?"

"The hearing has been moved up. Monday, the twenty-fourth." I smile, glad to have some form of happy news.

"This month?" I nod and Jonas pulls me in for a hug. "Thank god. That's less than two weeks."

His realization swirls in my head. *Less than two weeks.* Before the end of the month, all this will be over. I hope. *Please, let this be over.*

Maybe the hearing adjustment is the reason for all the quiet. No more signs of Leo. No threats or unannounced appearances. I have no plans on jinxing this, but I will take all the good news and positive energy I can get.

"Come on, let's go."

We file out to our cars. Although Operation Don't-leave-Autumn-and-Clementine-alone is still in full swing, it has been deemed safe for me and Clementine to be in my car if someone in the trusted circle follows us. A smidge more freedom while remaining safe.

At the apartment, we crash on the couch and settle in to watch a movie with Clementine. On the nights we stay at the apartment, Jonas sleeps on the couch. Initially, I protested and said he could sleep in bed with me. The gentleman his father raised him to be, he refused to uproot Clementine's normal bed space. It wasn't fair to her.

In the same breath, he also said if she fell asleep on the couch curled up with Spartan, he may reconsider my offer. I don't believe him.

While Clementine watches the movie, Jonas and I watch each other. He lays on his side—back against the cushions—while I lie on my back. With the softest touch, he slowly traces his fingertip over my skin. Following the motion with his eyes.

Over my collarbone, from shoulder to sternum. Up the column of my throat before brushing my hair aside. Along the sensitive skin beneath my ear. Around the shell of my ear. With each direction change, a shiver rolls through my body. When he reaches my temple, he draws small circles there. Drags his finger down my cheekbone. Encircles my lips, then presses the single digit in the middle before bringing his gaze back to mine.

Have you ever watched your lover as they intimately touch you non-sexually? I have never been so enamored with another person.

Without effort, Jonas loves me. Gives me every non-materialistic gift a woman desires and needs. Worships me. Cares for my daughter as if she were his own.

And he does all this without a single word said. His love is in his actions. The way he cannot keep his eyes off me. How he reveres me as a woman and a mother—strong and capable and exceptional. How he touches me—gentle and rough. The way he kisses me—as if every kiss may be our last. The way he breathes me in and hugs me close.

He leans down and I close my eyes as he presses his lips to mine. Slipping a hand behind my neck, he presses more of his weight into me. I pant when he sucks on my lower lip. Roll my eyes back when he dips his tongue in. Fist his hair when our bodies tangle like wild teenagers.

I really want to take him to bed. Strip him bare. Feel his steely-soft erection between my lips. Taste him on my tongue and swallow every drop when he releases down my throat. Grind my hips against his face and scream his name as I gloss the stumble on his jaw. Kiss him like a savage and taste my saltiness on his skin.

I want to do all of this and more. But not tonight. Not here.

In my apartment, we exchange simple touches. Touches that imprint your skin more than any tattoo ever could. Touches that express our fierce connection in other ways. The emotional and mental and spiritual.

Reason says all things never stay. But reality gives a swift kick in the ass to reason, telling her to shut the hell up. Because Jonas… he will always be around.

twenty

. . .

Jonas

As an adult, I have never celebrated Valentine's Day. Not in the sense of buying flowers and chocolates and gifts for a person I care about. My mom and sisters do not count in this equation. I'm strictly thinking of romantic interests. Considering the only other woman I thought of romantically never reciprocated, I never bought her anything.

For the first time, Valentine's Day is a big deal.

After I leave Autumn's apartment, I drop Spartan off at home and head to work. I relay my plan to Dad when I get to work and he tells me to take a half day so I can get everything done in time. I debate with him a moment, but give up after he tells me he will close the garage for the day if I don't.

Twist my arm.

Before arriving at work, I pictured the day going by slow. Excitement has me jittery and on edge. So, when lunchtime rolls around, I freak out. I let everyone take lunch, with plans to leave when they return.

"What if I don't get everything done in time?" I ask Dad.

"Most of the stores are right next to each other. Unless you have no idea what you're getting, you'll do just fine." Dad pats my shoulder. "Proud of you, son. And I'm glad you found someone who makes you happy. You deserve it."

"You trying to make me cry, old man," I tease.

"Would be a beautiful thing if you did. Shows how much they mean to you. Never be ashamed to show how you feel." Dad gives my shoulder another pat. "I'll be done in a bit. Then you get out of here and surprise those girls."

Dad takes his lunch and returns in no time. When I try to protest his twenty-minute break, he shrugs and tells me he ate. Conversation done. I finish the car I'm working on then prep to leave. After the tools are back where they belong, I ditch my coveralls and wash up.

"Sure you're good with me heading out this early?"

Dad shakes his head on a chuckle. "If you don't get out of here, I'll spill your secret plans to Autumn." He reaches for his phone.

The second time I brought Autumn and Clementine over for family dinner night, Dad gave her his number in case she ever needed help and she couldn't reach me. She reciprocated. Not only did the exchange shock me—our relationship still so young—it stirred up new admiration for my father. A man I hope to live up to.

"God. Fine. I'm leaving."

"Enjoy your weekend," Dad shouts as I exit the back of the garage.

"You too. Buy Mom some flowers."

I hop in the Jeep and drive toward the mall. Every store I need to hit is within a mile or two. And since it's still early in the day, traffic is light. Altogether, I have five stops. Only one stop will be challenging. So, I make it the first.

The second I set foot in the store, I question every reason behind the choice. But when a woman walks up to me and asks to help, I breathe a little easier. She asks open-ended questions and lights up when an idea strikes. In less than thirty minutes, I swipe my card as she bags up my purchase.

With an extra bounce in my step, I leave the store and go to the next. Fifteen minutes later, I exit the mall with the hardest part of my shopping done. I am in and out of the next stop faster than either shop in the mall. When I reach stop four, Shelly greets me with a goofy smile.

"Feel like I haven't seen you in years," she teases.

"Were you not just at my house last weekend? I swear you hung out, ate the food I grilled, and chatted with my girl."

A breezy smile kicks up her cheeks. "I love how happy you are."

The last time I remember blushing is middle school. So, the sudden heat on my neck and cheeks comes as a surprise. "Thanks, Shell."

After a quick hug, she slips into business mode. "What can I get for you?"

"Obviously, I'm here for flowers." Shelly rolls her

eyes at me. "But I don't know what flowers Autumn likes. Or Clementine. I'd prefer to not get roses."

"Too cliché?" she jokes, but continues. "Do you want to get the same for both of them?"

"No. Think it would be nice for them to have flowers they call their own."

Shelly taps her lips for a beat before her eyes light up. "Wait here."

She dashes around the floral shop so quickly it dizzies me. After stopping at several bins, she meets me back at the counter. One hand overflows with flowers while the other holds greenery. This is why I come here. Because Shelly and Elizabeth, Cora's mom, don't mess around when flowers are involved. I love their passion and how easily they can make an arrangement look like art.

"Blush ranunculus and eucalyptus greens for Autumn," she mumbles, setting them on brown paper. "And red poppies, baby ranunculus, daisies, and kumquats for Clementine." She secures the flowers for Autumn in the brown paper with black ribbon. Clementine's flowers are artfully arranged in a mason jar with the same black ribbon tied around the jar threads. Shelly sets a vase on the counter. "When you get home, add water to the mason jar. After you give Autumn her flowers, put them in this vase and do the same."

Although I am thankful for her step-by-step instructions, she talks to me as if I have never bought my mom or sisters flowers here. I let her do her spiel, though. "Thanks, Shell. They're perfect."

I pay for the deeply discounted flowers and we exchange one last hug before I leave.

Next and final stop before home; the grocery store. I breeze through the aisles, man on a mission, and pick up all the ingredients for the dinner and dessert I have planned. Once I check everything off the list, I load everything on the belt at the register and exchange Valentine's chitchat with the cashier. She tells me my lady friend is a lucky woman. *I consider myself the lucky one.*

Minutes later, I haul everything into the house and let Spartan out. I stow the food and flowers while I set up one of the gifts. Finished, I package up the only other present that didn't have a gift wrap option. I set out several candles and light them before filling out a card I bought for Clementine and writing a love letter to Autumn. Once that task is complete, I straighten up around the house and prep dinner and dessert.

Cutting the last of the strawberries, I check the time. Just after four.

"Whatd'ya say, Spartan. Should I tell the girls they can come over now?"

Woof, woof, woof.

"Will do."

I wipe my hands on a towel, then snag my phone from the counter.

Jonas: Whenever you're ready, come on over.

Autumn: Almost done prettying ourselves. Be over soon.

I smile at the screen. Neither of you needs to pretty yourselves, I mumble.

The buzzer on the stove goes off and I take the angel food cake out of the oven. I adjust the temperature of the oven and blend the ingredients for the baked five-cheese macaroni. Sprinkling it with bread crumbs, I place the deep dish on a sheet pan and slide it in the oven.

As I deposit the mojo chicken in the oven, Spartan barks like a loon. Which can mean only one thing… they are here.

I open the door to see my girls walking up and Penny waving behind the wheel of Betsy. My cheeks grow painfully tight as I wave back at Penny. *She's letting Penny take the car.*

Spartan tackles Clementine before they reach the door. "Come on, bud. Let them inside." After another lick or two, he runs back in the house, barking for Clementine to follow.

"Hey," Autumn whispers as she sidles up to me.

I lean down and kiss her. "Hey, scarlet." Another kiss. "I have surprises for you both."

We walk into the house. "Oh yeah…" Her voice trails off the moment she spots the flowers on the breakfast bar. "Jonas." My name rolls softly off her tongue. "You didn't have to buy me flowers." She pivots to face me, a gentle smile on her lips. "You didn't have to buy us anything."

I snake my arms around her waist and draw her closer. "True. But I wanted to." I drop my lips to hers and bring her hips flush to my body. "And there's still more." I step back and weave my fingers through hers, walking her to the bar. "For you." I point to the ranunculus and letter. "For Clementine," I say, pointing to the mason jar of flowers next to a card.

"Thank you." She lifts the flowers to her nose and inhales. "They're beautiful."

"You're welcome. Glad you love them."

"Clementine?"

Her head pops up from the couch where she and Spartan appear to be having a serious conversation. "Yeah, Mama."

"Come see the flowers Jonas got you."

I kiss the crown of her head. "You two enjoy those a moment while I check on dinner."

Autumn and Clementine ogle over the flowers and read the notes I left them. When I peek over my shoulder to see if they are still reading, I spot a tear roll down Autumn's cheek. Normally, I would worry. But the constant smile on her lips tells me the tears are happy ones.

"About ten more minutes until dinner," I announce. Autumn lifts her gaze to mine and I stop breathing. Her cognac irises swirl with admiration and passion and something powerful. Love. *She loves me.* The confession plain as day in her eyes and on her face, but I won't force the words from her lips. She will say the words when she is ready. "In the meantime… Clementine?" She glances up at me from her card. "Would you like your other Valentine's present?"

Her face lights up as she hops off the stool and bounces. "Yes, please."

I walk over to Autumn and lace my fingers with hers. "C'mon, scarlet." She slides off the stool and I lead us to the second bedroom. When I open the door and flip on the light, Autumn gasps and lifts her free hand to her mouth.

"Jonas…" she mumbles.

"Clementine." I squat down and look her in the eye. "This room is for you when you're here. Decorate it however you like. Hang out in here with Spartan. Whatever you want. This is your space."

Her little jaw drops as her eyes widen. "Really?" she asks in disbelief. I nod. She squeals and lunges forward, wrapping her arms around my neck. "Thank you, Mr. Jonas."

She releases the hug and I stand up. "You're welcome. Hope you like it."

She spins around and stares at the oak-framed twin bed. A khaki comforter with a punk version of Alice from *Alice in Wonderland* drapes the mattress. Two matching decorative pillows rest against normal bed pillows. On the floor, a shaggy five-by-seven red rug adds a pop of color to the room. The room still needs more work, but for now, it will do.

"I love it," she exclaims, running and hopping on the bed. "C'mon, Sparty." She pats the bed beside her and he jumps up.

My work here is done.

Autumn and I leave the room and return to the kitchen. She parks on a stool while I check the last of the food cooking.

"You didn't have to do all this," Autumn whispers.

I take what is left in the oven out and set it on trivets before facing her. "Yeah, I did." I circle the bar and step into her. "You and Clementine deserve to be doted on." Leaning down, I kiss her. "And I'm not done yet."

Once dinner is plated up, we call for Clementine. I have a sneaking suspicion we won't see much of her or Spartan, now that Clementine has her own space. While eating, we discuss what movie we should watch tonight. Being Valentine's Day, Clementine suggests a love movie. I laugh at her exaggeration of vowels in the word love.

While I clean up dishes and assemble dessert, I tell my girls to find us a *love* movie to watch. I tote dessert out to the living room and receive oohs and awes from Clementine when she spots my mom's version of chocolate-dipped strawberry shortcake—aka strawberry shortcake with chocolate drizzle. But before either of them reaches for their plates, I hold up my hand.

"Another present. Then dessert." Surprisingly, neither of them says a word. Hands folded in their laps, both smile and bat their lashes. "Actually…" I point to Autumn. "I have two more for you."

I take two velvet bags from my pocket and a small box. Autumn follows every move I make as she tucks her lips between her teeth. I hand the satchel tied with a red ribbon to Clementine. She opens it up and plucks out the silver link chain with a heart charm in the center.

"Look how pretty this is, Mama." Clementine holds up the necklace for Autumn to see. Autumn nods before tipping her head back and blinking rapidly. "Open your presents."

Autumn levels her gaze with mine. "You really didn't have to."

I cup her cheek and nod. "Both of you deserve nothing less."

She clamps down harder on her lips, then swallows. I tip my head at her gifts and she opens them. Inside her satchel is a matching necklace. The linked chain matches a charm bracelet I spotted on her wrist a time or two. I help them both don the necklaces before Autumn opens the final gift. The one I worry over more than the rest.

With trembling fingers, she peels back the paper and removes the lid. The second she sees the key inside the box, she grabs my wrist. Tears flood her eyes and spill down her cheeks.

"I'm not suggesting anything you may or may not be ready for. But I want you to have a key. In case you need to be here when I'm not. Or just to let yourself in. But Autumn…" I wait until she looks up at me. "There is no pressure. Please don't think I'm pressing you to move in. Not that I wouldn't love to have you both here every day."

She gingerly sets the key back in the box and replaces the lid. Leaning forward, she places it on the table without a word. Then she whirls around and hops in my lap, peppering me with kisses. I wrap my arm around her waist and haul her closer.

"Guess this means you're okay with having a key," I joke.

"Best gift ever." She crushes her lips to mine until Clementine pipes up and asks if we can eat dessert yet.

And just like that, life is perfect. Autumn and I scarf down dessert so we can touch and kiss and do anything except watch the movie. When Clementine passes out, I carry her to bed and we tuck her in. Spartan jumps up and lays at the foot, guarding her.

As we walk out, I leave the door cracked. Weaving my fingers with Autumn's, I guide us down the hall to the bedroom. *Our room.*

The moment our door closes, I step into Autumn. Frame her face in my hands. Kiss her without reservation. Her fingers trace up my biceps, along my clavicles, winding up my neck and into my hair.

Without hurry, we strip away our clothes. I guide her onto the bed and crawl up until her cognacs line up with my hazels. Sweeping the hair from her face, I press my lips to hers.

Today has been a whirlwind of adoration. Every glimpse, every touch, every kiss, every word. All of it swirls together in kaleidoscope fashion. A pattern of me and Autumn and Clementine. A life full of exhilaration and laughter and love. One I don't want to live without.

My heart gallops into a full sprint as my breathing spikes. Autumn reaches up, traces her fingers from my temple to my chin. I close my eyes and absorb the tingle she ignites under my skin. The burn that never fades away. The fire she blazes beneath my sternum.

I open my eyes and lock on to hers. Her breathing shifts; grows heavier. She sees it in my eyes. Feels it in my touch. Tastes it on my lips. And I won't keep it in any longer.

"I love you, Autumn." The admission soft and strong on my lips. "More than imaginable."

Her eyes glass over and she lifts her lips to mine. The kiss gentle. Heady. A proclamation. And for the first time, she breaks the kiss.

"I love you, too," she whispers against my lips.

twenty-one

. . .

Autumn

"I love you, too," I whisper against his lips.

Beneath my breastbone, the chambers of my heart contract in a vicious rhythm as the rest of my body catches up to this revelation. I drag in a lungful of air and tremble. Jonas ghosts his lips over mine and I close my eyes. A low-frequency buzz radiates off him and spills into me. I have never felt so completely vulnerable and alive in my life.

"You feel that?" he murmurs against my lips. "The energy vibration between us." I nod as the vibration sparks every nerve in my body to life. "Know what that is?"

"No," I confess, breathy.

"Love buzz." He presses his lips to mine. "The energy of two forces merging into one."

I slide my hands down the sides of his torso, past his waist, until I take hold of his glutes. Lean and muscular. I hold him in place as I gently rock my hips up. "Make love to me, Jonas."

His forearms planted on either side of me, he slowly drops his mouth. The soft caress of his lips on mine incinerates something deeper inside me. Love buzz, as Jonas called it. Deep in my bones. A low-frequency hum simmers in my marrow. Rocks my frame. Jars my strength. Stimulates every nerve ending from head to toe. The sensation starts at the epicenter between my lungs. Radiates until it reaches every possible end point. Then boomerangs back and blooms with fire and zeal and hunger.

I claw my way up Jonas's back. Rock my hips and grind against his length. He trails kisses along my jaw, sucking on my earlobe.

"Wanted to take this slow. Show you how much I love you. But you're making that a bit challenging."

Trailing my hands down his back, I squeeze his ass and press his erection between my thighs. "You do show me. Slow and sweet sex isn't the only way to express love. Sometimes, rough and fast is just as powerful."

"You're going to be the death of me."

"But what a good way to go," I growl in his ear.

Confession. I have never had rough sex. At least not what most people constitute as rough. Considering the last person I had sex with was barely twenty, neither of us had much experience at the time.

With Jonas, though, I don't imagine rough sex being something unenjoyable. I welcome the experience. Welcome the tinge of pain that marries with the pleasure. I may be less experienced in the partner department, but all women have needs. And I have done whatever necessary to satiate those needs over the years. But they don't hold a match to Jonas.

Jonas licks and sucks his way from my ear to my collarbone. Nips and marks my skin. Takes hold of my breast and kneads it in his palm. Drops his mouth to my nipple and sucks with teeth.

The pressure skirts the cusp of pain. Heightens the buzz low in my belly. Has me rocking my hips up, seeking relief. When he doles attention on the other breast, my eyes pinch shut as my back arches off the mattress. I fist his hair and yank. Hard. His responding growl with teeth has my breath coming harder. Faster. Heavier.

He kisses his way down my midline. Sucking and biting and marking me as his. When he drops between my thighs, I clutch his hair like a horse's reins. Rock my hips up to meet his tongue. Mewl as he teases and tastes. Moan as he builds me up and lets me fall.

And when he crawls back up my body, when he hikes my legs over his shoulders and locks me in place, when he clamps down on my neck… I groan.

He enters me slowly. Inch by glorious inch. And his eyes never veer from mine.

"Good, scarlet?"

"God, yes," I moan.

"Hold on. And let me know if we need to stop."

Stop? Holy hell. What did I get myself into?

Jonas leans in closer. Presses my thighs closer to my belly. Knees almost to my face. The position more awkward than uncomfortable. He kisses my calves as he palms my thighs. Then he rocks his hips forward. Fills me fully. And I bite my fist to stifle my cries.

In and out. In and out. Every movement fluid. Pulsing. With each new thrust forward, he picks up speed. Adds more weight. Hits that spot inside me harder. Builds me up and makes me cry louder.

He slides his hand from my throat to cover my mouth. Presses hard but doesn't mask my nose. "Let go, Autumn."

Sweat drips from his chin to my chest. My eyes roll back and I focus on every sensation he creates. The heat from our skin on skin friction. The sweat slickening our flesh. His girth and strength and stamina. His weight pressing down on me, pounding into me. But most of all, I focus on the love we share.

I fist his hair. Bite his palm. Cry out against his skin as my body has him in a viselike grip. And as soon as my muscles relax, he leans back. Drops my legs to the mattress. Peppers kisses wherever his lips reach until he lands on my lips.

And then he moves again. Slower. Measured. His palm caressing my cheek, my temple, my brow. Down my neck, my breast, the side of my belly, my hip. He makes love to me. Unhurried. Every touch and stroke and caress deliberate and tender.

"I love you, Autumn." He rocks forward. "More than I ever thought I could love another person." Forward again. "And I don't want a day without you by my side."

Reaching up, I frame his face in my palms. Meet him

stroke for stroke. "I love you, Jonas." My eyes roll back. "Never thought anyone would matter the way you do." I moan as he drops his lips and delivers an evocative kiss.

Our bodies move in synergy. Steady and unyielding. Constant and loving. Building. Blooming. Higher and higher.

"Look at me, scarlet."

I open my eyes and lock on his gaze. The orange near his pupil glows wild. My body on the brink and he knows it. Feels the way my body starts to grip his tighter.

"Love you, Autumn." His admission all I need to set myself free.

I quiver as my body grips him tight. "Love you, too." And Jonas releases inside me. Lips on mine. Our love sealing every crack our hearts ever held.

Jonas shifts to lie beside me, tugging me close. He envelops me in his arms and kisses my forehead, my nose, my lips. His touch adding a new layer of timbre or resonance to the buzz swimming in my veins.

No other time in my life compares to this. Loving Jonas is magical. Sublime. Irreplaceable. Before him, I never pictured myself happy with someone else. My priorities were set in stone and immovable. Or so I thought. Now, I never want to picture a day without Jonas. Without his joy and warm heart in my—and Clementine's—life.

I snuggle farther into Jonas's frame. Grip him tighter. "Good night," I whisper against his chest. "Love you."

He gently strokes my hair before kissing the crown. "'Night, scarlet. Love you, too."

The house is unbelievably quiet when I wake. No snores or tip-tap of dog nails or whispered conversations from a little girl and her dog. Which surprises me with how bright the sun filters through the blinds. Has to be past nine, although I have zero intention of moving to check.

While everyone sleeps, I decide to daydream. Fantasize over what life would be like with Jonas. Dream of sharing a bigger home and maybe the pitter-patter of more little feet. Going to weekly Wednesday night dinners and gaining a family. A family much larger and more loving than my own knew how to be. Affectionate people who love to see me and ask how my life has been. Remarkable people who don't criticize or judge who I am or what I enjoy.

They just care for *me*.

I picture a life with Jonas full of endless smiles and hearty laughter. Of sitting on the patio, cuddled in each other's arms, and listening to the cicadas chirp and fire crackle. Of teaching Clementine—and future children—how to ride a bike or grow gracefully into adulthood. I picture all of this and so much more.

And it stirs me to life. Heats my blood and quickens my pulse. Has me desperate for Jonas. To taste him on my tongue. Feel him skin to skin. Hear the hitch in his breath as he climbs higher and higher.

Without second-guessing, I dip beneath the sheet and wake Jonas with my tongue on his flesh. And I feel it. The moment he rouses from sleep. The moment it dawns on him I have my lips wrapped around him.

The more I lavish him with my tongue, the wetter I get. He swells in my mouth; close to climax. But before he releases down my throat, he hauls me up and positions my hips over his. Just as I start to protest, he lifts his hips and pushes inside me. The most unladylike groan rips from my throat.

I slap my palms to his pecs and rock back. Every thick inch of him stretches my walls. Strokes with precision. Drives me wild.

With his grip firm on my hips, I lift my hands to my breasts and palm them while I ride him. We set a relentless tempo. My fingers pinch and tug my nipples as I tip my head heavenward.

"Fuck, you're bewitching," Jonas grunts out.

Then he sits up, hands still on my hips. I wrap my limbs around him like tentacles and lock him in place. He fists my skin tighter, slams me up and down his length. Paints my skin with his breath. Groans in my ear. Dampens my skin. Presses his forehead to mine and holds my gaze. The room smells of sex and forever.

I weave my fingers in his hair, clamp down, and yank his head back. "I want you dripping down my legs."

He groans louder as his eyes roll back. *Slap, slap, slap.* Our hips collide with violence. His jaw slackens; opens wider. His cock grows impossibly thicker inside me. *Slap, slap, slap.*

Then he lets go. As do I.

Eyes open. Breathing stops. Mouth wide. He wraps his arms around my waist and bear-hugs me. Holds me still as he spurts inside me. Fills me. Marks me—again—as his.

And as our breaths quiet down and our heartbeats resume their normal pace, I imagine what it would be like to spend forever in his arms.

twenty-two

. . .

Jonas

I TOY WITH THE ENDS OF AUTUMN'S HAIR AS WE LIE ON THE lounger in the backyard. She sits nestled between my legs, her back on my chest as we watch Clementine and Spartan run around the backyard.

She sips her coffee before setting it down and twisting in my arms. Chest to chest, she bends her legs at the knee and crosses her ankles in the air while propping her elbows on me and resting her face in her palms. She looks like an old-school pinup girl. *My pinup girl.*

I sweep a few wayward strands from her cheek. She leans into my touch before kissing my palm. "I love sitting out here. It's peaceful."

"Lounging with you makes it a hundred times better than when I sit here alone."

"What, Spartan wasn't a good lazy day companion?" she teases.

I glance over to where Clementine points out flowers to him and tells animated stories. "He's only ever chill with her. Early on, I was worried he would knock her over being a spazz." I shake my head and laugh. "Guess he only reserves that for me."

Autumn smirks. "Maybe."

A week has passed since I redecorated the second bedroom and gave Autumn a key to my house. And not a day since has Autumn slept anywhere other than my bed. *Our bed.* Nothing official has been said regarding the two of them moving in, but the only time we spend apart is during working hours.

The more clothing and personal items Autumn brings of hers and Clementine's, the more like home this house feels. Small touches in the kitchen or living room. Clementine's *Jack Skellington* cookie jar on the counter. Autumn's current paperback is on the coffee table. A soft throw blanket draped over the back of the couch. Shifting my clothes in the closet and dresser to make room for Autumn. Her scent thick in the air no matter which room I enter.

"Did you want to do anything today? Go anywhere?"

Autumn shakes her head. "Just want to take it easy. With everyone coming over to hang out tomorrow, we should kick back today. Maybe go grocery shopping."

I hook my hands under her shoulders and drag her up my body. A half smile kicks up her cheek before she leans in and kisses me. She drops her hands to my chest and supports herself as we press our foreheads together and breathe each other in.

Having Autumn and Clementine here every day has been incredible. Not everyone pictures themselves cohabitating, but falling asleep and waking up next to Autumn every day feels natural. Right. How it always should have been.

"Might be a good idea to plan what to make for tomorrow," I suggest.

With the hearing on Monday, we thought it would be nice to have everyone over again tomorrow. A chance to hang with our friends and mentally escape the anxiety of the potential outcome.

As far as the case goes, things have been quiet. Too quiet. Almost eerie. Leo had thrown so much drama at us in the beginning, it was easy to assume his theatrics would continue. But since the note on my Jeep, there hasn't been a peep. Part of me hopes Leo has learned his surprise appearances, verbal threats, and shady notes won't rattle us the way he expects. But I am not naïve enough to believe he doesn't have other tricks up his sleeve. Men like Leo don't show up out of nowhere, make a scene, then drop off the face of the earth.

I stare up at my girl and check for any signs of worry. Look for tension in her jaw or the occasional twitch in her eye. Don't need her bottling up anything when it comes to Leo and this case. But as I study the smooth lines of her skin and fiery swirl of her cognac irises, I see nothing off-putting. All I see is happiness and warmth and love.

"Maybe we should do a themed cookout," she states with enthusiasm.

"Did you have something in mind? It is a party for you, after all."

A few days ago, Clementine came to me when

Autumn stepped away to use the bathroom. She talked in hushed tones and asked what I was getting Autumn for her birthday. I asked what day her birthday was because it had been top secret. Clementine eagerly shared everything. Not only was Autumn a leap day baby, but she also rarely celebrated her birthday.

That changes this year.

So, when the idea of having everyone together again came up, I suggested we do it as a birthday/we're-going-to-win-the-case party. The shocked expression on Autumn's face when she realized I had top intel on her birthday was priceless. She may not have enjoyed celebrating her birthday before, but I promise to make each and every one of her future birthday's memorable.

"Since it should be warmer tomorrow, let's do something tropical."

Winter in Florida lasts two months, if we are lucky. And this year is no exception. Winter may not officially be over, but the sun warms the air a little more each day.

"Tropical sounds perfect. Do you want to decorate? Or only make tropical foods?"

"Definitely food. Not so much of the decor. I'd rather spend the money elsewhere."

An idea sparks. "Let's figure out the food and drinks, then stop and pick up tiki torches. They're tropical and we can use them year-round."

"Deal."

We lounge out back a little longer before heading in and planning the menu for tomorrow. Once the shopping list is made, we shop early on so we can relax the remainder of the day. We purchase several tiki torches at the home improvement store to strategically place around the yard. Then leave the grocery store with four armfuls of bags.

The back half of the day is spent lounging on the couch with movies and books and cuddles. Lazy weekends had never really been my thing, but they are growing on me fast. Who knew just being around the right person made everything perfect?

After dinner and more movie time, we shuffle off to our rooms and call it a night.

Once Autumn and I wear each other out between the sheets, I tug her against my chest and easily fall asleep.

Bam! Bam! Bam!

I startle awake and glance at the clock. Four in the morning. Autumn shoots up and holds the sheet to her chest. "What was that?"

Bam! Bam! Bam!

Spartan runs out of Clementine's room and barks in the living room. Is someone breaking in?

I jump out of bed and throw on pants. "Stay here," I tell Autumn. Bolting to the living room, I peer through the blinds and scan the porch and yard. But I don't see anyone. The motion light kicked on and illuminates most of the yard. I scan every inch thoroughly, stopping when I see Autumn's car.

"What the fuck?"

Autumn peeks her head out of the bedroom but doesn't step out. "What is it? Is someone out there?"

I walk back toward the hall and point toward

Clementine's room. "Go lie with her," I tell Spartan. He jogs past me and runs into her room, jumping back on her bed. When I reach the bedroom, I search for a hoodie and my phone. I step into Autumn and frame her face in my hands. "Please stay inside while I check your car. Looks like someone busted your windshield."

Her chin wobbles as her eyes glaze over. "Please be careful."

I lean down and kiss her. "Always. Stay inside." She nods, following me to the living room and sitting on the couch.

Walking toward the front door, I grab the baseball bat I stash in the corner. I stare out the peephole before opening the door and stepping out. Everything is quiet as usual. With each step I take, I scan my surroundings again. The motion light flips on as I step into the sensory field. My eyes dart left and right. Ears zero in on the slightest sound. The closer I get to Autumn's car, the more the hair on the back of my neck rises.

"Fuck," I mutter as I get within feet of her car.

The windshield isn't just busted. In all honesty, it looks as if someone pummeled it with a sledgehammer. The glass isn't just webbed. It is thoroughly destroyed. Hammered so many times the glass is caving in. Bashed to the point that the glass is as clear as a blizzard.

I grab my phone from my back pocket and open the camera, taking several pictures. Pocketing my phone, I reach for the note under the wiper blade. Walking to the end of the drive, I glance up and down the street and see nothing out of the ordinary.

I unfold the paper and growl.

I warned you.

Throwing my hands up, I shake my head. "Too chickenshit to come at me? Not man enough to discuss this face to face? Breaking shit and leaving notes doesn't scare me. And you're no man. Just a fucking coward." I want to scream and pound my chest, but I maintain my composure before heading back inside.

In the house, Autumn runs up to me. Eyes scanning me head to toe. "What happened?"

I explain what happened to her car and the new note. She covers her mouth and shakes her head. "Come here," I tell her, opening my arms. I hold her a moment before bracing her at arm's length. "Need to call Dad in a bit, so we can tow your car to the shop. Should also update the police report with the incident."

"Why?" Autumn whispers. "Why do this? What does smashing my windshield gain?"

I take a deep breath and circle my thumbs over her shoulders. "Probably trying to rile us up."

Does this piss me off? You better believe it. Will I cave to this juvenile behavior and the cowardice threats? Not a chance in hell. There is too much at risk to allow my emotions to take over. No, I need to remain levelheaded. To be the real man in this scenario.

After checking the locks on the doors, I guide us to the couch and lie down. "Let's rest a little longer. Then we'll get up and take care of this."

I pull Autumn against my chest and hold her. Soon, her breathing levels out and I close my eyes, drifting off.

~

"Miss me already?" Dad says when he answers his phone.

"Ha ha, old man. Actually, wanted to ask a favor."

"What's up?"

I take a deep breath. "Someone smashed in Autumn's windshield last night. I need it towed to the shop, but I'm not comfortable leaving them alone at the house."

"What the hell?" When Dad starts cursing, you know a nerve has been struck.

I relay the alarming wake up in the early morning and explain the condition of the glass and the note left behind. He mumbles unintelligible words into the phone. Dad and I are similar creatures and right about now, he's working hard to keep his temper in check. Autumn may not be his daughter, Clementine not his granddaughter, but he protects and stands up for them just the same.

Dad agrees I shouldn't leave and tells me he will head down to the garage and drive the flatbed over.

"Really appreciate it, Dad. Thank you."

"We're family, Jonas. Wouldn't have it any other way."

After breakfast, we hang on the couch until Dad shows up. We chat while he loads the car on the flatbed. He tells me he knows where we can get a windshield to replace Autumn's and not to worry. Before he drives off, he promises to secure her car in the body bay of the garage. Thankfully, we have security cameras around the shop. If anything happens while we aren't there, we have "eyes" on the place.

When Dad drives off, I head back inside and sidle up to Autumn on the couch. "All taken care of." She tucks her lips between her teeth and nods slowly. I bring my thumb and forefinger to her chin and lift her gaze to mine. "Hey, there isn't much else we can do right now. So, as best we can, let's try to enjoy the day and our time with everyone later. Okay?"

She blinks back the tears fighting to escape. "Okay," she croaks out.

I press a chaste kiss to her lips. "This will all be over tomorrow. Let's focus on that and celebrating you."

We spend a little longer on the couch before hopping into action. We have a long list of things to do before everyone arrives—food, cleanup, setup—and divvy up the list so no one is overwhelmed. For obvious reasons, we give the simpler tasks to Clementine. But she will also help Autumn with a few recipes.

In no time, the house is clean and the kitchen counters are littered with bowls and platters of food. Going with the tropical theme, everything we have on the menu contains either fruit or Polynesian flavors. Autumn also messaged Cora before we went shopping yesterday and asked what to buy, so she didn't have to bring separate food.

Our friends slowly arrive at the house. No one asks where Autumn's car is, and we don't bring up the topic. Instead, we spend hours with our favorite people. Our family. We smile and laugh and enjoy ourselves.

Gavin, Rez, and Micah man the grill with me. Cora,

Shelly, Penny, and Tatyana lounge on the outdoor couch with Autumn. Rex, Erin, Iliana, and Trevor chat near the cooler and banquet table of snacks. And Clementine plays tag with Ashton and Spartan in the yard.

I love how we have all easily blended together. Four months ago, I never would have pegged this as my life. In love. A backyard packed with people who care about me as much as I do them. None of those people my kin. Each and every one of them there for me in a heartbeat.

Couldn't ask for a better life.

After we devour dinner, Clementine lights the candles on Autumn's pineapple upside-down cake and everyone sings "Happy Birthday". Cake is eaten and gifts are handed over. Autumn blooms under the attention and I vow to make each of her birthdays going forward better than the previous. She had no expectations of being showered with gifts, but doesn't turn a single one down.

One by one, our guests give us hugs and say good night. Penny, Cora, and Gavin hang around long enough to help us clean up. After the last farewells are given, we tuck Clementine in and get ready for bed.

"Thank you for today," Autumn says as she peels away her clothes.

I step into her and wrap my arms around her. "My pleasure, scarlet." I kiss the tip of her nose. "Next year will be even better."

She holds my gaze a moment. "As long as I have you, every year will be perfect." Her gaze drops to my lips as she licks hers. "Now, I'm ready for my favorite present," she whispers.

"Oh, yeah?" She nods. "And what's that?"

"You." She peels my shirt over my head and pushes me down onto the bed.

As she crawls up my body and presses her skin to mine, I wish her a happy birthday and lose myself to her.

twenty-three

. . .

Autumn

I SCOOP CHEESY SCRAMBLED EGGS ONTO A PLATE AND ADD a slice of buttered toast. Setting it on the breakfast bar for Clementine, I pour her a glass of orange juice.

Clementine swings her dangling feet as she eats her breakfast. To her, today is just a typical Monday. Breakfast before school. Getting dressed and gathering her backpack of school supplies.

But today is far from a typical Monday. Quite the opposite, actually. Today, my daughter's future is in the hands of a judge. A judge I have never met and know nothing about. A judge who reads over a stack of papers and listens to our attorneys as they plead our case. And there is nothing I can do except try to remain calm. On the outside, at least.

Jonas strolls into the kitchen in jeans and a T-shirt. Last night, we decided to dress as we normally would in the morning. We didn't want Clementine to go to school asking why we were dressed up or with worry in her heart. So, for now, we go about the morning as if nothing is different.

“’Morning, scarlet.” Jonas steps up behind me, wraps his arms around my waist and kisses my temple.

“’Morning. Hungry?”

He nods. “Little bit.”

I portion out the last of the eggs and make us each some toast. After we finish eating, we gear up and drive Clementine to school. She bops and sings in the back seat, and I can’t help but tear up a little. But I resist the urge to cry and swallow the wad of emotion lodged in my throat.

Just before we reach the drop-off point in the car circle, I spin around in my seat. “Hey, pumpkin. Hope you have a good day at school. Are you doing any fun projects?” Jonas rubs small circles on my thigh, trying to soothe me as I engage with Clementine.

I don’t want to consider this my last opportunity with my daughter, but what if it is? What if the judge sides with Leo and I am ordered to hand custody over to him before the end of the day? Doesn’t seem logical, but I have also never been in a situation like this. I have never had to think about the possibility of losing my child to someone who never cared until eight weeks ago.

“We’re making aliens in art class today,” she says with exuberance.

“How cool. Do you know what you want your alien to look like?”

Until we reach the drop-off, Clementine goes into animated detail on how she plans to create her alien.

When it's time to say goodbye, I choke back my words and hug her harder than normal.

"Have a good day, pumpkin. See you later."

"Bye, Mama. Bye, Mr. Jonas. See you after school." She hops out of the Jeep and walks past the gate into the school.

I stare after her until she heads into the building. As soon as she vanishes, I lose it. Tears spill down my cheeks and I sob at the plausibility of not doing this every day. Of not dropping my daughter off at school. Of not hugging her whenever I please. Or being able to enjoy the little moments. The animated conversations. Watching a movie with her every night. Witnessing her evolve from a girl into a young woman.

"Know it's not easy, but try to stay optimistic. Keep telling the universe you *will* get to keep her. Put it out there."

And I do. I pray to whoever listens and ask them to let today end well. To let Clementine stay with me, where she is loved and happy and healthy. To let today be the last day I hear from or speak to Leo again.

We get back to the house and rush to get ready. Jonas changes into gray dress slacks and a black button-down. Considering I see him in jeans and a T-shirt most days, I look forward to peeling his clothes off later.

"Quit looking at me like that," he states.

"Like what?" I play coy.

"Like you want to rip my clothes off." He chuckles when I shrug and my favorite dimple makes an appearance. "We'll have time for that later. When we're celebrating."

"Celebrating," I mumble. "Yes."

I finish getting ready. Apply a light coat of makeup and pin the top half of my hair back while letting the rest hang in loose waves. I lint brush my knee-length black and red dress, shifting the skirt a little to make sure the small pleats at the base sit over my knees.

"You look beautiful," Jonas says from the doorway. "We should get going."

We head out the door and drive toward downtown. The traffic is light heading toward the beach this time of day. Most residents are heading out, and it's still early for the snowbirds to drive to the beach.

By the time Jonas turns on Court Street, my palms are clammy. As he pulls into the parking lot, locates a space to park, and feeds the meter, my nails dig into my skin. My heart beats out of my chest as Jonas opens my door and holds his hand out.

"I've got you. Don't worry about what's going on around us."

He guides us into the courthouse and we go through security. Past the screening area, I spot Theresa and wave. Once we catch up to her, she shakes Jonas's hand before pulling me into a hug.

"Today is a big day. I know you're nervous, but I need for you to compartmentalize it as much as possible. Show your strength. Wear it on your sleeve. Do not bow or bend or show vulnerability. It won't matter to the judge, but if his defense sees it, they'll use it as ammunition."

I take a deep breath and shake my arms at my sides. "Okay. I can do this."

Theresa turns to Jonas then. "Glad to see you here, Jonas. Autumn will need your support here today, but do me one favor." Jonas's brows shoot up in question. "While in or near the courtroom, do not speak for Autumn. Although you may have good intentions, she needs to display her strength and not be outshone." Then she bounces her eyes between the both of us. "And both of you, try not to engage in any unsavory behavior. Don't speak to Leo or his attorney. Better to err on the side of caution."

Once we both agree, Theresa walks us through the courthouse and leads us to the courtroom where the case will be decided.

As we approach, Jonas speaks up. "Theresa, there was also another incident." Jonas looks to me briefly. "Autumn's windshield was smashed and a note was left."

Jonas pulls his phone from his pocket and shows Theresa shots of Betsy and the note.

"Were the police notified?"

"Yes," he responds, stowing his phone.

"Perfect. Hopefully we don't need it, but the evidence ways in our favor."

We sit on a bench just outside the room and hold each other's hands. No words are exchanged as I lean into Jonas. He draws small circles on my skin and soothes the anxiety ripping through my bloodstream.

Theresa clears her throat and we both look up in time to spot Leo and an older man at his side. I release Jonas's hand and sit up straighter. For the next however long, I shove every insecure thought about myself and losing Clementine in a closet in my mind. Leo's attorney steps up and shakes hands with Theresa. I suppose most attorneys in the area know each other and are cordial, even when they are on opposing sides.

Leo stares at me and Jonas. A wicked gleam on his face. He doesn't say a word, just stands beside his attorney with his hands shoved in his overpriced suit pockets.

The door to the courtroom opens and a man in security attire steps out. "You may come in now. Judge Walton will be ready to proceed momentarily."

Leo's attorney heads for the door, Leo on his heels. Before Theresa moves to enter, an older couple steps in line to go inside.

The moment I get a good look at them, I stop breathing. *What the actual fuck?*

Every muscle in my body turns to stone. I clutch Jonas's arm to stabilize myself. My throat runs dry and my mouth feels tacky. I blink a few times, wondering if my mind is playing tricks. But they are still there.

And when they sidle up to Leo, his wicked gleam grows tenfold. They enter the courtroom, and I hold us outside a moment longer.

"What the fuck," I whisper.

"Who are they?" Theresa questions.

"My parents. They kicked me out after learning I was pregnant and that Leo and I were no longer together."

"Why would they be here?" I shake my head at Theresa. "Either way, shove aside whatever you're feeling. Remember what I said earlier?" I nod. "Okay. Take a deep breath. Loosen your grip on Jonas. And let's go in there and win this."

I inhale deeply, over and over. When I loosen my grip on Jonas, I shake out my hands. With a few minutes left, we stroll into the courtroom and I keep my eyes forward, away from Leo and my parents.

A moment after we sit and Theresa takes out a thick binder, Judge Walton walks out. We rise from our chairs and stand.

"Be seated," she says. Judge Walton scans the documents in front of her. "Today's case is a petition of custody for Clementine Arianna Rooker." She glances at Leo and his attorney, then us. "Ms. Rooker. If I'm reading the documentation correctly, you have had sole custody of Clementine since birth?"

I glance at Theresa and she nods. "Yes, Your Honor."

Judge Walton nods then looks to Leo. "Mr. Parker. It is my understanding you have not formally met your daughter. Please tell me why."

Part of me jumps for joy when Judge Walton puts Leo on the spot. Although, no doubt he has been schooled in his responses.

"Your Honor, I was a young man when I learned I would become a father. I made a juvenile decision and walked away. I am here today to correct said decision."

Judge Walton hums and shuffles through the documents in front of her. She pins Leo with her gaze again. "Mr. Parker, your daughter is seven and a half years old. Why are you suddenly interested in her well-being? Why are you filing for sole custody when you have never interacted with her?"

Leo swallows. Beneath the table, I catch his leg bouncing. I give a mental victory fist pump at his nervousness.

Since this all started, these are the exact questions I have asked. No normal person files for sole custody when they have never made attempts to be in a child's life. When they have never shown signs of caring or wanting to get to know the child.

"Your Honor, there aren't many decisions in my life I regret as much as abandoning my daughter." His knee bounces faster. "I would like to make amends. Provide her with whatever her heart desires. Make sure she wants for nothing." He fidgets with the hem of his jacket under the table. "I want to get to know her."

Judge Walton purses her lips and doesn't look away from Leo. "I see." I don't miss how Judge Walton's eyes shift back to my parents before coming my way. "Ms. Rooker. Would you be open to shared custody with Mr. Parker?"

Theresa glances at me before speaking up. "Your Honor, when the initial suit began, Ms. Rooker agreed to allow joint custody so long as she maintained majority. She also wanted to include Clementine's opinion in the matter, seeing as she has never met her father and may be frightened to be left unattended with a stranger. Ms. Rooker stated she would allow supervised visitation with Mr. Parker and his family until Clementine felt comfortable being alone with them."

Judge Walton faces Leo. "Mr. Parker, did you refuse these terms?"

Sweat beads on Leo's temple and I beam inside. This

is not going according to his plan. *See, money doesn't always work in your favor.*

"I did, Your Honor."

"Why?" Judge Walton asks, bluntly. "Why do you feel your daughter needs to be fully removed from her mother's custody? Has Ms. Rooker done something untoward?"

"No, Your Honor. I just..." Leo shifts his face enough to side-glance my parents. And that glance answers every question I have asked since the day he stood in front of my apartment. It isn't Leo who wants Clementine. It's my damn parents. Again, what the actual fuck?

"Mr. Parker. May I ask your relationship to the man and woman behind you?"

Leo fists his suit jacket. The bead of sweat rolls down his temple and drips from the angle of his jaw. I am dying to hear his answer. "This is Burton and Kathryn Rooker. Autumn's parents."

"Ah, I see. And why are Ms. Rooker's parents sitting behind you and not her?"

This just keeps getting better and better. If I asked these questions, Leo would give me an angry rebuttal and storm off like an adolescent. But he can't be a loose cannon with Judge Walton.

"I'd like to rescind my petition for custody," Leo belts out. I gasp at the same time my parents turn beet red and sneer. "My choice to file for sole custody was irrational and hasty. My apologies to everyone."

"Well, this makes my day run a bit smoother," Judge Walton states. "But, you're not off the hook yet, Mr.

Parker. We will not discuss the details today, but your attorney will be receiving documentation from my office regarding missed child support."

Leo hangs his head. "Yes, Your Honor."

Judge Walton looks to me. "Ms. Rooker. I hear by award you sole custody of Clementine Arianna Rooker." She lifts her gavel and claps it to the base. "This hearing is adjourned."

We all stand as Judge Walton exits the courtroom. As soon as she enters her chamber, I spin around and hug Jonas.

"See, scarlet. Nothing to worry about." He hugs me tight to his chest. "It was great to watch him sweat, though."

I laugh. "It was, wasn't it."

twenty-four

. . .

Jonas

Autumn stands tall beside me, and I have never been prouder to have her on my arm.

While we wait for Leo, his attorney, and Autumn's parents to leave, Theresa talks softly about next steps. Paperwork that will follow in regards to back child support and any future support. Autumn disputes the notion, stating she doesn't want a dime of the money. But Theresa comes back with a better solution—a future savings for Clementine. Whether for college or a first car or when she decides to move out.

Leo and his attorney, as well as Autumn's parents, start for the door, but Leo pauses before exiting.

"Autumn, I apologize for all this." He rocks back on his heels. "And I want to forego any visitation. With me and my family. Sorry to have put you through all this. I will pay your attorney's fees."

Well, well, well. Mr. Hotshot is just full of surprises today. Either way, I am glad he had a change of heart. Not sure what provoked it, but maybe his morality kicked in. Thank god it did before the judge made a decision.

Autumn nods and gives a gentle smile. “Thank you.”

The four of them leave the courtroom. Autumn’s parents still appeared perturbed by the outcome, but I really don’t care. We hang back for a few minutes and allow them to get a head start on leaving.

“See, nothing to worry about,” I say, squeezing Autumn to my side. “I knew everything would swing in our favor.”

Autumn peers up at me with a sparkle in her intoxicating eyes. “Oh, did you now?”

I nod. “Yep.”

After a few minutes, we exit the courtroom. Before parting ways with Theresa, she tells Autumn she will reach out to her as soon as she receives the paperwork. Should be straightforward and only need signatures.

We walk down the steps outside the courthouse, hand in hand, smiles plastered on our faces. “We should definitely celebrate,” I suggest. “A nice dinner, or maybe a special dessert. Something.”

“I…” Autumn stops short and I follow her line of sight. To my Jeep. Where her parents stand, arms tight across their chests.

Not sure what their game is, but I kept an eye on them the entire time in the courtroom. They sat behind Leo, hands folded in their laps, expressions blank. Mostly.

As soon as Autumn told me who they were, something didn’t sit right with me. Why the hell would they show up to a custody hearing for Clementine? One—Autumn hasn't spoken to or seen them in almost as long as Leo. So, it's not as if they heard the news from her. Two—they sat behind *Leo*. Her parents sat behind *him* in silent support.

Why?

Not as if he and Autumn had been dating for several years and her parents developed a loving relationship with him. From what Autumn said, she and Leo had been together less than a year. During their time together, not much of it revolved around time spent with either of their families.

And then it clicks into place. The puzzle pieces lock together and form the bigger picture. I see it now. When their faces turned bright red in the courtroom as Leo forfeited. The way Autumn's father gnashed his teeth as the judge announced Autumn the sole custodial parent of Clementine. Their balled fists as they rose from the bench. The disgust in their eyes as they left the courtroom.

They did this. They went to Leo and orchestrated this whole mess.

Her father steps closer. "She doesn't belong with you," he seethes.

Pissed, I step protectively in front of Autumn and point a finger at him. "You need to back the fuck up."

"What are you going to do, boy." He steps closer. "You gonna hit me? Go right ahead. Plenty of cops around here to haul you to jail."

"Actually, I won't hit you. That's what you want. To see me hauled off in cuffs."

Autumn's mother comes to her father's side with a sneer on her face. "That's what you deserve, lowlife."

Behind me, Autumn's body tenses. Her nails dig into my biceps. Before I can stop her, she steps around. "No," she shouts. "You don't get to come here and act high and mighty. Not after sending your daughter to live on the streets. Not after you shielded yourselves behind a man who abandoned his child. Who the hell do you think you are?"

Her father steps within feet of Autumn and I shove him back. "Don't test me."

He throws his head back and laughs. "You don't scare me, boy." Then he faces Autumn. "You don't deserve her. What kind of mother works in a tattoo parlor and dates a mechanic? Don't you realize the damage you're doing to that girl? She won't live up to her potential."

"Think you can do better, *father*?" Autumn breathes heavily. "Because, in your eyes, I didn't turn out so great."

Her remark meant to make him falter has me wondering if she sees herself this way. As a failure. But I don't dwell on it now. There isn't time. Because he steps closer. Too close.

"How dare you speak to me with such petulance. Your mother and I raised you with good morals and faith. You best respect me, girl."

"Respect you?" Autumn inches closer to him. I remain on her heels. "Respect is earned, not handed over. Clergy collars don't make you righteous, *father*.

Nor do they mean you *deserve* respect more than someone else."

"I warned you," he sneers. *I warned you*. The note on Autumn's car yesterday. Moments ago, he said *she doesn't belong with you*.

Holy shit. Holy. Shit.

"It was you," I mutter.

Autumn faces me, brows pinched. "What?"

I meet her eyes. "The notes, your windshield. It wasn't Leo." I point at her father. "You did this." His smug smile all the response I need.

But before I react, Autumn's mother storms forward and backhands her. Autumn falls to the ground and everything around me goes red. I won't hit a woman, but I sure as shit won't stand for anyone hitting Autumn.

I reach out and grab her wrist. "Get your filthy hands off me," she screams. But I refuse to loosen my grip.

Her father steps forward and I glare at him. "Don't test me. I won't hit her, but I will gladly knock you out."

I glance around the lot, scanning for a police vehicle. Spot one in the distance, an officer sitting behind the wheel, and wave my arm high. The police cruiser veers our way and stops a few car lengths back. After talking into the radio on her shoulder, the officer steps out of the car and approaches us.

"What seems to be the problem?"

I lift Autumn's mother's arm. "This woman just assaulted my girlfriend. She, and this man, approached us in the lot after our hearing in the courthouse."

The female officer steps closer to Autumn, who hasn't stood up yet, and squats in front of her. "Are you alright, ma'am?" Autumn nods and the officer extends a hand to help her up. "Tell me what happened here." Her question directed at Autumn.

Autumn explains the reason we came to the courthouse today. How she was shocked to see her parents with her ex. Then, she gives a small backstory regarding her parents before explaining what happened as we approached the Jeep.

Before the officer begins questioning Autumn's parents, I interject about the harassment and police report she filed. I add how Autumn's father basically confessed to the notes and damage after I put the pieces together.

"You can't prove shit, lowlife," her father hisses.

Autumn steps up to her father. Gets in his face. Emboldened with the officer at her back. "Did you do this? Did you write those notes and trash my car? Try to take my daughter away from me by using her birth father as a scapegoat?"

His lip curls. Eyes narrow. He leans in, inches from her face. "You don't deserve to be her mother. Gallivanting around like a whore. Living a trashy life. No sign of God in your life. Worthless." He inches back and spits at her feet. "You're no daughter of mine."

The officer steps around Autumn, grabs his hands and yanks them behind his back. She reads him his rights and steers him to the back seat of her car. All the while, Autumn's mother thrashes in my grip.

"Who do you think you are?" she hollers at the officer. "How dare you arrest a man of the cloth. You'll burn in hell for this." She shifts her gaze to Autumn. "As will you. You disgust me. At least your sister knows what it means to be a good Christian woman. At least I don't regret her coming from my womb."

I tighten my grip on her wrist. "Best if you stop speaking now. Before you dig yourself in a deeper hole."

Autumn sidles up to me, takes my free hand and shakes her head. "No, it's okay. Let her say whatever she wants." Autumn turns her attention on her mother. "I've always known who you are, mother. Always known I wouldn't live up to your expectations. As a child, it hurt when I never made you happy or proud. As a woman..." she sighs, "I don't care. There has never been a day in my life where I felt your love. Ever. Growing up under your scrutiny made me feel small and meaningless. The day I left... that was the day I woke up. Came to life. I may have lived in a shelter for a short time, but even those people cared for me more than you ever did." Autumn wraps her hand around my waist. "And finding Jonas, discovering true love, has wiped away every ounce of hurt you and father inflicted upon me."

Caught up in her proclamation, I miss the slight shift as Autumn's mother swings her free hand forward. A crack ripples in the air as her hand connects with Autumn's face.

"You ungrateful little witch," her mother hisses.

The officer jogs over from the cruiser, yanks Autumn's mother's wrists behind her back, and cuffs her. As she walks her to the cruiser, she prattles off Miranda rights.

I face Autumn, framing her cheeks in my hands. "Are you okay?"

Her eyes glaze over as she stares up at me. "Yes. No. I don't know."

On the verge of tears, I hug her to my chest and turn her face away from the police cruiser. "Got you, scarlet." She fists the back of my shirt, trembling against my frame. "Shh, shh, shh. I got you." I sway her slowly in my arms.

As her grip loosens on my shirt, the officer approaches us. "Ma'am, I need to know if you'd like to press assault charges."

Autumn peeks up at me, seeking guidance. I want to tell her yes. Want to tell her she should not allow them to get away with everything they have done. But I don't. Instead, I give her a soft smile that says the choice is hers. I will never rob her of her choices. And this decision, although it weighs heavily, is one she should make on her own.

She swallows and meets the officer's gaze. "Yes." Her frame relaxes in my arms. "I want to press charges."

The officer takes out a business card from her breast pocket and writes on it before handing it to Autumn. "The case number is on the card. As soon as possible, we need you to come to the station and give a formal statement." Autumn nods. "If anything else occurs, call the number on the card." The officer smiles, the corners of her eyes crinkling. "Sorry this happened to you. Try to enjoy the rest of your day."

Turning on her heel, she walks to the cruiser, gets in, and drives off.

Autumn sighs and I steer her toward the Jeep. "C'mon. I know exactly where to go."

twenty-five

. . .

Autumn

WHAT THE HELL JUST HAPPENED?

Jonas helps me up into the Jeep. I buckle my seat belt and stare out the windshield, the world around me a clouded haze.

Today has been a roller-coaster ride from hell. And it isn't noon yet.

When my parents appeared outside the courtroom, confusion set in. The last time we spoke was the day they banished me from their lives. *"No daughter of mine will have a child out of wedlock."* Those were my father's final words to me. Literally disowning me with my mother at his side. She hadn't even flinched at his words. If anything, she appeared relieved I was leaving.

What kind of people do that?

Jonas gets in the Jeep but doesn't start it. We sit in silence as the last thirty minutes process. Their cruel words. Bringing a hand to my cheek, I rub against the sting beneath the surface. I zone out and scan memories over the last seven and a half years. Plucking out every oddity I couldn't explain. Wondering if my parents had been preying on me—preying on my daughter—all this time.

"How are you?" Jonas asks, breaking the silence. He reaches across the console and weaves our fingers.

I twist in my seat and face him, leaning against the headrest. "Freaked out. Puzzled. Hurt." I shake my head. "Relieved. Glad this is all over."

He brings my hand to his lips and kisses my knuckles. "Sorry you had to deal with all this in the first place."

"Not your fault."

"No, but no one deserves to deal with what just happened."

We stare at each other, his thermal pools a swirl of emotions. Sadness. Worry. Happiness. Hope. I grab hold of the last two and hug them to my heart. I fear the first two will linger if I don't tell him more about what happened with my parents. And the way I was raised.

"Hate to say it," I croak, my throat like sandpaper. "But I expected nothing less."

Jonas juts his bottom lip out, the corners of his eyes turning down. I lift my free hand and trace his lower lip from corner to corner.

"Growing up in the Rooker house was not like being around your family."

"You don't need to explain, Autumn."

I nod. "That's one of the things I love about you, ya know. How you don't hold expectations over my head." He smiles as I stroke my thumb over his cheek. "But I need to get this out."

"Okay. Just don't feel obliged."

I close my eyes and take a deep breath. Jonas turns into my palm and kisses the center. His touch buzzes under my skin and shoots a current straight to my heart. When my eyes open and lock on his, peace washes over me. Even with the pain of the past thrown in my face minutes ago, Jonas settles every anxiety-ridden memory.

Swallowing, I take one last deep breath and dive in headfirst. "When you're only exposed to one way to live for the first thirteen years of your life, it's difficult to believe another way exists. As a little girl, I looked up to my parents. Did as I was told. Took the beatings when I disobeyed. Listened to the constant verbal beat-downs. How did I know being treated as such was wrong? I had nothing to compare it to. Father enrolled me in the church's private school at age three. It wasn't a bad place. The teachers were wonderful, as were my classmates. With my father giving sermons several times a week at the church, everyone looked up to him. Saw him as a role model. Even me."

I close my eyes a moment and collect myself. Jonas tightens his grip on my hand, showing silent support.

"Even when he hit me. I was taught to believe disobedience equals punishment. Punishment in the Rooker household equals a hole-laden wooden paddle against your bare butt. Obviously, I avoided this as much as possible. But, sometimes, I received punishment simply because father had a bad day."

I tuck my lips between my teeth. Jonas caresses my

cheek with his knuckles. "Sorry this happened to you, Autumn." His voice soft and sad.

"Wasn't until I went to public high school that I learned how different my life was. Compared to my new friends, I was sorely lacking. Yes, I had intelligence. But only from textbooks. And even then, my education had been tweaked around scripture. Wasn't necessarily a bad thing, but it secluded me. Put me in a box with the teens labeled as weirdos or freaks by the popular students. I didn't let it bog me down, but I wished to make at least one friend who didn't look at me like I traveled through time from the 1950s in my handmade dresses."

Jonas laughs and my brows shoot up in question. "You still dress like someone from another era. Just look sexy as hell now."

I join in his laughter. "Touché." He makes a fair point. "Anyway… the longer I spent in public school, the more I opened up. Not just verbally, but in the way I expressed myself. Clothing, makeup, hairstyle. My parents never spent a dime on any of it, though. I had to earn it working at the grocery store near the house." Taking a deep breath, I lick my lips. "I remember the first day I wore makeup and my mother called me a whore. The first time I wore clothes that showed my curves and she backhanded me so hard I had a bruise on my cheek for a week. Every time I painted over it with concealer, I cried."

Jonas stares at me, glassy-eyed. "Wish I would've found you sooner." I love the way Jonas wants to heal all of my scars. Wants to replace every action that has blemished my life.

"Me too. But if you had, I may not be who I am today. And I love who I am. Especially with you."

He leans across the console and kisses me. So tender. So sweet.

"Esther—my sister—never received punishments. For whatever reason, she did no wrong. She was the daughter my parents always wanted. Obedient, quiet, subservient. When my parents threw me out, she stood by their side with disgust on her face. My parents had learned to keep her in private school after seeing how it changed me. Last time I spoke with her was about a year ago. Although she still feels my parents were doing what they thought was best, she is slowly being exposed to the world. Hopefully, in the future, we'll be in a better place. I'd love for Clementine to meet her cousins. And I pray one day to get to know her again."

"You will," Jonas states with confidence.

I exhale and release it all. My mother and her twisted version of love. My father and his rigid outlook on life. I breathe in fresh air and expel every ounce of the hurt they inflicted upon me.

"Thank you." Jonas scrunches his brows. "For letting me get that off my chest. For allowing me to shed weight I didn't know I still held on to."

He strokes his thumb over my cheek. "You're welcome." Leaning in, he kisses my forehead. "Can I take you somewhere?"

"Yes."

He kisses my lips. "Nowhere fancy. But after the day's events, I think it's the perfect place to be."

Jonas starts the Jeep and drives away from downtown. Billie Eilish croons through the speakers as the city zips past us. Every minute of the last two hours flashes in my mind. The worry and anxiety, joy and fright. Then I relax. Melt into the seat and close my eyes as realization hits.

This is over. And Clementine won't be going anywhere. Relief washes over me and I bask in it. Let it heal me and steal all the pieces of my past that threaten my well-being.

Before long, Jonas parks in front of his parents' house. I glance over at him and tilt my head.

"Only Mom is here. She wanted me to call as soon as the hearing ended. Since I didn't have the chance, thought this might be better."

For whatever reason, my nerves skyrocket. The few times Clementine and I have been over for family dinner night, his parents—the entire family—have been lovely. Treated me like I belonged. Hugged me like their own daughters.

So why are my palms sweaty?

We go inside the house and Jonas calls out for his mom. I clamp onto his arm, mirroring a timid child. His mom steps out of the hall, her smile bright, wide, and welcoming.

"Hey, you two." She pulls Jonas in for a hug, then me. She holds me at arm's length, eyes searching mine. "How'd it go?"

Jonas guides us to the living room and we all sit.

Over the next hour, we share the craziness of the morning. Along with the good news. More than once, Jonas's mom tugs me into her arms and just holds me. The second time she does, I cry on her shoulder. She holds me close, strokes my back softly, and tells me to let it all out.

Irene Thompson may not be my birth mother, but she is the most maternal person in my life. And she embraces me as her own. For that, I have never been more grateful.

When I finish spilling my heart, she drags us to the kitchen and we make lunch together. The simple sandwiches taste better than any meal I ate in my youth. We sit at the dining table and enjoy each other's company.

As it nears time to pick Clementine up from school, we exchange hugs and goodbyes.

"Hope to see you all on Wednesday."

I curl into Jonas's side. "We'll be here," I answer for us.

"See you then. Give that little girl a hug for me."

We say one last goodbye before leaving. Jonas drives us through the city and in the direction of Clementine's school. And the entire time, I ogle him.

How did I get so lucky? How did I land a guy as sweet and caring and desirable as Jonas? A man who doesn't just love me, but also my little girl. A man who goes above and beyond to make us happy. Who doesn't hesitate when it comes to our hearts and our happiness. Who will drop everything to be there for us.

I don't know what I did to deserve Jonas, but I will never take him or us for granted.

"What're you thinking about so hard over there?"

"How lucky I am," I answer without hesitation.

He reaches for my hand and brings it to his lips. "Think you're mistaken." When I continue to stare at his profile, unspeaking, he fills in the blank. "I am definitely the lucky one."

twenty-six

. . .

Jonas

CLEMENTINE DARTS ACROSS THE HOUSE, SPARTAN HOT ON her heels as they search for Lex. Giggles echo from the pile of blankets on the other side of the couch as Clementine keeps calling his name. When she finally lifts the blankets away, they both run off laughing.

I help Jasmine and Jillian make dinner while Autumn sets the table with Mom. They chat while placing plates and silverware and napkins on the table. But their conversation is too quiet for me to hear.

"Really good to see you smiling so much," Jasmine says, bringing my attention back to the kitchen.

"Thanks, I guess."

How can I not smile when Autumn and Clementine are near? They bring a joy into my life I never imagined possible.

Yet, it seems as if Autumn still has hesitations about living together.

Almost a month has passed since I gifted her a key

to my house. Since I set up a room for Clementine. And yet, I still don't have her in my bed every night.

Is it wrong for me to expect such things? Yes, I suppose so. Considering we have only been together roughly four months, asking Autumn to uproot her and Clementine's life for my own selfish needs would be a dick move.

Doesn't mean I don't want to, though.

Anyone else in my shoes would be grateful to have what I do. Autumn and Clementine stay at the house four or five nights a week. Practically full time. And on the nights they don't stay, I sleep in my bed alone.

Since the case closed with Leo, and since learning Autumn's parents were behind the damage to her car and the notes, there doesn't seem to be a need for extra eyes.

And it sucks.

Don't get me wrong. I am beyond grateful she and Clementine are safe. In fact, they are more than safe. Safer than before the trial began.

When Leo and Autumn's attorneys spoke after the hearing, something unexpected and surprising happened. Not only did Leo pay back child support, interest, and Autumn's attorney fees; he also signed away his parental rights. Theresa had to explain it to Autumn several times. We also learned Autumn's father threatened to throw Leo into a shitstorm with local media about his abandoned child. Leo is by no means a celebrity, but when you own a massive hotel chain, news spreads quickly in the community. The news may have ruined the life he'd built.

Basically, Leo told his attorney he didn't want a similar occurrence to happen to Autumn or Clementine in the future. He didn't want someone to try and use his paternity to hurt either one of them. He never had ill intent and honestly didn't realize what he was getting himself into. I don't know how much of that I believe.

Either way, at least Autumn sleeps better at night knowing no one can take her daughter from her.

"Is the roast ready?" Jillian asks as she finishes smashing the potatoes.

I open the oven and jab the pot roast with a thermometer. After the needle hits the temperature Mom deems as the perfect roast, I grab the potholders and take it out. "Ready."

We carry the food dishes to the table then holler for everyone to come eat. Dad, Anton, and the kids rush to the table. Once we are in our usual seats, Mom tells everyone how grateful she is to have them at the table again. Then everyone fills their plates.

Dad encourages Lex to be mischievous while Clementine giggles. He nonchalantly picks up a green bean with his finger and pretends like he will throw it at Mom. A minute later, Lex tosses a green bean and Jasmine snaps at Dad to not goad him. I don't remember Dad being such an instigator when we were kids. No matter, he loves making the little ones laugh.

Although it's only March, Jillian rambles on to Mom about the fall fashion line the store will receive soon. Turtlenecks and scarves and gloves. Wool jackets and thermal-lined pants. Honestly, fall and winter attire in Florida is a strange concept. The actual fall season feels like a mild summer. And winter resembles what northerners experience as fall. Most clothing stores in Florida sell swimsuits year-round. No joke, we could get away with wearing fall attire in the winter without discomfort.

Beside me, Autumn focuses her attention on Jillian. Every now and again, Jillian pipes up and asks what she wears during different seasons with her rockabilly style. Genuinely intrigued by Autumn's fashion. How she wears it with ease, although not many local stores carry her style of clothes.

I lean back in my chair, eat my dinner, and absorb the ease with which Autumn talks with my family. Autumn and Clementine both. As if they have been sitting at this table and sharing meals with the Thompsons for years. Watching them blend in without effort has my heart stuttering before it takes off in a sprint.

With each passing day, our relationship grows stronger. Our bond more inseparable. We gravitate toward each other like the moon does the earth. As if finally where we are meant to be. In synergy. Two halves of one soul coming back together.

In the same breath, I miss her. On the nights she and Clementine don't sleep under the same roof as me. When Autumn doesn't lie next to me in bed. I miss her weight on my chest and her breath on my skin. Miss her soft snores and the twitch of her fingers when she dreams.

Do I wish the two of them lived with me full time? Hell yes. Do I question why they aren't? Also, yes.

The last thing I want to do is pressure Autumn. Especially after the debacle with Leo and her parents.

But I also can't stand not knowing if she wants to take the next step. If she wants to move in together. Or if she wants to keep things as they are.

Is it too soon to live together? This question has popped into my head more times than I care to count. Perhaps timing keeps her hesitant. Four months isn't long in the grand scheme. Some couples live apart for years before moving in together. But some move in within weeks.

"What do you think, Jonas?" Mom asks, and I have no idea what I missed.

"Sorry, was zoned out a minute. What'd you ask?"

"If you wanted to join us for Easter. Nothing fancy. Egg hunt, sugary treats, and dinner."

I glance over at Autumn to see her watching me with a shy smile. "Sounds like fun, Mom. Just tell us when to be here."

She claps and rubs her hands together. "Wonderful."

Autumn curls her hand around my bicep and leans into my side, resting her head on my shoulder. I kiss her forehead then press my cheek to her hair. Taking a deep breath, I close my eyes and absorb every ounce of love she radiates.

Move in with me.

Beside me, Autumn stiffens. Minus Clementine and Lex, the entire room goes silent. *Shit.* "Did I just say that out loud?" I whisper, although everyone hears.

Autumn sits up straighter and faces me. She tucks

her lips between her teeth, eyes darting between mine. "You did," she croaks.

Dad sparks random conversation with Mom, thank god. Soon, everyone else chats among themselves again and pretends to ignore us.

I lean in closer to her, in the hopes of shielding our conversation somewhat. "Wasn't trying to put you on the spot. Sorry. The idea has crossed my mind before. And I'd love you both to be with me every night. But I didn't realize it came out of my mouth until you froze."

Passion mixes with fear and swirls like wildfire in her intoxicating irises. She clamps down on her lips harder and I have to fight the urge to graze my thumb over her chin, just beneath her lips. Beneath the table, her knee begins to bounce. Body stiff, her eyes dart toward everyone in her periphery.

"Can we discuss this later?" she whisper-squeaks. "In private."

I nod. "Of course. Like I said, it was a slip of the tongue."

Clamping down on her lips one last time, she releases them and spins in her chair to face everyone else again. She picks up her fork and pushes food around her plate, but doesn't eat much else. And for the next hour, she resumes prior conversations as if the subject never came up.

Just before eight, we exchange hugs with everyone and head out. Before heading over tonight, Autumn agreed to stay at the house. As she sits silently in the passenger seat, I pray she doesn't regret the decision.

I reach across the console and take her hand in mine.

She weaves her fingers with mine and I breathe a little easier. *Thank goodness.* Not sure how I would handle it if Autumn shirked away from me.

After I park the Jeep in front of the house and we wander inside, Clementine gets ready for bed while I let Spartan outside. The nightly routine goes much the same as usual. Autumn and I give Clementine kisses and hugs good night and ruffle Spartan's fur before we turn off the light and close the door halfway.

In our room, blanketed in darkness, I reach for Autumn and pull her into me. Kiss her forehead, between her brows, the tip of her nose, her lips. Her body goes lax, melts into my touch, my lips. She fists my shirt then releases the cotton, sliding her palms up my chest to my neck, lacing her fingers at the base of my skull.

Apple lingers on her tongue from dessert and mixes with the taste of her. Her cherry vanilla aroma billows around me. From shoulder to hip, she eliminates any measure of space between us. I hum against her lips, her tongue, as she threads her fingers through my hair and tugs at the strands.

With my slipup tonight, I worried—still worry—she would pull away. I have no intention of taking back what I said because I meant it. Just didn't mean to say it aloud. Yet. So much has happened since we started seeing each other, the last thing I want is for Autumn to believe I'm pressuring her into something she isn't ready for. Although, in my eyes, she is more ready than she realizes.

We take our time stripping off clothes and falling in

to the bed. Tonight, our kisses and touches and whispered moans weigh heavier in the shadows. Our bodies move slower, with more intention and adoration. This isn't just sex. Not just a physical need for release or routine activity. And when we climax, the energy around us radiates heart and heat and traces of forever.

My front to her back, arms holding her snug against my skin, we start to drift off. The last thought floating in my mind is how we never brought up the conversation from dinner again. Either of us. And I wonder if that is a good thing or bad.

twenty-seven

. . .

Autumn

Before Jonas and I started dating, I rarely went out. Not that I didn't want to. Penny tried several times to drag me out of the apartment to let loose. Clementine had always been more important. My sole focus.

Now with the custody case closed, I sleep better and breathe easier. Leo signing away his parental rights was the most selfless and unexpected act. Burton and Kathryn Rooker now have assault charges on file and are undoubtedly being ridiculed in their community with a restraining order on record. I have never been a vindictive person, but I do believe in karma. And several years' worth has unleashed upon them.

"Sure you're good watching her tonight?"

Penny tilts her head. "You act as if I've never had girls' night with Clementine before." A palm rests over her heart as her eyes go wide. "You wound me."

I throw my eyeliner at her. "Such a drama queen."

"Be glad your makeup's done, otherwise I'd be

holding this hostage until you groveled for forgiveness."

After applying my lipstick, I spin around and latch on to her neck. "You love me." Penny shoves me as laughter spills from both of us. "Say it. Say you love me."

"Will you get off me if I do?"

I peer up at the ceiling and pucker my lips, feigning contemplation. "Hmm… only if you mean it," I tease.

Penny surprises me and throws her arms around my waist, hoisting me off the floor. "Love you, Auti," she coos, delivering air kisses near my face and hair—careful not to mess up either.

With my feet firmly planted on the ground again, I blow her a kiss. "You're the best." Penny being Penny, she curtsies then saunters off to the living room.

In front of the full-length mirror in the bedroom, I do one last scan, hair to heels. The black and white plaid-print strapless crop top sits high enough to cover the girls, but shows two fingers of skin above my waistline. Charcoal slacks hug my skin from navel to ankle. A simple pair of black heels shine at my feet. My signature scarlet lips for an added pop and hair in a ponytail.

Jonas steps in the room and closes the door. He sizes me up, licking his lips. "Not sure if we'll make it out tonight."

I push out my lower lip and bat my lashes. "But I got all dressed up."

"Fuck, scarlet. Don't pout. I might mess up your makeup." He comes up behind me, staring at me in the mirror over my shoulder, arms slithering around my waist, hips flush against my low back. "Sure I can't convince you to stay in?" Jonas kisses beneath my ear and I roll my eyes closed.

"Our friends are waiting for us," I rebut huskily.

He kisses farther down my neck, hands roaming my abdomen. "They'll understand."

God, I want him to keep going. Explore my skin with his lips and tongue. Taste me. Heat ravages my skin as he kisses along the curve of my neck. "Jonas…"

"Yeah, scarlet."

"I want to." Spinning in his arms, I lock on to his otherworldly eyes. "But after we go out."

My favorite dimple appears as his lips kick up at the corners. His lips hover over my ear. "Hours of torture." He groans then releases me.

"It'll be worth it."

Before I change my mind about going out, I rush us out of the room. Jonas chuckles, his hand on my hip. Hugs and good nights are exchanged with Penny and Clementine. We buckle up in the Jeep and drive toward Tampa.

We crack the windows enough to let the cool night air sweep inside the cab. Salt and sand and earth perfume the breeze. Brilliant shades of tangerine and magenta dust the horizon as the sun dips below the water. "Level of Concern" by Twenty One Pilots plays on the radio as Jonas draws circles on my thigh with his thumb.

My eyes drift closed, amplifying every sense but sight. The whorl of Jonas's calloused thumb swirls on my thigh and stirs heat low in my belly. Hints of sunscreen mixed with Jonas's scent float in the Jeep cabin, and I take a deep breath. A brisk gust whips across my cheek and tampers the heat slowly building from his touch. And as the song on the radio fades from one to the next, I picture dancing with Jonas tonight, sweat dripping off our bodies.

Tonight celebrates a first, of sorts. Not the first occasion going out without Clementine. Jonas and I have gone on several dates. Gone out to hang with our friends and have fun—which is where we are headed now.

But tonight is different.

Because when we all go our separate ways tonight, Jonas and I will go home to his house. Alone. Without Clementine.

Part of me screams inside and waggles a motherly finger in my face, berating me for not being under the same roof as my daughter when I go to sleep. Another part of me hoots and hollers and jumps on the bar top whirling a towel over her head. She praises me, tells me *it's about damn time,* teases I won't get any sleep tonight.

"Should be there in five," Jonas states as he exits the highway.

I shoot a text to Cora and let her know our ETA. She replies and indicates where they parked. A few more turns and Jonas parks the Jeep one row back from Gavin's Range Rover. We stroll to the Rover hand in hand and meet up with everyone. After hugs and quick hellos, we enter the club.

Although I never experienced the clubbing stage of

my late teens/early twenties, I suddenly *feel* years younger. A rush of excitement fuels me as we walk through Roar. Bass and occasional treble pour from the speakers and rattle my bones. Sporadic flashes of colored lights illuminate the dark club while dim lights softly brighten the bars. Sweetness and salt filter through my nose as we pass people bumping and grinding on the dance floor. Jonas guides me through the club with his hands on my hips, provoking the urge to dance.

Gavin maneuvers the group toward a table near the bar. As we circle around, Micah waves then signals he will be over in a minute.

Jonas stands flush to my back, not a breath of space between us. His hands clasp at my belly as his fingers tickle the sliver of visible flesh near my navel. Light caresses fan the flame already heating my skin. Lips lightly nibble at my ear as I roll my eyes back and press my butt against his thighs.

"Mmm... definitely dancing tonight," he muses, breathy on my ear.

I tip my head back, rest it on his shoulder, and meet his gaze. His lips lower to mine and break away far too soon. When I display my best pouty face, Jonas shakes his head and chuckles.

Micah joins us at the table, exchanging hugs and bro back slaps. Although he works tonight, he promises to hang during breaks. He goes around the table and jots our drink orders on a napkin.

After he scratches the last drink down, Micah steps

between two people at the bar and hollers. "Peyton." A woman midway down the bar, blonde hair loosely pulled back in a ponytail glances up. Close to our age. She's tall—closer to Shelly's height than the rest of us. Her eyes scan the bar to find who called out. When her eyes land on Micah, she grinds her jaw. He tosses the napkin on the bar and slaps it. "Drink order," he yells.

She drifts down the bar to stop in front of him. From my vantage point, I can't hear the exchange. But hostility rolls off the two of them. Or is that sexual tension? He says something else to her and she shakes her head while grabbing a glass. When he spins around, she aims her middle finger in his direction.

I laugh and Jonas peers down at me. "What's so funny?"

He leans in close and I cup my mouth to his ear. "Little love-hate relationship between Micah and the woman behind the bar." Jonas looks to the woman in question and nods. "Not sure if they're dating or have dated, but there's definite tension."

Micah delivers the drinks to the table then darts behind the bar to help. We sip our drinks and catch up on life. Before long, everyone drifts out to the dance floor while Jonas and I hang back at the table.

Jonas faces me, snakes his arms around my waist, and hauls me closer to him. "Want to dance when they wear out?" Lacing my fingers behind his neck, I nod.

His gaze holds mine for a beat before dropping to my lips. Without preamble, he kisses me breathless. The flashing lights and thumping music fade away. Wet heat traces the seam of my lips and I open up. With hundreds of people nearby, Jonas kisses me wild.

Our lips break apart, but he peppers kisses along my jaw. When he reaches my ear, he sucks the lobe between his lips and growls. "Autumn." My moan in response vibrates my chest. "Move in with me."

I fist his shirt and bite near the collar at the base of his throat. He growls again, fueling the flame in me. "God, I want to."

Jonas leans back and I immediately miss his weight on my nipples. Finger under my chin, he tilts my head back. "Then say yes."

Music blares from every corner and hidden speakers in the ceiling. Sweaty bodies gyrate on the dance floor and near the tables. Upbeat energy bounces off every surface. And yet, it all disappears as I study how the blue marries gold in Jonas's irises.

This is the second time Jonas has proposed Clementine and I move in with him. The first was a slip of the tongue at his parent's a few nights ago. After I told him I wanted to discuss it in private, rehashing the subject hasn't happened. Until now.

Will Jonas be upset if I tell him I decided the very same night? That as he drifted to sleep, I imagined—not for the first time—what living together would be like. Waking up next to him every morning and falling asleep in his arms. I wanted to rouse him from sleep and tell him yes. But so many people say making rash decisions isn't smart. So, I simmered on it.

With each passing minute, hour, day, the desire to

say yes expanded in my chest. Consumed me. Begged to be let out.

I lift up on my tiptoes and press a kiss to his lips. "Yes," I whisper, breathy.

Leaning back, his eyes dart between mine. "Yes?"

I nod and, in a blink, he hoists me off the floor and spins me in circles. Glad I haven't drunk much. My feet hit the floor and he crashes his lips to mine. Tasting me. Devouring me. I fist his hair. Moan when he kneads my hips and grinds me to him.

"Get a room," Micah yells from the bar. Catcalls and wolf whistles echo around us as we peel apart.

As Jonas flips Micah off, the blonde bartender yells something at Micah I don't hear. But if the curl of her lip is any indication, she probably told him to shut up or mind his own business.

As our group trickles back to the table, we share our news. Cheers erupt as the ladies crowd around me and squeal. The guys exchange fist bumps or shoulder hug-slaps. Once the congratulations die down, we lose ourselves to the music.

Jonas threads his fingers with mine and walks backward toward the dance floor, tugging me along. His smile illuminates the dark club as he pins us chest to chest, palms flat on my low back. Our bodies grind and sway. Sweat slicks our skin and drips from our temples. Jonas drops his forehead to mine and holds my gaze.

"I love you," he mouths. His silent declaration louder than the thumping music.

"Love you, too."

He dips his chin and tastes my lips. One song bleeds

into another. Then another. All the while, Jonas and I sway in the middle of the dance floor, lips locked, tongues tasting, oblivious to the world around us.

When he breaks the kiss and we come up for air, he whispers in my ear. “Let’s go home, scarlet.”

Better words have never been said. “Let’s go home,” I repeat.

twenty-eight

. . .

Jonas

For someone who cohabitated in a small apartment with another adult and a child, Autumn has more shit than imaginable.

"We may have to add another room to the house," I tease, heaving another box from the floor.

Autumn sticks her tongue out. "Ha ha. If we fit everything in here" —she waves her arm around the bedroom— "we can fit it into the house."

My house—our house—may be small, but I have upgraded majority of it over the years. Done my fair share of walks through the Ikea showroom for innovative ideas in small spaces. Learned how to make the best of unused wall space. And although my belongings don't fill all the shelves and cubbies and rods in the closet, I made the most of the space when updating it.

Which means Autumn will have plenty of space for her clothes and shoes and purses and whatever else she owns. And if the closet fills, there is plenty of room in Clementine's closet.

Back seats laid down in the Jeep, I wedge the box between two others and go back for more. Everything leaving the apartment is small enough to fit in the Jeep or Autumn's car. After talking with Penny, Autumn opted to leave the furniture in the apartment for whoever rooms here next. Better it go to use than sell it.

In the apartment, I wander to the Jenga pile of odd-sized boxes. "This the last of them?"

Autumn pops up behind the open kitchen counter and brushes a stray hair out of her face. "Just packing up the last of the kitchen items. Everything else is done."

One by one, I carry out the larger boxes, followed by several small boxes labeled *bathroom*. As eager as I am to share the same living space with Autumn and Clementine, the number of personal care items going into the bathroom intimidates the hell out of me. What do I have? Maybe less than ten hygiene/personal care items in the bathroom. By the looks of it, Autumn owns the entire beauty care department in Target.

The bathroom may need revamping. Again.

Not that I am opposed.

Once everything is crammed inside the Jeep and Bel Air, we drive back to the house and haul everything inside.

The house looks like a war zone. Boxes in every room. Piles of wadded newspaper from unwrapping fragile pieces. We pile the boxes according to room then disburse accordingly.

Clementine spends the day in her room, putting away her own belongings as Spartan supervises. Every once in a while, we hear her direct him where something goes—although he isn't capable of putting it away. Or so I thought. At one point, I peeked in her room and watched Spartan carry a stuffed animal on the bed and place it by the pillows. Huh. Only for her.

We spend all of Saturday unpacking. Only taking breaks to eat and sleep. When Sunday morning rolls around, I glance around the house with fresh eyes. It's the same space, but not. The energy vibes differently. Feels more lived in. Comfortable. A home.

While the girls are still asleep, I cook breakfast. Our first official Sunday living under the same roof. And I plan to treat my girls.

Clementine wanders from her room first. Balled fingers rubbing her eyes as she yawns big. Spartan ambles lazily beside her. Before Clementine, Spartan was this wild child. Barking and running like his ass was on fire. Now, he peers up at her, docile and at her beck and call.

"'Morning, sunshine. Did you sleep good?"

She nods. "Can I let Sparty out?"

"Sure. Just open the back door. He'll bark when he's ready to come back in."

After she lets Spartan out, she sidles up to me in the kitchen. "Whatcha making?"

"French toast, sausage, eggs, and fruit."

Spartan barks to come back inside. Clementine tends to him as I finish cooking. When I spin around to grab plates from the cupboard, Autumn stands at the opposite end of the kitchen, ogling me.

Sleepy eyes rake over my bare chest and sweats. The

hunger in her eyes is a delicious assault that lights me on fire. Her tongue sweeps out and licks her lips. Chest rises and falls quicker. And I love how easily she is affected by me. Just as I am her.

Each morning, I am rewarded with her natural beauty. Although I love seeing Autumn styled to the nines—hair pinned to perfection, lips and nails scarlet red, outfit glamorous even when casual—seeing her fresh from sleep is my favorite. Tank top and pajama shorts hugging her curves. Face free of makeup. Hair frizzing in every direction. Feet and legs bare.

I saunter over to her, grip her hips to bring her flush to my chest as I kiss her. "'Morning, scarlet."

Eyes closed, a warm smile curves her lips up. "'Morning," she says, breathless. "Smells good."

"Was about to plate everything. Pull up a stool." I kiss her nose and smack her ass as she heads for the breakfast bar.

Maple, herbs, and citrus waft in the air as I deliver breakfast to my girls. As we eat, the topic of tonight's gathering comes up.

Although I have owned the house for some time, having Autumn and Clementine here makes it feel new. Our recent Sunday get-togethers with friends have been wonderful, so we opted to do a housewarming. As I see it, tonight's shindig is just another of our Sunday gatherings, just using the guise of Autumn and Clementine moving in as a reason to ask everyone over.

Once we clear our plates, I clean up the kitchen. Autumn and I sit down to write a shopping list while Clementine showers.

If there is one thing that will take time adjusting to, it's the fact I now have to share one bathroom with two additional people. Thankfully, the water heater holds enough to let us all shower without the water running cold.

Though we are slowly settling in to the idea of living together, I wonder how long we will be able to stay in this small house. Does it have everything we need? Absolutely. Will it be a struggle to live in a small space with one bathroom as Clementine approaches her teen years? More than likely. But we will cross that bridge when we get to it.

With the list made, we gather clothes for the day while waiting for Clementine to finish.

I sit on the edge of the mattress and follow Autumn around the room with my eyes as she plucks a shirt from the hanger and tugs jeans from the dresser. She lays them beside me and returns to the dresser for bra and panties. She twirls the minimal material lace panties around her finger and saunters over to me.

I look between the sexy as hell panties and her eyes, swallowing. "Don't think I've seen those," I squawk like a hormonal teenager.

Her knees bump mine before she plants each on the bed, straddling me. I stare up at her in complete fascination as she licks her lips. "You haven't. Bought them online a few weeks back."

My hands go to her hips, knead once, twice before dipping to her ass. I cup her cheeks and drag her closer to my chest. "Can't wait to see them on you." Her plump lips tug at the corners. "And to peel them off later."

She drops her mouth to mine and kisses me with fire on her lips. "Later." Hopping off my lap, she tosses the panties to the bed and takes my hand. "Let's go shower."

There are pros and cons to having a single bathroom and shower in this house. Con—you have to wait your turn. Whether to shower, brush your teeth or use the toilet. Con—you never know how long the wait will be. Pro—more joint shower time with Autumn to "conserve" water or time. At least that is the excuse we give Clementine.

Until today, I'd never had shower sex. Movies and television make it look easy. In reality, it's awkward and slippery and complicated. Guess we will have to practice until we get it right.

Won't find either of us complaining.

Lifting the beer to my lips, I swallow down the hoppy brew and glance around the back patio.

Everyone being here feels almost dreamlike. Six months ago, if someone would have told me I'd be head over heels in love with someone other than my best friend, I would've laughed in their face. If they also told me the love of my life came with the cutest little girl on the planet, I would've laughed harder.

Sometimes fate surprises you. Throws a wrench in your ideal plan because it has something better in store.

Seeing my friends and family together tonight proves you can't stay single-focused forever. You have to learn that people enter your life for a purpose. To show or teach you love so you recognize it when it enters your life. To tear you down so you learn how to rise and be the strongest version of yourself. And how to locate your own path.

For some, it takes a lifetime. Thankfully, I didn't have to wait so long. But I thank fate for the years I traveled down my path. Through the heartache and uncertainty. The friendship and laughter. Without them, I might not have met Autumn. I might not have been ready to meet her. Unwilling to open up or see the big picture. Feel the way my soul hums when she enters the room.

Tonight wouldn't be what it is without her.

Cora, Erin, Shelly, and Penny lounge on the outdoor couch with Autumn, laughing. Watching them whisper like school girls is a sight. Autumn snorts then smiles and I can't take my eyes off her. That woman belongs to me, and I am damn lucky.

Mom and Dad play with Clementine, Ashton, and Lex in the yard, chasing them around until they squeal with delight. Spartan is hot on Dad's heels, barking playfully. With Clementine living here now, I contemplate adding kid-friendly fun to the backyard. A swing set or trampoline or treehouse. Maybe Jasmine will bring Lex over to play more if I do.

Gavin, Rex, Anton, Micah, and Reznor are in what looks like an all too serious conversation. Anton animatedly tells them something and I am certain it is in regards to finances. Anton has always been a great guy, but as soon as someone mentions saving for the future or making significant life changes, he flips into the most passionate numbers man.

Jasmine, Jillian, Trevor, and Iliana sit opposite the couch near the fire bowl and talk softly. And, if I am not mistaken, Trevor glances a little longer than typical at Jillian, but I won't call him out on it. Trevor has been through some shit with his ex. Considering how long we have been friends, I know he wouldn't hurt my sister. Especially if he wants to keep his dick intact.

Cora rises from the couch and walks my way. Sidling up to the grill, she refills her drink then faces me.

"I'm happy for you."

After I flip the chicken, I glance at her. A smile I used to think I couldn't live without stretches across her face. The appearance brings me joy, but a form much different than it once did. So much has changed between us. It isn't often men and women remain friends. Usually, relationships or emotions meddle. At one point, that was almost the case for us. But it never felt right. Although I love Cora, my love for Autumn is a million times more powerful.

As Autumn once told me, maybe Cora came into my life so I could experience love and see it firsthand with her and Gavin. Cora was never fated to be mine, just a teacher to prep me for the future. For Autumn and Clementine.

"Thank you. Never thought this would be my life." I wave my beer bottle around. "But I'm damn glad it is."

Cora leans in and hugs me. "Knew she was out there. She was waiting for you too."

I break the hug and smile. "Yeah." I glance over to Autumn, who peeks up and smiles back. "Lucky I found her."

epilogue

. . .

Autumn

One year later

"I MISS YOUR FACE," PENNY WHINES AS SHE WANDERS INTO my booth.

"Just my face?"

She pops her gum and plops down on my freshly cleaned client chair. "Would you be mad if I said yes?"

"What's the matter, Rex not as pretty as me?" I tease.

A month after I moved out of the apartment with Penny, Rex and his girlfriend at the time got in a huge fight. Seeing as they were living together and her daddy paid the rent on their apartment, Rex got the boot. Thankfully, Penny hadn't found anyone to occupy the second bedroom. When Rex came into work "sobbing like a baby" as Penny so gracefully stated, she took pity on him and let him move in.

Over the last few months, I noticed a slight shift in how they act around each other. Small things.

The way he glances over to the reception desk more

often than before. Her obvious avoidance of him at work—overtly intentional. And anytime we all hang out, they stay as far apart as possible.

If I didn't know any better, I may believe they are sleeping together. Either that or they fight the urge.

Penny rolls her eyes on a huff. "Definitely not. He also isn't the cleanest human on the planet. And is it too much to ask for him to put the damn toilet seat down?"

I chuckle and she narrows her gaze at me. Taking a step back, I hold my hands up in surrender. "Sorry, but you have to admit, it's kind of funny."

She pops off the seat, plants her hands on her hips, and shoots me a pointed glare. "It isn't funny, Auti." Her hot pink fingernail aimed at my chest. "And you're supposed to be on my side."

"I am on your side," I cajole. "Sorry Rex is a bad roommate. Have you talked with him about it?"

Slowly, over the last year, I have lightened my schedule at the shop. Now working four lighter shifts, Tuesday through Friday, so I have more time with Clementine and Jonas. On a typical day, Jonas works until five and Clementine attends an after school martial arts program. And if I pick her up earlier than four thirty, I regret the decision all night.

In the not too distant future, I see myself working even fewer hours. But we will play it by ear.

"You're joking, right?" She shakes her head while tapping her Mary Jane on the linoleum. "Talking to Rex about anything is a lost cause."

I tuck my lips between my teeth to stop myself from laughing and focus on finishing my cleanup.

"Pen," I start with a headshake. "You need to talk with him. Even if he's a pain in the ass, you need to sit down and hash this out. It won't get better otherwise."

Tossing my gloves in the trash bin, I grab my purse from the cabinet and exit the booth with Penny on my heels. She plops down in her chair behind the reception counter on a huff.

"I hate it when you're right, Auti."

"Glad you still love me." I bend and bear-hug her. "Let me know how the talk goes. Love you."

"Yeah, yeah. Go be with your man." She shoos me away.

I hop in the Bel Air and drive to the dojo to pick up Clementine. As she gathers her belongings, Clementine brags about the instructor's praise on her kata technique. As girly as my daughter is, I never expected her to love martial arts the way she does. But it warms my heart she discovered something she is not only good at, but also loves enough to flaunt.

On the way home, I remind her we're going out for dinner. In the past year, having Jonas as a father figure and Spartan as a daily companion has been a good change for Clementine. Her sass has knocked down a notch and she interacts more with us than being glued to screens. Undeniably, my little girl has grown up so much.

As soon as I cut the engine, she darts in the house, loves on Spartan a moment, then takes off for a quick shower.

Not a foot in the door, Jonas has his arms around my

waist and his lips pressed to mine. "How was your day?"

"Uneventful, unless you count Penny flipping out because Rex is a slob."

He chuckles and shakes his head. "When I went out with the guys last weekend, he went on a tirade about her nagging. Seems like some love-hate going on there."

"Agreed."

We break apart as Spartan bolts past us and we stumble into the couch edge. Jonas scolds Spartan, then frames my face in his palms. "You alright?"

I nod. "Yeah. Just stumbled a bit. The house gets smaller the bigger he and Clementine get." Nonchalantly, I hint at needing more space for the second time this week.

Jonas shrugs it off and repeats the same line he said last time. "We'll figure something out."

Once Clementine finishes getting ready, we pile into the Jeep and drive to Red Robin. Instead of bopping and singing in the back seat, Clementine prattles on about how eager she is to earn her next belt in karate. Her hands animated while she talks about the new kata she learned today. Her enthusiasm pastes smiles on our faces. He clutches my thigh a little tighter as he steers us into a parking space.

No matter how gentle or firm, I love Jonas's touch. Live for the warmth and tingle it provokes. In the last year, every touch has held more meaning. Lit me on fire further. Had me falling more and more in love with him.

After a table full of appetizers, three burgers, and a

few drinks in funky cups, we decide to wander the mall to burn off the obscene number of calories we consumed.

In one of the department stores, we wander to the kid's section and stare after Clementine as she scrutinizes every item on the racks. As we steer closer to where her sizes butt up against the baby clothes, I get lost in the soft gray and subtle green onesies, sleepers, and outfits. Before I stop myself, my hand reaches out and grazes the delicate cotton.

Jonas steps up behind me, snakes his arms around my waist and whispers in my ear. "Everything okay?" His voice riddled with questions. "You've been quiet the last few days."

I drop my hand from the sleeper and spin to face him. "Yeah. Just been thinking."

His fiery hazels lock on to my goldens and study me with great intensity. "About?"

Clementine bounces over toward us with a rock band shirt in her hand. "Can we get this? Pleeeease."

I nod. "Sure, pumpkin. But that's it." As she skips away from us, I peer up at Jonas. "When we get home."

After we pay for Clementine's new "Girl bands rock!" shirt, we walk back to the Jeep. The ride home is quiet and heavy with questions. Out of the corner of my eye, Jonas peeks my way every opportunity he gets. I keep my eyes forward and my fingers curled with his.

At home, Clementine and Spartan lock themselves away in her room, leaving Jonas and I alone.

It's now or never, Autumn. Just tell him. No need to worry yourself sick. Everything will be fine.

Jonas guides me to the couch and we cuddle the moment we plop down. He strokes my hair and I close my eyes to focus solely on his touch. The heat of his skin on mine. His jagged breath as he hugs me closer to him.

"You can talk to me, scarlet. About anything," he croaks against the crown of my head.

No doubt my silence has him worried. Roles reversed, I would feel the exact same.

I tuck my lips between my teeth and take a deep breath before releasing them. "I'm late." Jonas goes still beneath me. Too still. I close my eyes and pray this won't be an issue. "And I took a pregnancy test a few days ago."

After a yearlong minute, Jonas scoots away an inch. I pinch my eyes until the corners hurt, until the warmth of his palms rest on my cheeks. Slowly, he tilts my head back until his eyes meet mine.

"Autumn…" he breathes my name as if it is his last breath. "Why didn't you tell me sooner?"

Tears sting the backs of my eyes and I question myself as to why I waited so long. Who the hell knows? I shrug and swallow the emotion swirling at the back of my throat. "Don't know. Guess I was worried how you'd react."

"Autumn, I love you. No matter what." He leans in and kisses me soft and sweet. "What did the test say?"

A tear spills down one cheek, then the other. "That you're going to be a daddy." I smile as his eyes dart between mine.

"Really?" he questions with wonderment in his

voice. I nod with my eyes on his. He kisses me again, this time greedier. "I-I don't even know what to say."

I grip his forearms and study his ear-to-ear smile. "Tell me that you're happy and you want this. A baby."

"Hell yes, I'm happy. And damn right I want this." He crashes his lips to mine and makes me breathless. When he breaks the kiss, he glances around the open floor plan before coming back to me. "Guess we will need more space after all."

I trace from his temple to the angle of his jaw before cupping his cheek. "I love you, Jonas."

His thumbs stroke my cheeks a moment before he drops his palm to rest over my lower abdomen. "Love you, too." His glassy eyes meet mine. "Thank you," he whispers.

"For what?"

My favorite dimple makes an appearance. "For loving me." He presses my hand to his sternum and covers it with his own. "And for giving me something I never thought I'd have." I scrunch my brow. "A family of my own."

bonus content

one

. . .

Autumn

"I DON'T KNOW," I MUTTER AS WE WANDER THROUGH THE third house this week.

Searching for a new house is not as fun as I once imagined. Definitely nothing like the reality shows on HGTV. And I swear I have told our realtor a dozen times exactly what we are looking for. Yet, here we are, staring at another house that meets none of the specifications either of us mentioned.

"What don't you like about it?" she asks, dumbfounded.

And because I am six months pregnant, I don't bite my tongue. "How about it isn't what we're looking for."

"Autumn," Jonas groans.

I face him and give a *don't you side with her* look. "Well, it's not. And I refuse to look at one more house if it doesn't meet our specs. I'm tired and my feet hurt," I bark out as I rub my belly.

The realtor goes red in embarrassment. "My apologies, Autumn. Just wanted to show you several houses in your price range."

"Under normal circumstances, I might appreciate your thoughtfulness. But now is not the time to lug me all around town."

"Yes, ma'am." She cowers and scurries toward the exit. "There is one more house to see and I promise it meets your requirements."

As soon as she is out of earshot, I mumble, "It better."

Jonas chuckles at my side as he wraps an arm around my shoulder. "C'mon, scarlet. Let's go see the last house. Then we'll head home so you can relax."

We drive north for ten to fifteen minutes before winding through a quiet neighborhood. I stare out the passenger window and eye the lush landscaped front yards and pale painted two-story homes. Kids run through the grass playing tag. A woman mows the grass while a man tends to the weeds near the flowers. And when we step out of the Jeep, the subtle scent of jasmine floats up my nose and relaxes me.

The house exterior is a steely blue with white and navy trim. Colorful shrubs line the front of the house along with native grasses and a variety of small flowers. At the base of two tall oaks, ferns form a thick diameter. A narrow walkway winds through the yard from the street to the porch. And off to the right of the main house is a two-car garage.

Unlocking the door, the realtor walks us inside. Ten feet into the house and I know we have found our new home—long as there are no issues.

We are shown the bottom floor first—living, dining, kitchen, breakfast nook, den, fourth bedroom, full bath, laundry room, garage, back patio and caged-in pool. As gorgeous as it all is, the enormity of it all overwhelms me. Then we trudge up the stairs and look at the three bedrooms and two full baths.

As I study the largest tub I have ever seen in the upstairs main bedroom, the realtor quietly leaves us to look and talk.

Jonas comes up behind me and rests his hands on my hips. "I can think of several things we could do in this tub."

I turn and play slap his bicep. "You're naughty." He laughs. "Which is one of the reasons I love you."

"What do you think, scarlet?"

Glancing around the room, I wish my growing belly didn't prevent me from jumping up and down. "It's perfect. Clementine will love it."

He bends his knees and levels with my line of sight. "Do you want to put an offer in?"

I tuck my lips between my teeth then release them. "Yes."

two

. . .

Jonas

"Only five more minutes."

Autumn screams in the passenger seat of the Jeep while she drains all the blood from my hand with her death grip.

"I'm not going to make it," she belts out between pants.

"Yes, you are." I steer the Jeep into the parking lot of the hospital. "See, we're here. Let's get you out."

I jog around the front of the Jeep and lower Autumn from the passenger seat. Tossing the delivery backpack over my shoulder, I wrap my arm around her and guide us toward the hospital entrance at her pace.

Once we check in, a nurse brings us to a delivery room, helps Autumn change into a hospital gown, and checks her dilation.

"You're doing good, Mom. At seven centimeters. Shouldn't be much longer. I'll page the doctor and be back to check on you."

The nurse leaves the room and I try to remember

everything from birthing classes over the past four months. At the moment, every single breathing exercise and soothing technique has flown the coop.

I hold Autumn's hand between mine. "How're you feeling, scarlet?"

"Argh!" Her grip on my hand intensifies tenfold. "Like I'm going to die."

"You're not going to die." I kiss her knuckles. "You're the strongest person I know. If anyone can get through this, it's you."

She grits her teeth in an attempt to smile. "I love you, but please don't hate me if I say mean things while this is happening."

"Say whatever you need to, scarlet. I'll be here, no matter what."

"Hey, Mom and Dad. I hear the little one is ready to come out and play," Dr. Heidi singsongs as she enters the room. "Let's see how you're doing, shall we?" The doctor does a brief exam and asks Autumn her pain level. After determining the contractions are a minute apart, she preps for delivery. "Dad, you should put scrubs on." I glance her way with a pinch between my brows. "Promise not to start without you."

I rush to the en suite bathroom and throw scrubs, cap, and booties on. When I reenter, the room is abuzz. Dr. Heidi barks out orders to the nurses while she sits poised between the stirrups at the foot of the hospital bed. Monitors next to Autumn's bed beep frantically and she pants on the bed.

Fuck.

I bolt to Autumn's side and grip her hand. "What's wrong?"

"My water broke and the alarms started going haywire." She pinches her eyes tightly, panting. "Dr. Heidi thinks it's rapid labor." My eyes widen as Autumn grits her teeth and numbs all the feeling in my fingers. "Basically, my body is ready to get the baby out now."

Over the next hour, Autumn bears down and pushes when the doctor tells her. Between contractions, she drops her head back and focuses on her breathing. I hold her hand and tell her to break my fingers if she needs to. The entire experience inspires me and shows me a strength I never knew a woman could possess. Leaves me absolutely awestruck.

And at seven thirty-one in the evening on January twenty-fourth, two days before my own birthday, I hear my son cry for the first time.

Seconds after I cut the cord, he is placed on Autumn's bare chest. I stare at the full head of dark hair and broad shoulders on his tiny human body. He curls his little fingers and lays his cheek above Autumn's breast. I have never seen a more beautiful sight in my life.

Swiping at the tears streaming down my cheeks, I lean in and kiss Autumn on the forehead. "He's perfect and beautiful."

Autumn smiles brighter than the sun as she caresses his cheek. "Hi there, handsome. So nice to meet you, Ryker Wade Thompson. Time to say hello to daddy."

I rip away my scrub top as the nurse scoots a chair

closer to Autumn's bed. Once seated, the nurse hands Ryker to me and I place him on my chest. And in this moment, the world stands still. His little fingers toying with my chest hair as I stroke my fingers along his back.

"Hey, big man." A tear slips down my cheek. "Mommy and Daddy have been waiting forever to meet you." I kiss his tacky skin. "So glad you're finally here."

Autumn reaches her hand out for me and I take it. I peek up at her through my tear-stained vision and see the tears running down her cheeks. "I love you, scarlet. Look what we did." I smile down at our son and kiss his forehead. "Best birthday present ever."

three

. . .

Autumn

April 21st — the following year

"Quit messing with my hair," I bark at Penny.

"Who the hell was that hairdresser? Do they even know how to pin up hair like ours," Penny huffs out.

When I asked Penny to be my matron of honor, I never expected her to be the bridezilla type. During the whole wedding planning process, I have remained calm and collected. Penny, on the other hand, has been a basket case.

I swat at her arms as she reaches for my hair to "fix" another bobby pin. "Stop it. My hair is exactly how I want it. Can we just focus on getting me in my dress, please?"

Click. Click.

Cora has the camera at her eye as she captures my big day. Too bad she has to witness matron of honor-zilla. But I trust her instinct to take all the perfect pictures today.

With a huff, Penny stomps over to the hook where my dress hangs. Cora snapped pictures of it on the hanger earlier before capturing my hair and makeup being done.

As I step into my dress, a knock raps at the door.

"I'll get it," Cora states.

She cracks the door open and peeks out. Then she opens the door wider and lets Jonas's mom enter. The moment she sees me, she gasps and covers her mouth before fanning her eyes.

"I will not cry. Not yet, anyway." She hugs me close. "You look ravishing, Autumn. Aaron will wait outside the door with Clementine."

Blinking back tears, I nod. "Thank you, Irene. Love you."

"Love you, too, sweetie. Whenever you're ready, everyone will start on your cue."

Irene exits and closes the door behind her. A minute later, Cora leaves the room so she and Erin can get in place to take photos from every angle possible.

"Ready for this, Auti?" Penny grips my forearm and gently squeezes.

I tuck my lips between my teeth and nod. "Never been more ready."

Penny stands in front of me, rests her hands on my shoulders, and locks eyes with me. "Remember to breathe. And hang on to Aaron." I nod and blink rapidly. "You look absolutely stunning. Love you."

"Love you, too."

Penny picks up my bouquet—baby pink ranunculus, soft green succulents, and hot pink berries—and hands it to me as she takes her own smaller version. Then she sweeps out of the room in a pink dress to rival her hair color.

Throughout my life, I never envisioned having a wedding day until Jonas proposed.

We had been in the new house just shy of four months. Ryker was barely five weeks old. And Jonas got down on one knee with the most stunning rose gold morganite and diamond ring. I wanted to scream with glee but didn't so as not to disturb Ryker. When he slid the ring on my finger, I stared at the stones for so long, smiling because it looked like a sparkling flower.

I glance down at the ring on my left fourth digit and sigh. Soon, the matching bezel diamond band will rest on the same finger, closer to my heart.

A knock at the door captures my attention. "Come in."

The door cracks open and Aaron peeks inside. "Hey, sweetheart. It's time."

I exit the dressing room, hooking my arm on Aaron's proffered elbow. In front of me, Clementine smiles so big it makes my face hurt. Her dress the same bright pink as Penny's. She waves and starts sprinkling rose petals on the pavers as she marches her way along the path into the wedding garden. Ten heartbeats later, Penny follows in Clementine's wake.

Aaron lays his hand on my forearm and meets my gaze. "From the first day we met, Autumn, I had a feeling you would be more than a woman whose car I towed. And when I saw the way my son looked at you, I instantly knew you'd be in our lives a very long time."

I smile up at his handsome face and pray Jonas will age as gracefully as Aaron. "Love you, sweetheart. And I'm proud to call you my daughter."

I tip my head back and bat my lashes at the sky. "Love you, too, Dad."

In my periphery, Cora snaps photo after photo of us. But I lose all focus.

"Here we go." Aaron steadies me as we march forward and head into the garden.

Cora darts in front of us and backs into the garden so she has a head-on shot of Aaron walking me down the aisle. The moment she shifts to the side and unblocks my line of sight, I gasp.

Fifty feet away, just past the rows of chairs where our friends and family sit, Jonas stands with his hands clasped in front of his waist. His charcoal suit snug on his broad shoulders and firm glutes, white dress shirt crisp, plaid pink and charcoal tie snug beneath his Adam's apple. But the most stunning part of my view is his smile and glassy eyes as he stares down the aisle at me.

Cameras click and flash all around us, but I ignore it all.

Everyone rises as Aaron and I approach. I hug him impossibly closer at the elbow as he guides me down the aisle, where I will officially become his daughter and Jonas will be my husband.

~

Jonas

Dear god.

I have never seen a sight more breathtaking than Autumn on my father's arm walking toward me in white lace and tulle. She looks like royalty.

With a sweetheart neckline, tulle billows down from her waist and dusts the grass as she shuffles her way toward me. A thin layer of rose embroidered lace decorates the skirt, bust, and sweeps down her arms to her wrists.

For as long as I live, I will never forget the way she looks in this moment.

My girl.

When she and Dad reach the arch, Dad gives her away and places her hand in mine. Her soft, warm skin steadies my jitters. Soothes every anxiety in my world.

But marrying Autumn doesn't make me anxious. Quite the opposite, actually. The only thing making me unsteady in this moment is that it didn't come sooner. And the minister isn't talking fast enough.

As the ordained minister reads the wedding script, I lock eyes with Autumn. Her cognac irises an intoxicating swirl of gold and cinnamon. Lips classic red. Hair pinned off her neck in whirls with a small rose gold comb encrusted with gems tucked in the back.

Just as I part my lips to whisper how gorgeous she looks, the minister pipes up and cuts me off.

"The bride and groom have prepared their own vows. Jonas…"

I reach inside my suit jacket and pluck out the paper. Unfolding it, I smile as I read the words.

"Autumn, from the first night I laid eyes on you, I

knew. I couldn't look away. Didn't want to. No one gives me solace the way you do. In a matter of minutes, I was bewitched. Enchanted. Enamored. Then I fell in love. Pictured every waking moment with you in my arms. And when I learned about Clementine, I was a goner. The love you both brought into my life is incomparable. And when I didn't think I could possibly love you more, you gave me a son." We both glance over to see Ryker tugging on Mom's hair. "If not for you, my heart wouldn't be full. My life wouldn't be complete. Autumn, you make every day better than the day before, and I cannot wait to see where life takes us next. Together."

Autumn tucks her lips between her teeth and tips her head back, blinking. She levels her gaze, swallows, and releases her lips before extracting a slip of paper from her bust. After a deep breath, she glances down and reads.

"Jonas… I remember the first night I saw you in the shop. You didn't see me that night as you flipped through artist albums on the couch. But I had trouble focusing on my client—Mr. Heaven." Penny snorts behind Autumn. "Anyway. I peered up every opportunity I had. There was just something about you. Something familiar. A piece of myself, dormant inside you, that I recognized. Then we officially met, and that was the most challenging tattoo I've ever done. Because all I wanted to do was look up at *you* and get lost in your eyes. After years of being on my own, you taught me how to love again. Not only love you, but also love myself. You have brought so much joy and compassion into my world. Lifted me up and held me steady. Given me a son as handsome as you and as silly as his sister." She pauses and takes a deep breath. "And today, Clementine and I have a gift we'd love to give to you."

Clementine pops up from her chair beside Mom and sidles up to Autumn. She sticks her hand in her dress pocket and fishes out a piece of paper, handing it to me.

"What's this?"

"Open it, silly," Clementine prompts.

I unfold the paper and scan the page. *Joint Petition for Adoption by Stepparent.* My eyes fly up to meet Autumn's and glaze over immediately. Mouth floods with emotion as I work to swallow past the golf ball in my throat.

"Jonas," Clementine states my name with confidence. I drop my gaze and hold the eyes that match her mother's. "Will you be my dad?"

Every guest gasps. I try to remember how to breathe as I squat down in front of her. "Clementine, I would be honored to be your dad."

Clementine leaps into my chest and wraps her arms around my neck. "Love you, Dad." I wrap her in my arms and rise up. Tears spill down my cheeks as I hug the life out of this little girl. *My little girl.*

"By the power vested in me by the state of Florida, I now pronounce you husband and wife. And family. Jonas, you may kiss your bride."

I lean into Autumn and kiss her sweetly. Clementine briefly hugs both our necks before Mom brings Ryker up and we walk toward our forever together. As a family.

four

. . .

Valentine's Love Letter (Love Buzz—Chapter Twenty)

Dearest Autumn,

Thank you. For coming into my life. For giving me a reason to smile each day. And for loving me. I can't imagine a better life than the one I have experienced with you by my side. And it is only just beginning.

I hope you don't get upset with all the gifts I give you today. And all the gifts I give Clementine.

I've never had someone to shower with gifts until you. I hope you don't think I'm going overboard. Because this is only our first gift-giving occasion. I have years to make up for—no arguing how we didn't know each other.

Having both of you in my life is the best gift you could have ever given me.

Yours always,

Jonas

up next in the bay area duet series

Who's story is up next? Micah and Peyton!

With his feisty and unsettled nature, Micah's story had to be the third duet. As challenging as Micah and Peyton were to write, their story is loaded with steam and witty banter, and I love it!

Enemies to lovers, former high school bully, and workplace romance!

I loathe Micah Reed. Yet, I can't keep my eyes off him.

Years ago, he opened his mouth in a room full of our peers. Said nine words and ruined my life.
My high school crush did exactly that… crushed me.

But I am no longer the quiet, loner girl from high school. The girl who let others trample her spirit.
Now, I take charge. Stand tall. Bend to no one. Never again.
Especially Micah Reed.

Peyton Alexander makes me question my sanity. Yet, I refuse to stop antagonizing her.

Since her first day at work, she has given me the death glare. Lipped off and verbally slapped me.
And every night, I go back for another round.

Not sure what I did to deserve her animosity, but I plan to find out. Plan to fix whatever mistake I made.
Although I live for her banter, I want more with Peyton.
The attention she gives other men, I want it for myself.
Call me presumptuous, but Peyton Alexander will be mine.

Micah wants me because I don't fall for his charms.
Peyton resists to deny herself the truth.

Will he figure out who I am?
Will she ever let me in?

Start reading Restless Night and A Love So Bright now!

thank you

Thank you so much for reading **Love Buzz**, book two in the **Inked Duet**. If you would take a moment to leave a review on the retailer site where you made your purchase, Goodreads and/or BookBub, it would mean the world to me.

Reviews help other readers find and enjoy the book as well.

Much love,
Persephone

more by persephone autumn

The Click Duet

High school sweethearts torn apart. When fate gives them a second chance, one doesn't trust they won't be hurt again. Through the Lens (Click Duet #1) and Time Exposure (Click Duet #2) is an angsty, second chance, friends to lovers romance with all the feels.

The Insomniac Duet

He was her high school bully. She was the outcast that secretly crushed on him. More than ten years later, he's her boss, completely oblivious to their shared past, and wants no one but her. More importantly, he doesn't understand her animosity toward him.

Transcendental

A musician in search of his muse and a woman grieving the loss of her husband. Two weeks at an exclusive retreat and their connection rivals all others.

Until she leaves early without notice. But he refuses to give up until he finds her again.

Depths Awakened

A small town romance which captivates you from the start. Two broken souls have sworn off love. Vowed to never lose anyone else. But their undeniable attraction brings them together and refuses to let go.

Distorted Devotion

Swept off her feet by love, life takes a dark, unexpected turn. Now the love of her life may be the cause of her death. Check out this gripping, romantic suspense.

Ink Veins

Persephone Autumn's debut collection, Ink Veins, explores topics of depression, love, and self-discovery with a raw, unfiltered voice.

Broken Metronome

When the music of the heart dies…

Broken Metronome is an angsty poetry collection full of heartache and the possibility of what may have been.

Sweet Tooth

Two people with the same rule. No dating. What happens when they bend the rules? A steamy standalone romance with a trigger warning.

inked duet playlist

Here are some of the songs from the *Inked Duet* playlist. You can listen to the entire playlist on Spotify!

Robbers - The 1975
Let Me Down Slowly - Alec Benjamin
Say Hello 2 Heaven - Temple Of The Dog
Pain Told Love - Tribe Society, Kiesza
Nathalie - Pepita Slappers
Fallingforyou - The 1975
Anchor - Novo Amor
Wrong Direction - Hailee Steinfeld
I miss you, I'm sorry - Gracie Abrams
this is how you fall in love - Jeremy Zucker, Chelsea Cutler

acknowledgments

Loved ones first!

Thank you to my wife, dad, and daughter for constantly being my biggest fans, cheerleaders, and motivators. Without your support, my writing journey wouldn't be where it is now. We've had ups and downs, but every time, we come out on the other side. I know I do because of you three in particular. I love you!

To the best editing team a lady could ask for… Ellie and Rosa, you always make my manuscripts beautiful and perfect. At least with this one, my commas were practically spot on. Must've been a good day lol. And Rosa, your insight and feedback is invaluable. You always pick up on stuff I missed or didn't wrap up 100%. I can't wait to hug you both one day!

To Theresa… First, I miss your face. Most importantly, thank you for letting me use your first name and physical likeness for a tertiary character in this book. When I wrote her, I tried to picture you (minus your super tall heels). All the hugs! And I can't wait to hang out again when the world is less chaotic.

To the early readers and promo peeps… thank you for reading my books! Thank you for wanting to read my future books! This author gig isn't the easiest, but you make it so much better. Much love!

To my author friends… I look forward to squeezing you all one day. Thank you for any and all support you give. For letting me share my covers and releases in your groups or on your pages. For sharing my books in your newsletters. For answering any questions whenever I bug you. We have to stick together through all this author madness, and I'm glad to have you in my corner.

To everyone who's read my previous books… THANK YOU! Thank you for loving my work enough to read more than just one. Thank you for not throwing my book away. Thank you for looking forward to the next book.

To every person new to my books…. THANK YOU! Thank you for taking a chance on me and reading my work. Writing is wonderful and crazy and frustrating. But for every person who reads my words, writing is worth it every single time.

connect with persephone

Connect with Persephone

www.persephoneautumn.com

Subscribe to Persephone's Newsletter

www.persephoneautumn.com/newsletter

Join Persephone's Reader Group

Persephone's Playground

Follow Persephone Online

- instagram.com/persephoneautumn
- facebook.com/persephoneautumnwrites
- goodreads.com/persephoneautumn
- bookbub.com/authors/persephone-autumn
- amazon.com/author/persephoneautumn
- pinterest.com/persephoneautumn
- twitter.com/PersephoneAutum

about the author

Persephone Autumn lives in Florida with her wife, crazy dog, and two lover-boy cats. A proud mom with a cuckoo grandpup. An ethnic food enthusiast who has fun discovering ways to veganize her favorite non-vegan foods. If given the opportunity, she would intentionally get lost in nature.

For years, Persephone did some form of writing; mostly journaling or poetry. After pairing her poetry with images and posting them online, she began the journey of writing her first novel.

She mainly writes romance, but on occasion dips her toes in other works. Look for her poetry publications and a psychological horror under P. Autumn.

www.ingramcontent.com/pod-product-compliance
Lightning Source LLC
Chambersburg PA
CBHW021620030826
48979CB00034B/487

* 9 7 8 1 9 5 1 4 7 7 4 8 6 *